"With its excellent pacing and beautifully complex plot, *Shifter* is a peach of a novel. Think you know what reality is? Steven D. Jackson will convince you otherwise. *Shifter* is a superb debut novel that will pin you to your seat."

- Cas Peace, *Artesans of Albia* trilogy

Published by Rhemalda Publishing
P.O. Box 1790
Moses Lake, WA 98837
http://www.rhemalda.com

SHIFER

Edited by Diane Dalton

Cover art by Melissa Williams
http://mwcoverdesign.blogspot.com/

Author photo by Alexander Melhuish

ISBN: 978-1-936850-49-5 Paperback
        978-1-936850-50-1 EPUB

Library of Congress Control Number: 2012938443

Visit author Steven D. Jackson on Facebook or at his website http://thecerberusarmchair.blogspot.com/.

For Daf.

Acknowledgements

In many ways, *Shifter* represents my attempt to shoe-horn my life into the shape I wanted it to be and celebrates the fact that I eventually managed it, but I couldn't have done it alone.

I have to start off my acknowledgments with a massive thank you to Cas Peace, author of the *Artesans of Albia* series. Without you, Cas, this would not have happened and *Shifter* would not exist. I know my original draft over-used the word "slightly" so much that you nearly had a heart attack, but I'm eternally grateful to you for sticking by me and getting me through.

To my friends, many of whom served unwittingly as inspiration for the characters in this book; I hope you don't mind my amalgamating your various attributes into new individuals. It was too funny an opportunity to miss, so if I've stuck bits of you in with bits of other people, I make no apologies. Kudos for working out which bits you contributed, though I'll never ever confirm it.

I couldn't have made it through the process without JP. His unfailing dedication to pub-related support sessions is something to which we should all aspire. So thanks, JP, for getting me back on my feet every time.

A big thank you to my family for putting up with my obsessive secretiveness about the book in the early stages and for being so supportive. I know I can be a bit weird when I'm doing a project! I reserve a special thank you for my brother, for being the source of endless enthusiasm that he is and always has been, and for helping me develop the creative mindset we share that others mistake for insanity.

As for Rhett and Emmaline and everyone else in the Rhemalda family, words cannot describe my gratitude to you all for your help in making this a reality.

SHIFTER

STEVEN D. JACKSON

CHAPTER ONE

The fragments of a coffee cup stared up at John from the floor. He glared back, trying to suppress the urge to kick them across the room. It made no sense to get annoyed with a coffee cup, however maliciously it had jumped off the kitchen counter. He sighed, not taking his eyes off the ceramic pieces scattered on the worn-out lino, which was now covered in coffee. It would probably stain.

I should really do something about that, he thought. Staring wouldn't help. A cynical inner voice suggested that yet another stain on the floor didn't really matter. He ignored it.

He turned carefully on the spot, keeping his elbows in and surveying the cramped kitchen area while trying not to knock anything else off the counter. To call it a kitchen was laughable. It was just a couple of appliances and a sink shoved in a corner, symbolically separated from the rest of the living room by the lino that replaced the carpet. It served its purpose. He didn't need anything better since he lived on his own, but sometimes it felt a bit too pokey. He could barely move without knocking things, mainly because there were too many plates and cups piled up on the scant counter space.

"Gotta do more washing up," he muttered without conviction as he surveyed the kitchen. His hand hovered over various piles of dishes as he tried to find something suitable to soak up coffee. "Sponge … sponge … nope, the sponge is rancid." He pulled his hand back before it touched the sponge, concerned that it might now be home to some form of mold.

"What the hell can I use?" he muttered again, just as the thought struck him. Paper towels.

The paper towels were in the cupboard under the sink, which meant he had to reach down to get it. Pleased that he at least had something he could use, John forgot about the expanding puddle of lukewarm coffee. He stepped right into it.

"Oh, what the—" He lifted his foot to stare accusingly at the utterly soaked sock, as though it had been in league with the puddle all along. Ripping it off, he threw it across the room, not caring where it landed. "Damn thing," he mumbled as he heard it hit the floor. Now he needed a new sock, and he doubted he had time to deal with the puddle. He had to concede defeat.

Abandoning the coffee cup, he headed back through the connecting door that led to his bedroom, the only other room in the scandalously tiny flat. Stain or no stain, the clock was ticking and he would be late if he didn't hurry. Events this morning had conspired to make him as late as possible, from the mystery of the missing wallet, to the shirt he thought he had ironed which was instead a crinkly mess, to the broken cup, and now, of course, to a soaked sock.

Squeezing past the bed, which took up most of the room, John recovered his last clean pair of socks from the drawer. It was handy, he thought, that he only ever bought black, work-friendly socks. He glanced hurriedly at his clock which sat on his chest of drawers, noting that he needed to leave now if he was going to be at work on time.

"Plenty of time, plenty of time," he chanted under his breath as he finished with the sock and stood up. It was partially true. He would have plenty of time if he left quickly. He chuckled to himself as he ran a hand through his dark hair, shaking it a bit so would look less slept in. He knew he ought to get up earlier so he had time to deal with his appearance before

SHIFTER

STEVEN D. JACKSON

work, but it was still difficult to accept that he was supposed to be a responsible employee now. Worrying about being late and looking presentable had yet to become routine. He still felt like a student, but at the age of twenty-four he knew it was time to get used to seeing himself as other people saw him. As a professional person, suit and all, albeit a suit that was a little worn out to the trained eye.

He smiled as he glanced in his mirror. He looked alright. Other people wouldn't guess that he lived alone in a hovel surrounded by piles of laundry and coffee cups. The question, as always, was whether he could pull off the air of authority required by his title. That was something they didn't teach at law school, the idea being that once you made it you should naturally acquire the traditional mannerisms. However, the term 'lawyer' still didn't ring true with John. When people asked him what he did, he was often inclined to deflect the question, saying 'office work', or 'the usual', and avoid going into details. He squared his shoulders, watching his reflection adopt a collected and professional pose that he was happy to note looked quite convincing.

"Well, hello," he said to the reflection, his voice as low and posh as he could manage, his eyebrows forced into a serious expression. "John Davis. Pleased to meet you. Won't you sit down? Oh, not at all"—he began to gesture wildly with his arms while trying to keep his expression grave—"not at all. Frightful weather, isn't it? Oh, indeed, blah, blah, blah, I'm terribly important, don't you know?"

He couldn't keep it up, it was too stupid. John laughed sheepishly as he pulled himself together. He needed to get going. His shoes were by the front door. That, at least, he knew. What he hadn't remembered was the pile of clothes sitting behind his mangy old sofa, ostensibly awaiting the attentions of the washing machine but never seeming to make it any closer to the kitchen area. Perhaps it was providence that made him trip over the pile on his short walk across the cluttered living room, reminding him to sort the mess out.

9

"Bloody—gahhh!" he said, kicking at the heap of clothes as he pulled himself back to his feet. He knew it was no use swearing at a stack of stuff he had shoved there himself, so he ignored it and pulled on his shoes. The cramped conditions wouldn't be forever. Soon he would be able to update the box-like television, which was so out of date it was hard to find a DVD player it would connect to, and maybe get another chair. No, scrap that, a new house. Of his own. He wondered briefly whether he would live in a tidier manner if the place was bigger. Nope, he conceded, probably not.

The door handle was cold under his hand, but he didn't open it just yet. Outside he could hear the rain driving against the building, battering the windows relentlessly as the wind howled. Once again, John remembered his decision to buy an umbrella. He made this decision almost every day, and every day he forgot. It had been pouring down off and on for some weeks now. There really was no excuse for putting it off except for maybe the thrill of getting soaked in the rain. Once he managed to get his boss to give him a raise he could buy whatever he liked, within reason. An umbrella certainly wouldn't be a bad investment.

John headed to the car, his face down as the wind whipped through his hair and threw rain in his eyes. He didn't need to see where he was going anyway. He had walked this way a hundred times. As he glanced up he couldn't help but smile at the little blue Metro. However old it was, the tiny car was still his and he loved it. How it had managed to keep running all this time he had no idea, but he'd had it now for a good two years despite it threatening to die on a regular basis. Somehow it was still alive, which was a source of great pride to John. His father had a similar take on cars. He preferred to keep them running at all costs despite being a respectable, middle-aged man who would look far better in a decent car, as opposed to one that was literally falling apart as he drove. That was one debate John knew he would never win with his father. Logic and reason flew out of the window whenever replacing his Dad's little green death-trap came up in conversation. His mother didn't mind since it left more cash lying around for her fancy sports cars. After all, she would say with a wry smile, we need something to put the shopping in.

John smiled to himself as he followed the familiar route, barely even noticing the road. Perhaps after he convinced the senior partner to raise his salary, as he certainly should now that John had qualified, he could think about getting a new car. He looked around the Metro's interior fondly as he drove, feeling guilty on some level for wanting to replace it when it had served him so well, but resolving not to let himself slip any further into the eccentric thinking that his Dad so enjoyed. Not that there was anything wrong with it, of course, but it might not look too good if he was driving around in a heap when he was supposed to be a hotshot lawyer. He smirked. "Hotshot in a Metro," he chuckled. "Awesome."

John parked and sat in the car, unwilling to exchange its comfort for the storm outside. He was the only one in the car park. Everyone else must be stuck in the inevitable traffic jams that swept Britain whenever it rained. He gazed up at the building, noting that it didn't look like much from the back. At the front was a huge sign which proclaimed proudly that this was Macleod, Gunn & Hensford LLP, together with a predictable slogan and some fancy lettering. It was almost sad that they hadn't invested any time or effort in the back of the building. What must clients think when they parked here? John supposed that the firm just couldn't afford to waste money on another huge sign, but then why not change the name of the firm? He doubted that Macleod, Gunn, and Hensford would care. Whoever they were, they were almost certainly dead by now. Very dead, probably.

He had worked here for nearly two years. He liked the location of the place, just over the river from the town center and with some decent views out of the windows. The impressive façade made John feel proud to work there. There were too many employees to allow him to get know everyone properly, but it wasn't a vast, faceless corporation like some others he knew. It would be a shame to leave, but he had made his mind up that if he couldn't get a significant pay rise, then he would have no choice. He would miss the place, especially in the summer when the sunlight glittered on the river and the people visible from the windows went around in sundresses and T-shirts. He could almost share their carefree attitude for a while as he watched. In weather like this, though, with the torrential rain hammering against the building and the steel grey river churned by wind, no one would be out and about. It was a good time to make plans; a good time to look to the future.

John glanced at the clock on the dashboard, resigning himself to the fact that he couldn't put it off any longer. He opened the door and stepped into the tempest outside.

As he stood fumbling for his office keys in the car park, getting progressively wetter and cursing the weather for making everyone else late, John was startled to hear someone calling his name. He could just make out that it was Jenna, a colleague who worked for one of the other partners. John knew her name, but he was mildly surprised that she remembered his. She was huddled under her umbrella which looked, he decided, pretty ridiculous. It was the kind that resembled a bubble and encased the person's head and shoulders, except this one had tendrils attached to it. As the wind buffeted the oddly shaped bubble, it seemed to undulate. The whole image was distinctly jellyfish-like.

Jenna and her jellyfish, John's mind randomly volunteered. Obviously he wasn't fully awake yet. Or maybe he was being soaked into madness.

Jenna was one of those people who rarely said anything at all, and on the odd occasions when she did speak, it sounded either well-rehearsed or completely out of control. Today was probably the latter. Jenna called to him and waved frantically from beneath the umbrella, the generous invitation to share wildly out of character for someone so shy. John thought of this as he hurried over to her, seeing her distorted face within the umbrella distort a little further with the realization that he wouldn't be able to stay a fair distance away while benefiting from her jellyfish. Changing tactics, he jogged past her, pointing toward the office door and making sounds of encouragement which were lost in the relentless barrage of wind and rain. He gripped his keys and opened the door as quickly as he could, stepping inside to admit Jenna.

Smiling at her, he struggled to think of something to say to cover the slightly awkward situation. In the end, he settled for a quick laugh and a gesture to the vile weather. "Seriously wet out there …." He trailed off, cringing inwardly at the lame comment.

Jenna smiled at her shoes while fiddling with her bizarre umbrella, wrapping it up in its tendrils. On reflection, thought John, it was a pretty good design. "So I'll see you later, then," he said lightly, dropping his keys back into his sodden pocket and wondering whether the remote for the lock would be damaged by the water. Jenna flicked her eyes up and smiled back, mumbling a similar reply.

It really was such a shame, he reflected as he walked down the corridor with its stark white walls toward his office. She was probably a really nice girl, but her shyness was sometimes exasperating. He found that his smile faltered within moments of people muttering at the ground while he was trying to talk to them. That, he reflected critically, was definitely one of his flaws. After all, it really wasn't their fault. They couldn't help what they were any more than he could.

His desk, as always, looked like an artistic commentary on the untidiness of the average office worker. Papers were strewn about, some in piles attempting unsuccessfully to appear orderly, others balancing on files which were likely to collapse onto the floor at any moment. He thought he knew what and where everything was, though, and he was quite happy to have everything accessible. The most important bit of paper was the hastily scribbled list of 'things to do' he had compiled the day before, back when he fully intended to make fresh start on everything. He knew very well that the first two things on the list would get done and be replaced by two other pressing things for tomorrow. Items near the bottom stood very little chance of ever getting done at all and were merely repeated on each revision of the list to ensure they weren't forgotten.

Today's items were decidedly uninteresting. There were letters to answer and things to draft, nothing to make a day pass quickly. A bizarre picture of a very angry man shouting at a small guy in a suit provided the only amusement, but that had been drawn while on the phone to the angry man yesterday. He would, no doubt, be in contact again today. "Joy," muttered John as he put the list to one side to look at his emails. "Kill me now."

Mr. Grady was a tall man with a penchant for garish shirts. He also happened to be one of the partners at the firm and was John's immediate superior. John owed him quite a lot, given that Mr. Grady had given him a training contract, trained him, and then let him run his own caseload largely unsupervised. Still, a boss was a boss, and John couldn't help but feel apprehensive when Mr. Grady came into his office with a piece of paper clutched in one hand and a smile on his face that looked nothing if not predatory.

"Ah, John, good morning. How're things?" His smile widened and John thought he looked like a cat enjoying playing with a mouse.

"Yeah, not bad, thanks." John decided to play the game as though he had some choice in the matter. "What's that?"

Mr. Grady's smile folded into a carefully practiced look of consternation, although it didn't meet his eyes. John tried not to groan aloud. He had seen that look too many times. Grady consulted his piece of paper, his eyes narrowing a little as though he saw something on there he hadn't expected. "Well," he began, as if distracted, "I think you're going to have to get up to speed with my files this week, John, since I'll need you to cover for me when I'm off. I wish I'd had more time to let you get to grips with it all, but things just come up so suddenly …." He fell silent as he scrutinized his piece of paper.

John had covered Mr. Grady's files more times than he could remember over the last two years, so this was nothing new. What was new was that he was actually being told in advance and in person. While strange, this was not exactly sinister. He relaxed. Perhaps there was nothing more to this after all. Maybe the guy was so excited about going on holiday that he wanted to start talking about it early. Fair enough. But what was on that piece of paper?

"Okay," said John feebly, "no problem." He wondered if his confusion showed. Mr. Grady gave no sign of noticing it. He simply stated his thanks and headed back to his office, whistling. John's eyes narrowed as he watched his retreating figure. Perhaps there *was* a reason to be concerned after all. He hadn't been given the piece of paper.

———————

"You're just too damn suspicious for your own good," Chris, lifelong friend and outspoken antagonist, declared later that evening. "If you didn't over-think everything anyone ever says or does, you might actually enjoy your life a bit."

Chris took a long drink of his beer for emphasis, then set it back on the gnarled wooden table and looked around at the pub's other occupants. The Old Bill was reasonably empty tonight, but then it always was midweek. Only the local older residents were in, huddled around the open fire or leaning against the wooden beams, staring at the odd assortment of farmers' implements inexplicably hanging on the walls. "Anyway, stop whining. Everyone hates their boss. Most people just keep it inside."

Chris looked at him imperiously, obviously missing the irony that he himself was the world's most malcontent employee, and a vocal one at that.

"I don't hate my boss. I was just saying it was weird that he mentioned it all before he went. I think maybe there's something important happening this week that he hasn't told me about …."

Chris was no longer listening. He was staring unashamedly at the girl who had just sauntered into the pub. She was wearing something akin to cling-film. Closely following her was an enormous guy in a tank top, a decidedly murderous expression on his face. To distract his friend before he got them both killed, John tried to think of a way to change the subject.

"So what exactly is this new job of yours all about? You do something with maps and computers, like a computer map maker?"

"Yep, like a computer map maker. I am the modern equivalent of Francis Drake, the difference being a chronic lack of danger and excitement and no money. But yeah, I do map stuff with those mysterious machines we in the modern world call 'computers'. You should probably look into them, they're pretty useful."

John ignored the snide remark about his lack of computer knowledge. It was one field of expertise in which he could never compete against Chris. He was just glad that the mismatched couple had disappeared and the chances of a violent death as a result of his friend's staring had reduced considerably.

"You aren't listening to a word I'm saying, are you?" Chris asked mildly as he finished the last of his beer and immediately checked his wallet for more beer money. "Give it up, she's gone. I saw her wander off with that giant bloke." He smiled faintly as he got up to head to the bar, apparently amused by the surprised look on John's face. Although he misunderstood the intention behind John's strategy, Chris had accurately deduced exactly what had distracted him. John regarded him suspiciously. Since when was he so astute?

"Another drink?" Chris asked, missing or ignoring John's expression.

"It's Tuesday."

"So tomorrow will be Wednesday. Well done. I'll get them in."

———————————

It was one o'clock in the afternoon, which meant it was lunchtime, and John was feeling quite smug. He had found himself an empty office with a view of the countryside in which he could hide from Mr. Grady while not appearing to be hiding. He wasn't feeling particularly marvelous after last night and didn't want to run into anyone if he could avoid it. His chocolate bar was in various bits on a plate. It had been carefully dissected with a blunt knife. The rain was still falling mercilessly outside, but it felt strangely cozy to be looking out at it from a dark room with the only light being the day's faint grey illumination.

The sound of the door opening behind him made John turn his head. Jenna wandered into the room, apparently unaware of his presence. He sighed inwardly. Privacy was something you couldn't insist on in a public place. Jenna saw him and jumped, her hand flying to her chest as she let out a yelp of surprise. The image would have been comical if John hadn't at the same time realized he looked like a lunatic, sitting in the dark with a knife and a mutilated chocolate bar.

"Oh, hey, Jenna," he said cheerily, trying to cover the astounding strangeness of his appearance with levity. "Care to share my darkened room? Got a brilliant view of absolutely nothing from here."

To his great relief, she laughed. "It's great, John, what a find. Hey, what've you done to that chocolate bar?"

Her surprise at finding him, coupled with genuine intrigue about his odd eating habits, seemed to have released her from her shyness. Or perhaps, he thought, it was just that no one else was around and he could barely see her. Either way it was an improvement. "Erm, yeah, I tend to cut up chocolate bars. Don't ask me why, it makes no sense."

"Oh, really? You sure it isn't a tragic cry for help?" She smiled and wandered to the window, where she stood staring out at the weather.

"Well, no one would normally see, so I'm obviously keeping it to myself. I guess I'm probably past crying for help and well on the way to true self-destructive madness."

She laughed again. John was enjoying himself. This was weird, he thought. Jenna had never really spoken like this, at least, not to him. That knowledge made him feel like he was helping her or something, and despite the nagging doubt in his head which was accusing him of outrageous egotism, he liked it. Jenna had visibly relaxed too. She was looking out the window with a lingering smile on her face. John had the distinct impression that she was thinking very hard about something. He looked closely at her, or as closely as the gloom would allow, and noticed that she wasn't actually bad looking. She was reasonably slim, with dark hair which might look quite good if it was cut a bit shorter, maybe styled a bit rather than left to hang there. He wondered fleetingly if she was single and realized that he knew absolutely nothing about her, not even what she did.

"Hey Jenna, what exactly do you do here? I've seen you around loads of times but never actually asked."

She glanced at him as if weighing her words. Then she appeared to remember her shyness and glanced at her wrist, mumbling that she had to get back and she would see him later. It did not escape John that she wasn't wearing a watch.

Alone in the dim room once more, John stared out at the storm. He resolved to make more of an effort with Jenna, or at least to find out her surname. "Nice name, Jenna," he muttered to the silent room. He had never met anyone with that name before.

The rain did not reply as it thrashed against the window.

CHAPTER TWO

As John headed back through the deluge to his car, his hair plastered to his skull, he wondered why he didn't mind rain until it got into his shoes. Having wet feet felt like a horrible violation. To him, it was the ultimate invasion of personal space. He decided not to think about it, pondering instead Chris's words from the night before.

Obviously I do over-think things, he thought. He had been told that on more than one occasion, and by a doctor too. It was mildly disturbing to think that Chris, of all people, should be able to form such an accurate picture of John's mental failings. He put it out of his mind, resolving never to allow Chris to believe John thought he was right about anything. That would just set a bad precedent.

The car's pedals made his sodden socks squish against his feet, which was a very odd sensation indeed. It was not exactly uncomfortable, though, and within a few minutes he had quite forgotten about it. His head began to ache as he drove, distracting pressure building inside his skull. He shook his head to clear it, blinking his eyes as he tried to concentrate on the road ahead. The feeling receded after a moment or two, allowing him to return his attention to the world outside. It had finally stopped raining, albeit rather suddenly, and the sun had managed to come out from wherever it had been hiding over the last few days. Something struck him as odd as he made his way through the residential district. Something about the sunlit world nagged at him, but he couldn't quite put his finger on what it was.

People on the street were clearly enjoying the change in the weather. Everyone looked happy and light-hearted. It was nice to see after so much rain and so many miserable faces. There were women in slinky dresses and the odd guy with his T-shirt off, as though it was his duty to show his over-muscled torso to the world just because the sun was out. John felt happier than he had for some time, amazed at how the collective public mood could change simply with the weather.

The weather that had changed so very suddenly.

John frowned. The feeling that something didn't quite add up was growing stronger. Where had that woman got her slinky dress from when she had been huddled under an umbrella and wearing a raincoat only a few minutes ago? Come to think of it there were no puddles on the road, no scent of freshly fallen rain, and no one looked at all wet. Shaking his head to clear it, John indicated left and turned off into a residential side street. Abruptly stopping his car, he ran a hand through his hair and rested his head against the steering wheel.

Dry hair ....

"No, it can't be." He ran his hand back over his head and was forced to conclude that yes, his hair was dry. Not conclusive, he reminded himself, since he had been driving for a couple of minutes. It could have dried in that time. Couldn't it?

Unlikely ....

The voice in his head was not being particularly helpful. John opened the door and stepped out of the car, noting that his shoes felt perfectly dry. The world suddenly appeared to be in the height of summer, and no one had noticed that it was totally impossible.

Except him.

Feeling his grip on sanity slipping, John made his way down the street, leaving his car where it was. He briefly

STEVEN D. JACKSON

considered parking it properly, but since he was going insane he decided he had more important things to think about. He passed a wheelbarrow in someone's garden which had clearly been there for some time. It was bone dry. Not a drop of water had collected inside. His mind reeled and he grabbed onto the garden fence for support as he tried to make sense of it.

Concussion ...?

That had to be it. He must have hit his head at some point and lost track of time. How much time, though, and how had he managed not to crash his car? What day was it, in fact? He looked around, taking stock of where he was. He couldn't be far away from the doctors' clinic and it ought to be open for another few hours. Even if his estimation of the hour was wrong, he still had time until the end of the day, judging by the position of the sun. He would make his way to the clinic and speak to someone. "Maybe I'm just crazy," he said with a nervous laugh. "That would solve the whole dilemma about my future."

Not wanting to compound his problems by hanging onto someone's fence while talking to himself, John forced himself to turn around and take a deep breath, his eyes shut tight against the madness outside.

Transition Recall Detective Sarah Kendra sat unmoving in her office. It was early evening and the sun was still out but fading fast. She thought it must be about 6:00 p.m. Papers and files sat in strictly ordered piles to either side of her working space, a meticulously maintained haven of orderly efficiency. The space itself consisted of the only patch of her desk which was not covered in documents or equipment, but it served its purpose. Keeping the space clear was often a fulltime job. It gave her a reason to spend time shuffling things around, making sure there was always somewhere to put things. It made her feel there was a purpose to the clutter in which she lived every day.

Today, the working space contained her elbows. Kendra sat with her head in her hands, eyes closed. Her fingers pressed against the sides of her head, hiding beneath the sleek blonde hair which she had left loose that day due to having spent last night in the office. This was not a common occurrence for the normally pristine and presentable TRD Kendra, who was highly respected, if slightly aloof. She smiled faintly as she squeezed her eyes even tighter. If only they knew her mystique was only a by-product of her lack of interest in being friendly with her colleagues. Somehow, it made people pay even more attention to her. Perhaps it gave them something to talk about in the canteen. Strange, though, that she actually didn't know any of them except for their names, which she had deliberately learned as soon as she had joined the organization.

Kendra suffered a minor sense of confusion. How long had she been here now? Ten years? Since leaving school, anyway, that much she did know ....

Shaken out of her reverie by a squeal of hinges, Kendra slowly opened her eyes. She really ought to have that door oiled before it gave her a heart attack. Raising her head, she leaned back in her swivel chair and turned to face the door. Her new Recaller was peering in and feeling guilty, by the look on her face, for disturbing Kendra. Catherine "call me Cat" Reynolds was young, only in her late teens, and decidedly deferential around Kendra. It probably didn't help that the guys in the organization referred to their new partnership as a bit of a joke, but given the vast difference in their levels of experience it wasn't so surprising. Then again, it wasn't important that Cat was inexperienced. She was easily the most talented new recruit Kendra had met, and that was precisely why she had chosen her.

Cat made her way into the room, glancing at the various piles of paperwork littering the floor. It was a look Kendra knew well, one of surprise and concern. Surprise that Kendra lived in such a mess and concern that Cat obviously didn't understand Kendra the way she thought she did. When someone came to that realization, Kendra knew it added an extra touch to her air of mystery. She didn't mind. A bit of uncertainty made for a better relationship because it gave a certain amount of control back to her. She smiled to herself as Cat finally made it across the room to the other side of the table and sat in the rarely used chair tucked behind it.

As she reached across the desk for the paper file Cat offered her, Kendra studied the young Recaller's face. She was visibly strained and wan-looking, but then she offset this impression of illness with a smile that gave Kendra's heart a jolt. It lit up her whole face and made it obvious that she was bursting to say something. Procedure and politeness, however, meant that Kendra had to be given time to read the report before being subjected to the Recaller's interpretation of its contents. Whatever it was, it was probably big. That would explain Cat's sickly pallor, at least, and meant that the report should probably be given more than a cursory glance. Cat pushed her lank, reddish-brown hair back behind her ears, her smile wavering as she waited for the TR Detective to read her report.

Kendra began to read aloud, her practiced eyes picking out the salient points of the report without having to read the headings, prefaces and general comments that made up its bulk.

"... Category 5 ... approximately 650km diameter ... meteorological with consequential cognitive and physiological readjustment ... possible background radiation increase limited to 15% ...."

She lowered the paper and locked eyes with Cat, who had been holding her breath. Letting it out, the Recaller launched into her theory, her eyes glinting with excitement as she spoke. Kendra tilted her head slightly to one side, adopting an expression of open-minded interest, her eyebrows furrowed slightly as if in thought. She had, of course, already decided exactly what the report meant and what she needed to do, but simply leaping into action and giving orders was no way to forge a partnership.

Cat had clearly felt the transition keenly as it occurred earlier that day, shortly after 5:00 p.m. Kendra reflected briefly on this as she scanned the paper again, wondering why she hadn't been aware of the transition. In so doing, she missed the first part of Cat's tale. The Recaller's impulsiveness was something they needed to work on.

"And it had been raining, like, all day, hadn't it? And the last few days. I remember that it's been terrible weather for absolutely ages ...."

Part of this was clear enough to Kendra. She could recall that there had been some bad weather, but not for a few days now, or so she thought. The transition had been near perfect, then. Sometimes the pieces didn't fit completely once they were exposed, but this time they were seamless. This one, evidently, was powerful.

"... and then, all of a sudden it just stops. Completely dry. My clothes, my car, even the umbrella I was holding. And everyone around me, *everyone*, was the same. Not a cloud in the sky, it was incredible. It's always so strange feeling one, but this one hit me hard. My brain felt like it was going mad and I actually felt pretty shaky. It was like I could feel the memories trying to adjust inside my head, like someone had stuck a spoon in there, you know, and was just stirring it around."

Cat broke off with a nervous laugh and glanced at Kendra to see if the Detective was in the mood for a light-hearted version of events. Not wanting to ruin the girl's moment, feeling that it was important for her to make the most of this, Kendra smiled back. They could discuss proper procedure and delivery at a later date. Confidence was the key for Cat now.

Reassured, Cat continued, looking away again and frowning at the nearest file as she related the tale. "Anyway, I thought I would turn around and come straight back to work. When I arrived here a couple of the other Recallers had the same sort of feeling, but they weren't as sure as I was what had happened." Cat allowed herself a shy smile. The girl clearly knew her worth. "So then I went through the computers, looked up the readings from the sensors, and it turns out the weather was good over most of the UK yesterday and today. The only areas with awful weather are up near the top of Scotland and way out to sea. You can almost draw a circle around the good weather, and according to the systems it's been like that for a few days now. *But I know it hasn't.*"

She gestured sharply with her left hand to emphasize that point, almost knocking a pile of papers over. She was clearly still trying to make her case. She hadn't had time to get used to people believing her yet. Something else to work on.

"I ran it through the simulators and the probability machines, or rather I got Brice"—she shuddered slightly—"to do it. I still don't get those things, and I didn't want anyone to have any doubt."

Another nervous laugh and a glance at Kendra. This time Kendra didn't smile back, she wanted to get to the end of this story and didn't want to encourage any more tangents. Cat cleared her throat and composed herself before adopting a more serious tone.

"The results make it clear, Detective. It was a major transition covering almost the entire United Kingdom, affecting every person within the diameter. Aside from the simultaneous weather change, the memories of every single person affected have been altered to the extent that they don't remember any bad weather for a few days. Most disturbing of all is the clothing. People were out in rain and wind, then suddenly had skirts and summer tops on with their umbrellas stashed at home. It's so sophisticated it's like it was carefully planned for every individual, but that's got to be impossible, hasn't it? We wouldn't even have noticed if it wasn't for me and the others working it out."

Kendra had to concede that the magnitude of this transition was incredible. It far exceeded anything she had encountered before. Well, not for a long time, she corrected herself mentally.

"Location?" she asked, knowing it was probably a little optimistic to get a fix on something so large.

"Sorry, Detective, there's simply no way I would possibly feel where it was coming from. It was all I could do to hold on to my memories and my umbrella. A transition this size, covering the country, could have come from anywhere."

"You said that you could almost draw a circle around the affected areas," Kendra replied.

"Yes, Detective, it goes up as far as the lower end of Scotland and out to sea and into France, but it's a very crude circle and not particularly reliable."

"What is the rough central point, Recaller Reynolds?"

Cat eyed her apprehensively, obviously not keen on using such crude methods. *Perhaps she thinks I'm going to interview everyone below the M4*, Kendra thought, amused.

"Somewhere between London and Southampton is most likely, I'd say, but I don't think—"

Kendra cut her off with a raised hand and a smile. "Don't worry, Cat, we aren't going door to door. I want you to look into hospital admissions throughout that target region. Mental health admissions too. I want reports of any increased behavior disturbance resulting in people being institutionalized or people admitting themselves. You know what I mean, headaches, seizures, inexplicable sense of displacement. That kind of thing. Something of this magnitude would almost certainly have had an impact on the health of a sizeable number of people near the epicenter. Even if they don't remember anything, they might be suffering the effects. Look into that, and we will have a smaller area in which to work.

"I also want you to review the reports from the planted psychiatrists and doctors, anything out of the ordinary for the next few days. It's possible that someone suffering the effects may approach a professional."

Kendra paused, wondering whether to add in the next part. Erring on the side of caution, she gave a final instruction.

"Whatever you do, Cat, you are not to approach anyone

you find in those reports for a follow up. Not even the doctors themselves. If one of the patients is the subject, then it is entirely possible they don't know it yet. That does not make them any less dangerous. If we are to have a chance of locating the subject, they must not have any hint that we are looking for them."

Even as she gave these instructions, Kendra was conscious of their cold-blooded undertones. Viewed through Cat's eyes, they would almost certainly seem unreasonable. Despite the fact that their network was extensive and perfectly sanctioned, Cat would not be comfortable in the beginning with the steps they had to take. Kendra had gone through the same transition, as had they all. She was not blind to the moral difficulties that their job presented. She kept her thoughts entirely to herself as she watched Cat for signs of wavering resolve. Kendra's first priority, next to locating this subject, was training Cat to be the best she could be, and that meant teaching her to be careful, even ruthless, when occasion demanded it. It was now about 6:30 p.m., though, so they could resume all this tomorrow.

"Cat, leave it for now, okay? We will sort this out tomorrow when we're rested. Go home."

Cat nodded and rose, making her way to the door. Kendra saw her hesitate and turn her head slightly. She waited, wondering whether the Recaller would say what she was so sure she would say.

"Sarah? If we find the Shifter …," Cat turned to face her, trailing off as she did so. Her eyes were wider than usual, as if knowing what answer she would get if she completed the question.

Kendra kept her composure and her voice cool. This was perhaps the most important point to make and it would not do for Cat to have any doubts. Doubts, Kendra knew well, led to terrible mistakes.

"A *transition* this large," she began, deliberately using the correct terminology to contrast with Cat's colloquialism—

she wanted to make this hard truth sound like it came from a textbook—"implies a subject of remarkable, possibly uncharted, capability. Moreover, the fact that only one of our Recallers was able to detect the transition suggests sophistication beyond usual levels.

"The report suggested an increase of local background radiation of up to 15%. Now, however temporary that might be, it is still incredibly alarming. The strain placed not only on the local affected but on what we loosely regard as 'reality' during such a transition, plus the increased threat from the resulting radiation increase, is unacceptable. Should this subject continue to perform transitions similar to this, the results could be catastrophic. Once located, the threat must be neutralized. You understand that, Recaller Reynolds?"

Cat stared at the floor. She understood well enough. Perhaps she had only wanted to point out that she didn't like it much. Perhaps the poor kid would rather be on the analysis side of things than the enforcement side, but unfortunately for her the two were inextricable when dealing with a subject of this magnitude. She nodded and left the room, closing the creaky door behind her.

Kendra was left to consider tactics. Once the reports from the hospitals came in, they might need to move quickly and decisively without hesitation. She caught the reflection of her eye in the clock opposite her. She stared back at it.

Without hesitation.

CHAPTER THREE

ohn's gait was steadier now that he had accepted the idea that he probably had hit his head. Ironic that he was actually thinking hitting his head was a good thing. It was also amazing he hadn't crashed. The pavement stretched out before him, reassuringly straight and unyielding. Whatever had happened before, at least his mind was clear now. Even so, he couldn't help glancing to one side occasionally to check that his fellow pedestrians weren't secretly dripping wet, although he was doing this less frequently now that he had accepted his own explanation.

He still needed to get to the clinic. This wasn't an occasion to call his psychiatrist, especially after he had been doing so well recently. Besides, Dr. Macava only really dealt with mental conditions and emotional problems like depression. He probably wouldn't appreciate John contacting him about a bump on the head. John's fingers absently touched his mobile phone, his resolve faltering slightly. What if it wasn't a bump on the head? *No,* he thought, *you've been doing great recently. Keep it together.*

A woman in a supermarket uniform gave him a sidelong frown as she passed, making him wonder if he had been muttering aloud. *Let her look,* he thought, being sure to keep the thought inside his head.

You weren't muttering ....

John stopped. Why had that woman looked strangely at him if he hadn't been doing anything odd? He stood staring into the distance for a moment, trying to make sense of the peculiar feeling that he was missing something. The answer suddenly hit him like a slap in the face. He was still wearing his raincoat on top of a full suit. No wonder it was so hot. He hadn't changed his clothes after the storm passed like everyone else had.

Like everyone else who managed to get home and get changed within seconds?

Pushing the cynical voice aside, he reminded himself that he must have lost a bit of time through hitting his head, which was why he was still in his wet weather gear. He clawed at his oversized coat, pulling it off and savoring the cool air which hit him like a much needed dose of reality. Slinging the coat over his arm, he made his way around the corner into the car park of Stokelake Family Medical Practice. He even managed to put a spring back into his step; if he was suffering from a head injury he could easily take a few days off work. Maybe he should go mad more often.

Stokelake was a reassuringly traditional brick building. It was all on the ground floor and nestled a little way back from the road among carefully placed trees and shrubs. The impression was distinctly serene, as it was intended to be. People were meant to feel comforted simply by being inside the grounds, which looked like a pleasant haven of effortless medical expertise. The reality, of course, was somewhat different. The place was quiet today, but the atmosphere inside a doctors' office is never the alluring sense of tranquility found outside. John pushed open the glass door, frowning at the cheaply made sign which reminded people not to abuse their workers. Why would anyone abuse a doctor?

The interior was similar to all doctors' offices ever built. The wooden reception desk was at one end next to the door, with a bored looking girl sitting behind it staring at a computer as though it wasn't there. In front of her stretched a large, open-plan waiting room, wallpapered in a dull yellow which could have been there since the seventies, and filled with low, cushioned seats. At various increments between the chairs were even lower tables, piled high with out of date magazines and completed coloring books, plastic bricks which didn't fit together, and a few random newspapers. Mercifully, there were very few people in the waiting room.

Trying not to wrinkle his nose at the disinfectant-covering-something-unpleasant smell of the place, John made his way over to the receptionist, wondering exactly what he was going to say. The girl looked up, apparently startled. Her eyes darted to the clock hanging on the wall to her left as she drew her chair in and then glanced back at John. It was deftly done. He wouldn't have noticed if he hadn't already been looking at her. Looking at the clock himself he was mildly surprised to see it was coming up on 6:30 p.m. It had taken him longer to walk down here than he had thought.

"Er … hi. I was wondering whether ... you are still open, aren't you?" The idiocy of what he had just said hit him a millisecond later. Of course they were open, there were people in there.

The receptionist regarded him with an unreadable expression. She was clearly practiced at keeping a straight face, otherwise John felt sure she would have sneered as she spoke. "We're open until seven on weeknights. Do you have an appointment?"

"No. It's just that I'd really like to see someone tonight. You see, I hit my head ...," he trailed off. She had stopped listening at the word 'no' and turned to her computer. She tapped on the keyboard, her face remaining expressionless. Clearly she didn't care one iota what was wrong with him. And why should she, he reasoned. Some bloke comes wandering in at the end of the day, asking stupid questions. Why should she care even if his head was falling off? From her manner, he almost felt she wouldn't mind if his head exploded where he stood.

She turned back to him, her eyes surveying the room behind him with some distaste. "We don't usually let patients see the doctors without appointments," she began, looking at him sternly as though this was an extremely important lesson for him to learn, "but Dr. Evans will be free in a few minutes. His 6:40 has cancelled." Her eyes narrowed as she spoke the word 'cancelled', as though the perpetrator of this particularly heinous crime would do well to stay out of her way. "You can see the doctor once he is free, Mr. ...?"

"Davis."

"Alright then, Mr. Davis, please have a seat and the doctor will be with you shortly." She typed a few words into her computer, pressed the return key with a flourish, and settled back in her seat as John turned to face the waiting room.

He had never liked waiting rooms. His psychiatrist's waiting room was a world apart from this, furnished with old leather sofas and antique looking tables, a smell of new leather pervading the air. There was almost never anyone there, as far back as John could remember, though he hadn't started seeing Dr. Macava until a couple of years ago. Back when his fear of the future and perceived lack of control over it had begun to unravel his confidence in his ability to get on with life.

A preoccupation with the future, Dr. Macava had explained, can cause you to lose focus on the present. When you lose focus you begin to lose control, so it is the very act of worrying about the future that makes it more difficult to cope with the present. You end up in a cycle where the more you worry, the more you seem to have to worry about.

Whether or not any of that was true was not the point. Having someone to talk to and explain his feelings had been the real help as far as John was concerned. Dr. Macava had become a confidante, and despite the fact that John no longer needed to see the doctor professionally, he still took comfort from having that resource in his life. He almost never used it these days because Macava was a psychiatrist and decidedly expensive, as were all private health care professionals, and John no longer got free sessions. Macava was a private patient kind of doctor, except for when he did occasional National Health sessions at the hospital on the outskirts of the city. John respected the man a lot for that. Macava took immense pride in doing as much work as possible for the NHS and even did pro bono sessions on the side, which John suspected he wasn't supposed to. Macava was the sort of man who wanted to help people who needed it, and he was rich enough not to care about the loss of revenue.

John took a seat opposite an elderly lady. Her feet were encased in boots lined in a thick, fluffy material. John supposed it could have been real fur, since the lady was probably old enough to have bought those things decades ago. She looked healthy to John, but his mind was racing, performing that strangely entertaining process of trying to work out what might be wrong with her. She wasn't sniffing or coughing and her skin looked okay, but she was shifting her weight a bit too often as though uncomfortable. Suddenly realizing that she might be uncomfortable because he was staring at her, he looked elsewhere. It probably wasn't the best way to entertain himself after all.

A mechanical female voice followed a cheerful chime from an overhead display. "Mr. Davis. Dr. Evans, please."

John rose, smiled awkwardly at the elderly woman, hoping she hadn't been too unnerved by his scrutiny, and made his way down the short corridor at the end of the waiting room toward the door marked 'Dr. Evans'.

Dr. Evans was a short man who appeared to be in his forties. He had a pleasant smile and an approachable manner, and John decided he liked him as he walked in and sat opposite him. "So, Mr. Davis, quite a last minute appointment according to my note. What can I do for you?"

The doctor leaned his elbows on the desk before him, fixing his face in a mask of sincerity. John decided not to come out with it right away. Somehow being in that office opposite the doctor made it suddenly seem all the more real.

"Well, I was driving home today and I looked out of the window and it was sunny. It was raining before, but then it was sunny, really quickly. It ... that is, I sort of ... I think ...," John trailed off, suddenly confused and lacking in conviction. "The thing is it was like I had lost time. I think maybe I hit my head as I was going along. I think I might have hit it pretty hard, maybe I got a concussion."

The doctor stared at him over the top of his clasped hands. He was obviously puzzled. "So you think you hit your head while you were driving?"

"I think so."

"You were lucky not to crash."

John laughed nervously. The moment stretched and John couldn't think of anything else to say.

"Mr. Davis, a concussion can bring on confusion and some memory loss, but ordinarily it would have to be a very heavy blow to the head to cause that. I don't mean to make light, but had you suffered such a blow I suspect you would not have been able to continue driving. For that reason, I doubt you have a concussion, which is a good thing, of course. A concussion can be a very nasty business indeed."

John stared at the floor, feeling foolish. What had he been expecting?

"Mr. Davis, what do you do for a living, if you don't mind my asking?"

John looked up. Where was this leading? "Oh, er, I'm a lawyer." It still felt strange to him, saying that aloud. He had felt much safer saying 'trainee'. He definitely wasn't feeling particularly mature or adult right now.

"And are things stressful at work?"

Ah, the point emerges. John was with him now, and perhaps he was right. He nodded, averting his gaze and feeling even worse now that the probable truth had hit him.

"Well, Mr. Davis," the doctor said quietly, leaning forward

and smiling in a sympathetic manner, "perhaps you just need some time off. This sounds very much to me like a case of an overworked young man who could do with a bit of relaxation. What do you think? I can have a note filled out for you. It would all be above board. You needn't feel honor bound to go to work if it is affecting your health."

John summoned a smile from somewhere, cast it in the doctor's direction, and muttered his acquiescence. He was not at all happy with this explanation. It was stress or an emotional problem, just like his anxiety. It had probably been brought on by his earlier brooding about his prospects at Macleod, Gunn & Hensford LLP. What had Dr. Macava specifically told him not to do? Exactly that. And now here he was, being told he had a stress problem by a kindly doctor who thought he was overworked. It was his own stupid fault. He should probably speak to Macava.

The doctor was studying him, a sympathetic and concerned look on his face. Apparently taking John's silence for embarrassment—which it was—the doctor began scribbling a note. John could hear the pen moving as he scrutinized his shoes, feeling wretched. He looked up as the doctor was finishing the note for him, a smile on his face which was the smile of a person who has just done something altruistic. He passed the note over and whispered conspiratorially that if John needed a few more days, he only had to come back and let him know. John was genuinely glad to take the note. It was a very nice gesture on Dr. Evans's part and he intended to make a point of seeing him again whenever he needed a doctor. Of course, that would mean speaking to the unnamed receptionist again, but he could probably cope with that.

John left the surgery feeling happier but disappointed in himself. He needed to talk to Macava now and get his head straight. As he fished his phone out of his coat pocket, he wondered if the psychiatrist would mind being bothered at home at this hour.

The firelight was beginning to sting her eyes. She could feel liquid collecting in the corners as she stared into the flames. Under normal circumstances, Kendra would never have allowed tears to form, but she was lost in memories at this moment. She had sat immobile for what felt like an age, hardly aware of her surroundings until the heat from the fire became too much to bear. Blinking, she tried to pry her thoughts out of the past and back to reality. How long had she been sitting alone in her front room by the fire? Rarely did she allow herself time to reflect on the past, but now that she had started, it felt as if she couldn't stop.

Something about that conversation with Reynolds earlier had caused it. The girl's willingness and eagerness had been like a glimpse into her personal history that was both welcome and painful. Had she ever been so eager? Perhaps. She had trained hard and tried to come up with theories that others had missed. She had quickly made a name for herself and she knew she had gained respect for her easy assimilation of information and ability to grasp the more outlandish concepts that went with the job. But was any of that enthusiasm genuine?

Some of it was, at least. Some was born out of a desire to succeed in that field, or at least to seem to succeed. What she could not deny was the work she had put in, the hours of graft and toil to make a name for herself as the best in the department. The only thing in question was her motive, and where there is ulterior motive there is room for confusion. Too often the lines are blurred, she reflected. One path merges into another for so long that you forget which one you were supposed to be following when they finally diverge. The hardest question of all, when you reach the fork, is which way do you choose when all you really want is to go back?

"No," she muttered, still staring into the flames behind the grate, "not back." She was here again, just like before.

So similar, but so vastly different. The old motives, the old causes, had long since fallen away. Now, all that remained was the job. The life she had chosen for herself, for whatever reason, was hers to live still.

Kendra looked down at the crumpled paper in her hand, her glazed eyes re-reading the same section she had stared at so often over the last few hours. '… Category 5 ... approximately 650km diameter ….'

It no longer mattered how she had gotten here. She was in a unique position to prevent the catastrophe that Recaller Reynolds had no idea could be coming. It was her duty, and she would be letting more than just herself down if she flinched again. She could feel somewhere inside that the situation required the ultimate response, just as she had said to Reynolds.

The TR Detective turned her unseeing gaze back to the fire, letting her thoughts join the swirling flames. She steeled herself, breathing slowly in through her nose. The cold knot in her stomach relaxed. If this was what needed to be done, then it had to be done. She would devote herself to it utterly as she always had, and she would be the one in the end to resolve the situation. This time there was no question; the subject was too dangerous to deal with in any other way.

But when was there ever a question?

Kendra closed her eyes, her jaw set. A muscle twitched in her cheek. No question.

———

"Hello, John. It's been a while. How are you?"

Dr. Macava's voice was genuinely warm. It was a voice John knew well and it never failed to cheer him up. The doctor was an older man, probably in his seventies, John thought, and his voice had that resonating quality that older people's voices often had, like an old Shakespearean actor doing a heartfelt monologue. Tonight, at least, he sounded happy to hear from John.

37

"Hi, Nicholas. Yeah, I'm fine. I just needed to talk to you if that's alright? I know it's quite late."

"Not at all, my boy, not at all. I've told you before you can call at any time, and if you happen to take me at my word when I happen to be watching *Absolutely Come Dancing,* I can hardly blame you for that, can I?" The doctor laughed lightly.

John relaxed. Whether or not he actually was watching the dancing show was neither here nor there if he was willing to talk for a while.

"So, what's on your mind, John?"

"Well, I just went to see a GP about what I thought was a head injury."

Macava gasped. "Dear God. Are you alright?"

John waved the concern away, quite forgetting that he was on the phone. "Fine, I'm fine. That's actually part of the problem, believe it or not. The doctor said I hadn't hit my head at all and that I was probably stressed at work. He even offered to write me a note so I could get a few days of rest."

"Well, John, I don't think that's ever a bad idea, but I have to say I am a little concerned that you thought you had a head injury when you didn't. Is that not a little strange, even if you are stressed?"

"That's kind of why I called you, Nicholas," John said dryly, thinking that Macava was being deliberately obtuse.

"Yes indeed. Indeed." The doctor sounded distracted. "Listen, John, I don't think I entirely follow you. It might be a little too much dancing on the brain, but would you mind starting somewhere nearer the beginning to help an old man keep up?"

John hesitated. He didn't want to leap in with the full story as he was still a little unsure of it himself. He didn't want to give Macava too much cause for concern. "Well, I was driving home earlier today and I sort of lost some time. It was like I came around from being knocked out but without noticing I'd been knocked out, and it seemed like I had lost a couple of minutes. I don't know for sure, but it was like I had been hit on the head and woke up a few minutes later. So I went down to the doctor to get checked out, but there was nothing wrong. He said I was probably stressed."

The psychiatrist was silent for a moment before replying in a low, measured voice that sounded a little out of character. "You lost time. I'm still not sure I follow you. Tell me exactly what happened."

John's blood ran cold. The doctor had rarely sounded so serious. Part of his success was that he was always able to take his patients' stories in his stride and deal with them without giving his true thoughts away. John knew how psychiatrists like Macava worked, and this wasn't how they tended to talk to patients. Keeping his voice as causal and unconcerned as he could under the circumstances, he started again.

"It was like I had fallen asleep at the wheel and missed things. I don't know how much time it was, but the weather had changed when I came to." John broke off, terrifying thoughts wheeling through his fevered imagination. What if Macava thought this sounded more like a condition brought on by something much more sinister, like a tumor or a stroke? He could feel himself beginning to sweat.

"The weather had changed. Lost time." The doctor sounded as though he was writing the words down, his voice low and barely audible. "Listen, John, I have a few theories about this, but I have to say I agree with the GP. You were probably stressed out at work. Tell me, have you been doing what I said and keeping your thoughts in the here and now? You haven't been tormenting yourself with thoughts of the future and worrying yourself to death?"

Now that Macava was warming to his subject, some of his old character was coming back into his voice. John did not believe that Macava thought it was stress—that much was obvious from the way he had first reacted—but it was not like him to lie or deflect the subject.

"Well, now that you mention it, I have been catching myself

thinking about those kinds of things," John began truthfully, "but not much. Certainly not as much as before. I thought I was doing pretty well until this, to be honest."

"Hmm, well maybe you should come in and see me. I'm at the hospital tomorrow afternoon for some NHS work and I can easily slot you in afterwards. Would that be alright, John? We can really get to grips with this then. I do think it's a psychological effect, almost certainly brought on by or associated with the trouble you have had recently. It is perfectly natural that you'd need a bit of help every now and then following our last sessions. The mind doesn't just suddenly heal, you know. It has to be nurtured and conditioned, and you and I can help yours get back into shape. Alright, John?"

The doctor's voice had taken on its usual soothing qualities again and John felt himself relaxing at the sound of it. Pushing away his paranoid thoughts about brain tumors, he agreed to drop in and see the doctor about six o'clock tomorrow. As Macava hung up the phone, John wondered whether the psychiatrist was just making an effort to seem unconcerned. John's fears began to nag again. What kind of condition might the doctor be thinking about that would drive him to make light of it so as not to frighten John? *But wait,* he cautioned himself, *Macava is a mind and emotion kind of doctor. He doesn't deal with physical maladies, so he won't be thinking about things like that. Whatever it is can't be life threatening. He is probably just concerned that you've actually gone mad on his watch.*

John shoved his phone back in his pocket and headed back to where he had abandoned the car. "If I'm crazy," he muttered, "I'm suing that shrink."

CHAPTER FOUR

The world seemed lighter than before. The blank nothing into which John was staring suddenly appeared a shade of brown rather than black. He could feel warmth on his face. Slowly opening his eyes, he turned his head away from the window's glare. He remembered leaving the curtains open last night, hoping that the sun would wake him up reasonably early. It hadn't.

John rolled over in his bed toward the darker side of the room, thinking suddenly of a vampire as he squirmed away from the beams of light happily streaming through the window. He reached out for the clock perched precariously on the box that served as a nightstand, casting a frown at it as he shifted onto his back, holding it above his head. As the numbers and hands came into focus, his memories of last night suddenly made no sense.

9:30 a.m.

A jolt of cold panic coursed through his body. He threw off his blankets and sat up, blocking out the protest of his skin as he rudely thrust it into the morning chill. Why hadn't he set his alarm? How come he had merrily sauntered into his room and left the curtains open thinking the sun would get him up in good time when it was a *work* day? As he feverishly groped for his work clothes hanging on the bedroom door he suddenly remembered that he had a sick note and had decided not to go in today.

"Ahhhhhh."

He grinned at himself in the mirror. He wasn't well. The doctor had said so. Whether or not it was strictly true, he could use that note he had been given. He would have laughed if his legs hadn't felt so cold.

Kicking unceremoniously at his trousers which had almost made it onto his legs, he flopped back onto the bed. Now he remembered why he had wanted the sun to wake him. It was still early enough to call work and explain, but he hadn't had to get up at the normal time. Thinking about it, he actually felt pretty good this morning, so maybe the extra rest had worked. A voice in his head tried to remind him that his psychiatrist had not sounded overly happy about his mental state, but he shoved those thoughts back down. He had already decided to enjoy his day off as much as possible while trying not to think about the reason for it.

John slid off the bed and made his way into the living room where he had left his phone. The unholy chill he had felt in the air on first waking had disappeared. The air was cool, but he was getting used to it, and it felt strangely liberating to be wandering around the flat at 9:30 in the morning in nothing but his boxers when he knew he ought to be at work. He smiled to himself as he picked up the mobile and wandered over to the socket by the sofa where his charger was permanently plugged in. Slumping down on the old sofa, he found the number for work and called it, carelessly shoving the charger cable into the phone.

"Er, hello," the voice on the end of the phone stammered. "Good, erm, good morning. Macleod, Gunn & Hensford."

John chuckled. Bad luck for Jenna to have been passing reception when he called. Apparently she wasn't used to doing reception. He wondered where the usual receptionist was.

"Hi, it's John. Is that Jenna?"

"Oh, hey, John. Yep, it's me. God, I am so rubbish at

reception!" Jenna laughed somewhat breathlessly. She was obviously glad she hadn't screwed up the simple greeting for anyone important. "So how come you aren't here?"

John was taken aback. Jenna worked in another department. He was surprised she had noticed his absence. He wondered if he would have noticed if she wasn't there. Probably not, he thought, putting it down to another character flaw. He made a mental note to take more notice of his colleagues.

"I sort of hit my head yesterday on my way home and the doctor said I should take a couple of days off. Kind of a concussion. Could you tell Mr. Grady I won't be in today and maybe tomorrow? I don't think there is anything that needs to be looked after right away. It can all probably wait until I get back. And tell him that I won't get a chance to look at his stuff before he goes away, but I can do that as I go along. I've done it before, after all." John smirked, imagining the look on Grady's face when Jenna relayed that particular part of the message. It was true, though. His training had been more or less a 'sink or swim' operation and he had been covering Grady's files on and off for the better part of two years now.

"Sounds pretty serious, you sure you're okay?" Jenna sounded genuinely concerned.

"Don't worry about it, Jen. I've got a crumby old sofa to sit on, some DVDs, a skanky old flat to watch them in, and a battered old car to go and get more in, so I'll be fine." He tried to say it light-heartedly. After all, there wasn't really anything wrong with him other than stress and emotional stuff, and he was going to see Dr. Macava about it anyway. Just as he said it, however, he knew he had utterly failed to sound convincing. His honest feelings about his awful flat were too heartfelt to fake. As he glanced around at the walls he felt his mood sink a little. When was he going to improve this dump? A start would be to move the various piles of clothes which still sat in heaps about the place, along with a few empty beer cans from who knew when.

"You really don't like it there, do you?" Jenna's voice was

full of pity. He sighed inwardly. He hadn't meant to sound self-absorbed and after sympathy. Nothing was going right at all.

"It's not so bad, to be honest." John paused, thinking about what he had just said. "Hey, did I call you Jen just now? Sorry about that, it just sort of slipped out."

Jenna laughed softly. "I wondered if you'd noticed. I guess it's the head injury, huh?"

John chuckled. "Yeah, I guess. Anyway, I'd better be going before I do any more damage. See you in a few days, okay?"

"Sure. See you. And John? Now you're qualified you can get a better flat. It'll be okay. Hope you feel better soon. Bye."

He hung up and tossed the phone on the sofa, reflecting on what Jenna had said. Maybe she was right and he just needed an opportunity to tie Grady down to a meeting and ask for a higher salary. Something, at least. He rubbed at his forehead, trying to massage away the muggy feeling that had come over him. His head felt too heavy and it was aching. Closing his eyes, he gradually became aware of the coldness of the material under his bare legs. Hadn't he just been thinking how warm it was in the flat? Come to think of it, his back was cold too. His eyes snapped open.

What the hell ...?

Something was definitely wrong here. The lounge looked the same, except the door to the kitchen looked a little cleaner.

Kitchen. Door.

There was no door to the kitchen. Or rather, there hadn't been before. Yet there it was in all its glory, a wall with a wooden door standing open, a wedge holding it back as though it had always been there. Through the open door he could see the kitchen beyond, clean and orderly, as if he had just had an entirely new kitchen built onto the living room.

John launched himself off the sofa, colliding with the coffee table in his haste. Cursing vehemently, he picked himself up, looking around the floor for any more unseen obstacles. He moved slowly backward into the corner of the room, which was distinctly longer than it ought to be. The backs of his legs touched the TV stand which contained his DVD player and Sony Playstation. That at least was where it was supposed to be. He reached out his hand to touch the TV behind him, just to make sure, snapping his head around to stare at its vastly extended screen as his fingers failed to reach the far edge. He couldn't tear his eyes away from it. He clamped them shut instead, feeling his heartbeat racing wildly as he tried to rationalize what he had seen.

His mind was blank as he stood in the corner, breathing too heavily, his hand clutching the television while he forced himself to open his eyes and survey the subtly altered room. He could hear the rasping sound of his breath as though it came from a vast distance, as utterly unconnected to him as this room felt. His thoughts were a jumble as he tried desperately to remember whether this was how it had always been or, if not, how long it had been like this. Part of him felt this was how he had bought the place and that his reasonable salary was more than capable of supporting large, flat-screen televisions, leather sofas, and fully separate kitchens with large worktop surfaces and no coffee stains.

The dominant part of him screamed that it wasn't true, it couldn't be true. His salary was abysmal, he had just that minute been thinking about it, telling himself to speak to someone about it. His flat was a disgraceful hovel. He had just been talking about it on the phone, sugar coating it so people wouldn't think it was so bad. He closed his eyes, willing himself to be rational. The fact was that his psychiatrist had told him he was suffering emotionally and that what he was suffering could account for yesterday's blackout, the one that could have killed him. He was under a lot of strain, and to be perfectly honest he couldn't exactly recall why he had felt the flat was so bad before. Or even why he thought it was so different now.

As he relaxed, the idea that this was real took hold. Rationality washed over him like a refreshing wave, gently pressing him to accept what he could see. After all, it was probably just leftover emotional baggage that had made the world seem bleaker. When he came to that conclusion, he was suddenly able to accept reality for what it was. The strange fog of uncertainty lifted from his mind. He knew that this was new to him, but he reasoned that he was finally seeing it without the veil that had colored all his previous thoughts about the place. He must have been depressed, very depressed, and now he was okay, so everything looked fine.

A doubt nagged at him, that same subconscious voice he had suppressed earlier. *You were stressed, yes, but you weren't depressed. No one mentioned depression ... and none of that makes any sense.*

It was true, he had to admit. His explanation didn't quite fit because he hadn't been depressed about anything. He had actually been pretty happy. As Dr. Macava had said, he was doing really well, hence his surprise at hearing from John yesterday. John pushed the nagging doubts aside and decided instead to simply make a note of his thoughts and feelings. He would talk to Macava about them later on. It wasn't his job to diagnose himself, it was his job to enjoy his free sick day. Getting it all on paper and then retiring with some DVDs ought to do it.

"**D**etective? Another one just happened."

Kendra looked up from the computer screen as Reynolds came hurrying toward her from across the crowded room. Straightening up, she turned away from Recaller Brice, whose computer she had been looking at, and took a few paces to meet Reynolds.

Brice, clearly glad to have control of his computer back, pulled his chair in toward the desk and began tapping on the keys. Kendra was vaguely aware that the Recaller couldn't possibly be typing anything of significance that quickly. It was too obviously a cover for eavesdropping, but she didn't care. Brice was one of the house-bound Recallers who rarely, if ever, got actively involved in anything. A late recruit in his forties, he was very good with machines and readouts, but he wasn't so hot on strategy, contact, combat, or anything that really mattered. In fact, he wasn't much of a Recaller, but he was a keen, eager worker and extremely useful in the computer department, so his tendency to eavesdrop was something she could overlook. None of her subordinate TRDs made use of Brice, having a certain scorn for those with little or no actual Recall potential, so she had him to herself. In any case, the others did very little groundwork these days. If only they knew how useful Brice was, perhaps they would change their minds about him, but Kendra had no inclination to enlighten them. Among other things, Brice was a key component of her highly respected success rate and her position as senior Transition Recall Detective of the South East.

Glancing uninterestedly at Brice, Reynolds handed over a piece of paper. It was still warm.

"Location?"

"North of here, my guess is between here and London. It can't be too far, though, or we wouldn't have felt it. It wasn't a wide range transition this time, from what I can tell. The locality must have been extremely small for the vibrations to be so weak, but I know I felt it and the signs point north."

The report in Kendra's hand was virtually useless. It simply reiterated what the Recaller had said. Kendra wondered for what must have been the hundredth time why they bothered with reports at all if the Recallers were just going to blurt out all the information as soon as they got the chance. The point was discipline; the Recallers needed to learn that they had to keep a lid on these transitions. It simply would not do for other people to find out what was happening or had happened in the past, and learning not to blurt things out even within the organization helped them to avoid problems outside. Feeling that she had given Recaller Reynolds that particular lecture a few too many times, Kendra refrained from delivering it again, especially in front of all the other house-bounds and Recallers wandering about and pretending they weren't listening.

"Narrow the search accordingly. It won't be long before something shows up, and when it does, we need to be ready to move."

Kendra handed back the report as Reynolds grinned excitedly and hurried off to recheck the hospital and medical reports for the Surrey and Kent areas. The Detective wondered if they would find anything after all. If the first transition had been an accident, it might also have been an awakening. This second one may have been an experiment or a specific transition, in which case the subject was becoming aware of his or her abilities. The more aware they became, the more difficult they would be to find, and the last thing Kendra wanted was to turn this into a full-blown hunt and containment exercise. That would display an astounding lack of control over the process in the early stages and simply wasn't acceptable.

She just needed a name or a place, something specific so that she could get on with containing the subject. This episode was fast becoming high profile. She had already received calls from the North East and North West divisions, and it was only a matter of time before the other two called. It was clear to all five regional divisions that the epicenter of the last transition was somewhere within the South East. At the moment she had exclusive jurisdiction to operate, along with her two superiors who did little more than liaise and direct the more mundane aspects of the organization. This was her operation and she had to acquit herself with commendation, especially with the four other divisions watching. Whoever this subject was, they were exceedingly strong. If she missed the chance to catch them early on then she might find herself unable to do so at all, which would at best be humiliating, at worst a disaster.

She had often wondered exactly how strong the subjects could get. Was their strength limited at all? This one had managed to change the weather over an entire country and alter the perception of everyone within that country to a greater or lesser degree. The phenomenon had essentially passed unnoticed by the general population and indicated a level of power she had not come across before. For the second time in her professional career she was unsettled.

Brice was watching her, perhaps wondering what the significance of the troubled look on her face was. She tried to ignore him. "So, Detective," he said lightly, easing back in his chair and abandoning his recently reclaimed computer, "are we any closer?"

Kendra looked down at her hands, wondering how much she should tell Brice. His skills would be needed shortly, of that she was sure, but knowing when to explain and when to withhold information came down more to instinct than training.

"The search has been narrowed, Brice. Reynolds feels that we are looking around the Surrey area or maybe Kent. Somewhere north of here, but lower than London. There are still a lot of medical reports to come in, but we can at least focus on the more likely places now."

She turned to face Brice, perching herself on the desk beside him and adopting a look of concentration as though she was oblivious to the signals of trust and confidence she was giving off. Brice pulled his chair closer, obviously happy to be included and eager to help out. Kendra almost felt guilty about the ruthless manipulation of the man's ego, but she cast the troublesome sentiment aside before it took hold.

"What we need ideally," she said in an undertone as though trying to keep the conversation between the two of them, "is some detailed background radiation data to corroborate Reynolds's assessment. If this subject is found, we will need something concrete to justify what action we take."

She paused meaningfully and looked hard at Brice. She knew very well that the action they would need to take was serious and decisive, and it would need justification. Retrospective justification was fine, as long as the evidence was there. The civilian police would find a way to explain the event, there was no chance of the organization being implicated, but the internal policies had to be met regardless. When the cases were reviewed at the higher levels, the use of force would be scrutinized. Should something be deemed excessive or unwarranted, then the remit of the organization might be called into question. This was something they could not afford. Autonomy was everything, and accountability was the key to Kendra's autonomy.

Brice's eyes brightened at the prospect of data gathering, his delight something Kendra would never understand. "If the sweeper teams report directly to me, I can tabulate the data immediately. I can narrow the location a bit more and run it through to see if the danger levels have risen ...." Brice trailed off, looking at Kendra. He knew she understood what he would be doing. Her demeanor simply said 'do it.'

"I want you to use any data you can find floating around in public records and get as much as you can to indicate the levels in the past ...." This time it was Kendra who trailed off. Brice was nodding laconically. They had been through this before. Kendra smiled. It was professionally expedient to be on good terms with her support staff, but she was beginning to genuinely like Brice. Despite his sycophantic demeanor, he was good at his job, and she was glad she had invested enough time in him to make him eager to help.

"Thank you, Recaller Brice," she said sincerely as she slid off the desk. With a final glance and a quick smile she headed back to her office. She had to call the civilian sweeper teams and get them to bypass normal procedure, go straight to the new location, and report directly to Brice. She could not afford any delays or incorrect tabulation with this, and she trusted no one on the sweeper teams, having never met them. It was risky having the teams bypass their director and make direct contact with the organization, but she felt that time was short. She needed the readouts quickly, and bending some rules was the best way to get them.

Closing the office door, she collapsed into her chair,

propping her feet on her working space among the piles of paperwork which she had long since forgotten following the start of this case. She pulled her phone from the inner pocket of her jacket and began to make the necessary calls, trying to ignore the growing certainty that this case was like none she had dealt with before. She hoped she had the strength to see it through. Her eyes fell on her gun, lying on its side partially concealed by its holster. It stared impassively back at her, mocking her faltering resolve.

Her gaze hardened. If it came to such measures, this subject wouldn't have a second chance. She would make sure of it.

FIVE

CHAPTER

John's notes sounded ridiculous. When he read them back, they made no sense. How was he supposed to explain this to Macava if he couldn't get it right on paper? The trouble was that he couldn't quite recall the certainty he had felt earlier.

"I give up," he declared to the empty room, throwing the pen down and lying back on the leather sofa. The chill of the material hit his neck, reinforcing his utter certainty that it hadn't been leather before. How profound must his mental problems be if he couldn't remember his own sofa? He had a vague recollection of a tatty old thing made of some dull material, but he couldn't quite reconcile it with the piece of furniture under him.

He lay on his back and stared up at the ceiling, one hand stretched out across the seat and the other resting on his stomach. He could vaguely feel his ribs, which reminded him of two things. One, he wasn't dressed yet and it was nearly ten o'clock in the morning. Two, he was pretty hungry. It was weird, being off work. He felt he ought to be doing something or making use of the time he had been given today. His thoughts turned to food. Chris wasn't working on Thursdays or Fridays anymore and normally slept until some insane hour of the afternoon. He wouldn't be awake right now, but he might agree to come out for breakfast somewhere if John woke him up.

John wandered back into his bedroom and pulled on some jeans and a tattered T-shirt. He had a mental image of his mother telling him he ought to get some decent clothes now that he was a lawyer, and another of him agreeing while knowing full well that he would resist buying new clothes until the old ones actually fell to bits on him. Clothes shopping was definitely not his strong point. Something about the process struck him as abhorrent.

He retrieved the phone from where he had thrown it after speaking to Jenna. When Chris answered, his voice was thick and slurred. He had clearly just woken up. "Yeah? What do you want this time of the morning?"

"Nice to talk to you too. It's ten o'clock, my chirpy friend, so I thought you'd appreciate a wake-up call."

There was a pause. "I hate you," was the belated reply.

"Yep, I know. So anyway, do you fancy breakfast? I was thinking of heading into town." John dropped his voice and adopted an enticing tone. "There's still time for a SlammieBurger breakfast ...."

Chris was awake now. He was quite the fast food fan. "Okay, sure. When are you picking me up?"

John had intended to pick him up anyway, so he could ignore the deliberately presumptive manner with which Chris had broached the issue. "I'll be there in about ten minutes."

"Fine. I'll be ready."

John hung up and shoved the phone into his jeans pocket, reflecting not for the first time how a friendship that had spanned fifteen years could actually end up resembling, to an outsider, not so much a friendship but a relationship of mutual antagonism. He chuckled as he headed out to the car, jangling his keys as he went.

"So, tell me again how it happens?"

Chris was valiantly attempting to stem the flow of liquid yolk from his fried egg, apparently determined to prevent it from contaminating his hash brown. John watched with raised eyebrows while simultaneously pondering the mechanics of yolk flow and how exactly to explain what he was going through. He didn't want to ask why the hash brown could not simply be moved. Such things were not polite to say in the face of such monumental effort. He furrowed his brow and started to explain, realizing about halfway through that the garbled explanation was not especially good.

"It's like I suddenly notice that what is there is actually there. Whereas before it was something else, only I know it's always been how it is …." He paused, rallying his thoughts for another attempt. "Or at least I think it was something else before, and the realization suddenly hits me that it's different now, but that it might always have been like it is now. Couldn't you just move the hash brown?"

Chris looked up indignantly. "It's not about moving it. It's about not having to move it because I can—" He returned his attention to the plate just in time to see that he had in fact failed to prevent the yolk from inexorably reaching its destination. He sighed, flicking an accusing look at John.

"Not my fault. Anyway, look, I was in my flat and I suddenly realized how sort of big and clean and new it was. The TV was big and the kitchen had a door."

Chris was listening now. "You realized all that. Like you hadn't known it for months?"

"Exactly. It was as though I suddenly noticed things, but at the same time remembered that they hadn't always been there. It was as though someone had reached into my head and put in memories of the past that were wrong, memories of a flat that was old and crumby."

"So you were imagining what the place would look like old and crumby. That's not so weird. I used to do that at college, with those girls who wandered about like they owned the place."

"But it wasn't that. I had the memories of the place looking like that a few seconds before. Vivid memories, as clear as the memory of walking in this place today. It was like the whole thing had changed all of a sudden and was pretending it had always been like that. *But I knew it hadn't.*"

Chris regarded him silently for a moment before picking up his plastic fork and absently prodding the burger on his plate. "Did you talk to your doctor about it?"

"Yeah, and I'm going to see him today."

"And what did he say?"

John hesitated. The fact was that he hadn't spoken to Macava about this at all. The psychiatrist had been concerned enough about the weather change problem from yesterday. There was no doubt in John's mind that the two were connected, which meant he had more serious issues than he had thought.

"I haven't told him about this one, only the one from yesterday."

Chris abandoned his burger and looked up. His eyes betrayed his concern although he kept his tone conversational. "Oh, yeah? You didn't mention yesterday."

"I was driving my car and it was raining." John paused to glance at Chris, who was frowning, obviously thinking of yesterday's sunny skies. "It was raining," he repeated, "and then all of a sudden I realized it was sunny and that it had been for a while because everything was dry. I was totally shocked and I ended up nearly crashing the car. I went to the doctor and told him I thought I'd knocked my head in the car and lost a load of time, which I thought would account for the fact that I missed the transition from raining to sunny."

Chris was staring at him. Trying not to imagine what he must be thinking, John continued. "So anyway, I explained that to the doctor and he thought I must be under a lot of stress because if I had actually hit my head, I probably would have crashed. I guess he felt that I couldn't have lost time and managed to keep driving. I called Dr. Macava after that and he told me to come in today. He said I'd been fixating on the future and that's what had probably brought this on. So now I'm thinking that this thing today was just a follow on from yesterday. All I can think is that whatever the emotional thing was that I was having trouble with, it was coloring my perceptions. When I stopped moping around and over-thinking every tiny thing, nothing was as bad as I'd been thinking it was."

Chris pursed his lips and looked away, mulling the whole thing over. Finally he said, "That doesn't account for the fact that it didn't rain yesterday. What did the doctor say about you thinking it had?"

John stared at him, confusion warring with panic in his brain. "What do you mean, it didn't rain yesterday? Of course it did. I went to work with my raincoat and everything. I missed the rain stopping, that's all. Don't mess with me, okay? It's really not funny."

Chris snorted. Grabbing his cup of tea, he leaned back in his chair and grinned. "Ah, you had to go and spoil it, didn't you? You were doing pretty well up to then. I almost believed you had proper nut problems." He shook his head and laughed.

John's head was spinning. Neither doctor had said it hadn't rained at all yesterday. Why would they have left him thinking it had? He ran through the conversations in his mind, realizing he hadn't told Macava he had thought it was raining, and that Evans hadn't really addressed anything he had said at all. Evans had been sure he was confused and stressed, but hadn't really listened to the story he had told. Could it really be that it hadn't actually rained?

Chris's grin had faded and he was looking intently at John. "Wait, are you ... were you being serious?"

John ignored him, staring down at his long since abandoned fried egg. It had congealed and looked decidedly unappetizing. "I need a second opinion, Chris, no offence or anything."

He pulled his phone from his pocket as Chris raised his eyebrows in surprise. Calling work, he asked to speak to Jenna.

SHIFTER

STEVEN D. JACKSON

"Hi, John, feeling any better?"

"Hey. Look, I need to ask you something, okay? You remember the other day, when I met you outside?"

"Yeah?"

"Well ...." He hesitated, trying to think of a way to get the answer without alerting everyone at work to the fact he thought he was losing his mind. "What do you call that crazy jellyfish umbrella you've got?"

It was a long shot, but definitely worth a try. John waited for her response. Chris was giggling into his tea, making noises that John supposed were meant to be jellyfish sounds. Waving a hand at him to shut him up, he turned his attention back to Jenna. She had been silent for a while now.

"I don't think we were talking about my umbrella, John. I think we were talking about your car, weren't we? Or was it your flat?"

"No, it was the flat, but I should probably have mentioned the car too," John replied as lightly as he could, making a huge effort to maneuver the conversation to where it needed to go. "That's pretty awful too. A blue Rover Metro that's about a million years old." That much was true. He really needed to get a new car, as he had been thinking only recently. "But I'm thinking more about the umbrella, what kind is yours?"

He wanted to scream at her that she had used it only yesterday and it shouldn't be too hard to remember, but he needed to hear it from her own lips.

"Okay, well, let me think. I haven't used it for a while, what with the weather being so good ...."

John's hand felt like it wasn't connected to him anymore. The room in which he sat seemed too big, too bright. He sat unmoving, a blank space filling his head where normally thoughts should have been dancing around. He couldn't understand it. It made no sense. He was utterly sure it had been raining, hard, for days on end. He had seen Jenna's mad umbrella only yesterday. It was the same as the flat today. It couldn't be merely perception. It felt so undeniably real.

57

The flat had changed and the weather had changed, but to everyone else it had always been as it now was.

A concept from a film he had seen once came floating back to him. The principle was that madness and sanity could switch places if madness became the majority. People who considered themselves sane would end up in padded cells, railing against the madness of the world. Of course, in that instance the person had been talking about the entire world becoming possessed by insane entities from another dimension, but the principle was similar. That was obviously how crazy people saw the world, that it was the world that had gone mad and not them. That was certainly how John felt at this moment. The only spanner in that particular theory being that the mad wouldn't actually have the presence of mind to wonder if they were mad.

Jenna had hung up and Chris was staring at him again. He smiled weakly at Chris and muttered something about being really tired and needing to go home. Rising awkwardly from his seat, John left the restaurant and stepped into the mocking sunshine outside, trying hard to keep from screaming at the madness of the world.

———————

He heard the hospital doors slam open as the trolley was shoved through them, the paramedics struggling to keep pace as it was piloted toward the Accident and Emergency operating theatre. The commotion around him was intense, people scrambling around with tubes and needles in their hands.

Half-heard commands flew over John's head as he peered out at the world from a long, dark tunnel. The echoes of his own name being repeated made their way to his ears as he tried to make sense of what was happening. The voices were insistent, demanding answers, but to questions he couldn't understand. Too many echoes and too many vibrations clouded his hearing. People in his field of vision looked like semi-formed shapes rather than solid people.

STEVEN D. JACKSON

He tried to open his mouth to speak, but something was pressing against his face. He couldn't manage to make the sounds. Nothing seemed to be working and he couldn't understand why his arms felt so heavy until he realized they were strapped to his sides. His head was similarly strapped, and as the visions grew blurrier, the noises tinnier and more distant, he began to think he was in serious trouble.

There was the sense of something warm on the top of his hand, a creeping sensation making its way up his arm. His vision darkened until he could see no more. The last sound faded out.

He woke quite suddenly. His dreams had been disturbed, unconnected, and he tried to grab at them as they faded. He felt tired, like he hadn't slept, and his head hurt as though he had a hangover. Groggily he looked around the room. It was still light outside, but heavy curtains were drawn and the only illumination in the room came from a beeping machine at his side. He wasn't cold, but a quick inspection revealed that he was wearing nothing but a hospital gown. Without thinking, and in the grip of a mild panic, he ran his hands down his body, pleased to find that none of his body parts were missing.

So he was in a hospital. He knew that the sensation he was feeling was the grogginess of a drug-induced sleep, possibly a general anesthetic. He once had his wisdom teeth taken out under general, and the feeling the next day had been much like this. He felt fine except for a pain in his left shoulder. He raised his hand to rub at it, discovering that the shoulder was wrapped in bandages.

He settled back against his pillow, trying to piece together why he was in a hospital. What had happened yesterday? Or was it still today? He couldn't tell. Slowly the pieces reassembled into a coherent chain of events. After leaving Chris at the restaurant, he had gotten behind the wheel of his car in the sunshine, feeling almost numb. The realization that his loss of time was far more serious than he had first thought had hit him hard. As far as he could tell, there were only two explanations. Either he was actually losing his grip on sanity, or the world was moving around him, reshaping itself but leaving him behind.

He remembered wondering whether that was the way the world worked. Was nothing ever as it seemed? Did everything change and move around constantly with everyone carrying on afterwards as though it had always been that way? If so, it struck him as supremely unfair that he had suddenly fallen out of kilter with it. Was he somehow being forgotten? Maybe he should just try to adapt each time.

However, during the second incident only the flat had changed. Would the world reshape itself just to give him a bigger flat? Probably not. If change was the natural way of things, then it would happen to everyone and not just him, as it had with the weather. He had contemplated these thoughts over and over on the way back home. He supposed he was lucky that he knew the roads backward or else there was no way he would have been able to concentrate.

"So how did I end up here?" Frowning, he stared into the semi-lit room. He must have crashed the car, but not at any great speed or he would be in a far worse state than he was. An ache in his shoulder as the sole result of a car crash was unlikely.

The door to the room opened and a young man in a doctor's white coat entered, carrying a clipboard. He went to the window and drew back the curtains, letting in the sunlight which appeared to be waning. The room, now that John could see it clearly, was generally white or off-white. Its minimalist furnishings included a small table with a chair and a machine to which he did not appear to be connected but which was merrily beeping away nonetheless. John had little time to contemplate his surroundings, however, as the youthful doctor approached the bed with a wide smile which reminded John of the waxworks in Madame Tussauds.

"I'm glad to see you're awake, Mr. Davis. I am happy to inform you that you are absolutely fine. Well, except for that," the doctor pointed at his bandaged shoulder, "but that's no more than a muscle sprain, really, so you can leave as soon as you're feeling okay."

"Thanks, Doctor. Do you know what happened to me?"

"Apparently you were lucky, Mr. Davis. A witness said someone came out of a concealed entrance and hit your car. You lost control and spun across the road. You were knocked out, but I think your car is okay, and you seem to be fine too." The doctor smiled again, and this time the expression looked far more genuine. John let out a relieved breath. It sounded like it had been a close call. Then again, the story didn't ring any bells in his head.

"I don't really remember it. How is the other guy?"

The doctor's smile wavered and he looked uncertain. "Oh, he wasn't brought here, maybe he drove off. I'm really not sure, Mr. Davis. Anyway, it's good to see you're okay. I'll be back in a few hours. You should probably stay here for observation, but you've got a TV up there," he gestured into the corner of the room where an old television was perched precariously on a wall bracket, "and if you need anything you can call the nurse with your call button behind you."

The doctor turned back on his way to the door, finger pointing in the air as though he had just remembered something. "Oh, we found your business card in your wallet. We thought your office would know how to contact your family, so we gave them a call. You might be getting some visitors from there soon. It's coming up to four-thirty now, though, so they need to hurry if they're coming."

John wasn't really listening. He was only vaguely aware of the doctor leaving. He was trying to recall yesterday's events.

In a flash the memory returned.

He had been driving the Metro back home, his head still full of what he had just discovered, staring out of the window, noting absently that the sun looked nice reflecting off the shiny black of the car's bodywork. His attention had snapped back to the present and he had stared stupidly at the side mirrors edged in polished black where there ought to be tired blue, not even noticing his foot on the accelerator as the car picked up speed and hurtled down the road. His thoughts were a jumble of unconnected phrases: *It can't be ... the wrong car ... my keys fit ... my car isn't black ... it's happened again ... I'm going mad ... my car can't go this fast ... I'm going too fast ... going to crash!*

He jumped with the memory of the crash. He could feel the phantom pain where his ribs and collarbone had cracked against the seatbelt as he plunged forward. He remembered the crushing feeling as the belt gave way and threw him into the windshield and the ear-splitting sound of the glass shattering as the weight of his body destroyed it; the horrifically unnatural feeling of his legs lying in a tangled mess underneath him as he sprawled across what was left of the bonnet.

He had crashed, badly, as a result of another mental episode. His car had changed from a Rover Metro into something else, something shiny and black and powerful which had leaped forward with a greater speed than he was used to, causing him to lose control. There had been no side road, no mysterious other driver, and his injuries had not been superficial.

John lay in the bed mulling the facts over, his heart beating too fast. A thin sheen of sweat was quickly covering his skin. The weather had changed after he had been caught without an umbrella. The flat had changed after he had been moaning about it on the phone. The car had changed after he had complained about it. His injuries, the circumstances of the crash, had been rewritten completely to save him from almost certain disability or even death. He fervently hoped that his car was alright, whatever it now looked like. He took a deep breath, letting it out slowly and trying to force his body to calm down.

"What if it's me," he asked the empty room, trying to inject a tone of rationality into his voice and not entirely succeeding,

STEVEN D. JACKSON

"what if the only explanation that makes any sense is that it's me?"

Could he be rewriting his life as he went along? It wasn't possible, and yet it was the only answer he had. However it was happening, whatever the reason, the fact seemed inescapable. As plain as day, the answer glared at him, and he stared back at it, unable to deny it yet utterly unable to accept what was an absolute impossibility. The only reason for these things to be happening was that he was somehow doing them for his personal benefit. *How* he was doing it he couldn't say, but the evidence supporting the argument was difficult to refute.

As he reflected on this revelation, the initial shock began to escalate into panic. A sinking feeling of dread settled into his stomach, congealing into ice as he began to realize exactly what he was considering. He stared unseeing at the room, feeling utterly alone.

CHAPTER SIX

The door of John's hospital room swung open and Jenna burst in. She was clutching a crumpled envelope. He smiled as he watched her fiddle with the door, glad to have company and for the opportunity to put aside his bleak thoughts. She hurried to his bedside, a manic look in her eyes. She was breathing heavily as though she had been running, and her makeup was smudged around the eyes. *Funny*, he thought, *she doesn't usually wear much make up. Bad day to start.* He let out a giggle, belatedly realizing that he was making it look like he wasn't entirely connected to reality. Why this tended to happen around women he would never know.

Aha, his inner voice whispered, *but perhaps now you can change that, yeah? Maybe this strange new twist to your life isn't so bad after all?*

He was suddenly reminded of countless superhero movies where the main character, upon discovering his amazing potential, decides to create an entire code of conduct which seems designed to make his life miserable. This was reality, though, and if he had the ability to rewrite his life for the better, he would damn well do it. What was morality when morality could be rewritten?

Jenna was looking at him with serious concern. Her

agitation was obvious as she looked his body up and down, as if worried he might fall apart at any second.

"Hi, Jenna. It's really nice of you to come down here to see me. Some guy came out of a side road and knocked me across the road, but it's alright. I'm okay. I guess I was pretty lucky, huh?" He smiled happily at her. It felt good to be the one in control. As far as he could tell, things could only get better from here on. The ice in his stomach had melted.

"So you're not hurt?" She looked doubtful, kept casting furtive glances down his body which made him feel uncomfortable. After all, he was covered only by a thin bed sheet and it was pretty revealing. He tried not to think about it, concerned that he might end up accidentally giving himself something to be really embarrassed about. He was glad he was sort of in shape.

"Nope, not hurt at all except for a sprained shoulder. I have no idea how you sprain a shoulder in a car accident, to be honest, but there we go. I'm actually feeling pretty good."

"Oh, thank God! Here, we all got you a get well card ...." With a breathless smile, Jenna brandished the envelope she was carrying.

He took the card, turning to the window to make use of the light. The card was nicely done, and most of the guys at work had signed it. He was touched. He had no idea any of them genuinely cared. His gaze lingered over Mr. Grady's note, wondering whether the boss had found it strange that John had been out in his car while off sick.

'Hell of a way to get your illness taken care of, John. Get well soon. Mr. Grady'

Translation, John thought, *if you were ill you wouldn't have been out, it serves you right for faking, and you had better get back here quick before I go on holiday.* It was clever. To an outsider it would simply be a funny comment on the irony of ending up in the hospital on a sick day. John scowled in spite of himself.

He closed the card and looked out the window again. He

was vaguely aware that Jenna was talking, telling him about how worried she had been and how long it had taken to get there, how she had feared the worst and how she had been concerned since his strange phone call that morning. John wasn't listening. His mind was still full of amazement at the conclusion he had come to and at his new positive outlook on it. He supposed there was a chance he was wrong, but he couldn't think of an alternative explanation. He couldn't wait to tell his friends about this. Especially Chris. He would be jealous beyond belief.

"I've definitely got to talk to Chris," he said, thinking aloud as he gazed out the window. He slowly became aware of silence in the room. Bringing his thoughts back to the here and now, he looked around at Jenna. She was staring at him, her eyes wide and a frown on her face. She looked affronted.

"What did you say?" she asked.

"Oh, sorry, Jenna, I didn't mean to interrupt you." John offered her a wan smile, trying to play on the fact he was a hospital patient despite having said he was fine. "It's just that my thoughts are all over the place at the moment."

She looked slightly mollified, but not much. Her expression softened a little.

"I was just thinking I need to tell my friends about this, especially my mate Chris. He'll be so jealous!"

"Jealous that you got in a car accident?"

"No, no, jealous that ...," he trailed off. There were levels of crazy stuff he wasn't prepared to discuss with certain people, and he barely knew Jenna, after all.

Jenna regarded him coldly. He had obviously failed to placate her. In fact, it looked like he had made things far worse. Her eyes had narrowed and she somehow looked dangerous. John stared at her as the moment lengthened, wondering exactly what he could say. The silence was broken by the doctor re-entering the room with his clipboard. He had his head down and was talking before he even got into the room.

"So, Mr. Davis, the word is that you can go. There's

absolutely no need for you to be here anymore. After all, there isn't anything all that wrong with—." The doctor stopped halfway through the sentence, glancing from his patient to the dark-haired girl sitting across from him. He moved forward carefully, as if sensing something wasn't quite right.

"Madam, if you wouldn't mind, I would like a moment with Mr. Davis alone, please."

Jenna stiffened and stood up, her eyes on the floor. She had fallen back into her submissive, quiet demeanor again, and she left the room without a sound or a backward glance. The doctor turned back to John. "What was that about?"

"I kind of screwed up by not listening when she was talking, I think."

The doctor threw back his head and laughed, startling John. "Ah, yep, I know what you mean. Bad move, mate, bad move." Apparently, he had forgotten his professional bedside manner and was chuckling away to himself as he flipped through the notes on his clipboard. "Anyway, you can go now, if you like." He paused, his professional manner resurfacing as he looked at his notes. "Although, if you don't mind, we'd like to keep you here until tomorrow morning."

"Okay, great, thanks. Do you know if my car is okay?"

The doctor frowned. "Yeah, I think it's alright. You didn't need to be cut out of it or anything." He looked through some more notes. "Oh, wait, here we go. Yep, your car is here, actually. Someone must have brought it over for you. You can get your keys from reception."

This struck John as odd. Who would have moved his car, and why didn't the police have it? Unless of course he had done this for himself, written it in to assist him. It could be a rational explanation, given how rationality had changed so dramatically in the last few minutes.

"Oh, there is something else, Mr. Davis." The doctor finally let the papers on the clipboard fall back into place. "One of the local private psychiatrists does a turn here at the hospital every now and then, a Doctor Macava. He says you had an appointment with him today which you missed or were going to miss. He's here now and has asked to see you, if you feel well enough. Actually, I think he was the one who got you this room, so I reckon it's worth seeing him. Friends in high places, mate." The doctor winked and left the room.

John smiled. It would be good to see Macava again, although he didn't in all honesty know what he was going to tell him now.

When Dr. Nicholas Macava entered John's room, he was wearing everyday clothes. He smiled a greeting. John wondered whether consultant psychiatrist types wore white medical coats at all. He had yet to see Macava in one. Then again, he had never seen him on his NHS days, so he hadn't been sure what to expect. A woolen sweater over an open shirt and plain trousers were the flavor of the day. John was the sort of person who wore jeans pretty much at all times when he wasn't in his work suit, and he had no idea what to call the trousers favored by the older generation. All he knew was that the Americans called them slacks.

He returned Macava's smile. He knew very well that Macava should have charged him an awful lot more than he had done in the past, and that the kind of consultancy service he was happy to offer John was not something he offered to all his patients. John considered himself very fortunate to be one of those people who liked his doctor and who treated him more as a friend than a shrink.

"Hey, Nicholas, I was just thinking of leaving. That doctor who looks about my age said I could go if I wanted, although they'd like me to stay."

Macava frowned, but John knew him well enough to detect the slyness in his eyes. The frown was clearly not a mark of genuine disapproval. "Now, John, you mustn't be prejudiced against the younger professional," he began piously. "They went through the same training as everyone else ... they just haven't killed enough people yet to take the job seriously." Macava chuckled. "After all, you must have clients who

STEVEN D. JACKSON

suspect you of not knowing what you're doing. Being so obscenely young and all that."

John laughed and nodded. It was true. He once even had a client remark to his receptionist that he didn't appreciate being 'passed on to a mere boy.' The professional relationship had soured somewhat after that, with the man managing to find fault with everything John did, to the point that his very name was anathema to John. It was a common joke in the office.

"So you didn't quite manage to miss our appointment after all. It's about half past five, so if you want to tell me what's happened, I'm happy to hear it."

John really didn't want to talk about it now. It had been a long, complicated day and he wanted to be alone for a while. He started to tell Macava that he didn't feel like talking when the psychiatrist interrupted him.

"John, I think I need to insist. What you said yesterday needs to be discussed." His tone brooked no argument, and John resigned himself to telling the tale. He started with the weather, moved on to the flat, and then finally the car and his injuries. Macava listened in silence, sitting in the chair by the table, his head turned away from John. His odd posture made John nervous. This was not the usual way in which a psychiatrist discussed things with his patients.

When John finished speaking Macava turned his head, still not facing John directly. "But I know for a fact that you were brought in here with no more than a shoulder strain. I asked them to bring you into this room. I wouldn't have done so if you'd had more serious injuries, would I?"

"No, but that's just it. It's different now, the past is different. It's like a train that's been diverted down another track, but when you look back, the track you've been on all the time is different to how you remember it."

Macava closed his eyes and nodded. He looked as though he had made up his mind about something. John waited for his diagnosis in anxious silence as the moment lengthened.

"Listen, John. I think I know what this is, but I don't want you to worry about it, okay? I need to go make a few calls. You go back home and stay in bed for a few days, alright? Try not to leave the house for any extended period."

Macava still hadn't looked at him, and John felt a chill moving up his spine. What the hell was Nicholas thinking? Whatever it was, it sounded serious and only compounded the fears that had been growing since speaking to the psychiatrist the day before. Macava had been cagey on the phone, but it was worse to see him so guarded in person. For someone as open and approachable as Nicholas, he was acting in a decidedly unnerving manner.

"I'm really sorry I can't hand the answers out on a plate, John," Nicholas continued, finally looking at him, "but some things need time. Now tell me one more time. Each and every thing that has happened has altered the world or time?"

"Yes."

"And you felt like it was a realization of the *real* world, a kind of awakening to another time or reality?"

"That's right. It was like something reached out and cleared my vision for me and made me see everything for what it was, at least until the car accident and the injuries. After that I started to wonder if it wasn't me doing it."

"*You* doing it?" Macava's voice was sharp and he was looking hard at John. Something about this entire conversation sounded wrong, and John finally decided that he didn't trust Macava anymore, however much it might go against rational thought. He changed tactics to end the exchange.

"Well, you know. Me or God." He said it as disingenuously as possible. He smiled, raising his eyebrow.

The psychiatrist's expression relaxed and he leaned back and smiled broadly. "Ah yes, well, you could always blame God for everything."

"Not a believer, Nicholas?"

"Once, maybe, but then I discovered that people didn't have teapots in the years zero to thirty AD."

John stared blankly at the doctor, sure he had missed some deeper reference somehow linked to teapots. He sighed inwardly. There was no way he could compete with Nicholas on this one. "So?" he said as seriously as he could manage, watching the psychiatrist smile. The smile was decidedly condescending.

"Well, I suppose you wouldn't know about the 'teapot in orbit' argument, being an outrageous philistine, but put quite simply, I feel you can't run a universe without a good cup of tea."

John raised his eyebrows at the doctor in the best expression of indifference he could manage. His mind raced as he tried to remember anything he could about teapots in orbit, finally concluding that he had no idea what Nicholas was referring to. He gave up and lay back, feeling a lot better for having had his train of thought jolted off track. He chuckled softly. This was why Macava was so good at what he did and it would be a mistake to let his guard down. He had to be careful not to suggest, or let Macava suspect, that he believed he was actually changing the world around him. When, in a day or two, the psychiatrist came up with his theory of what kind of delusions were plaguing John's mind, he could then quietly see if this newest development fitted his diagnosis. No sense making himself sound even crazier at this point, no matter how true he felt it was. *When I get home I'm going to practice*, he thought, wondering how it worked.

Macava made some parting niceties and left, apparently feeling a bit better about John's mental state, having witnessed the re-emergence of his sense of humor. *As soon as I'm out of here*, John thought, *I'm telling Chris all about this.*

The reports were in. The sweepers had done their jobs quickly. Gillworth, Surrey. Background radiation had risen in that area almost imperceptibly, but markedly more so than in other areas. This subject had apparently not put anyone's life in danger as a result of radiation, but Kendra knew full well that there were a lot of ways a reckless or even calculated transition could claim lives.

She shifted her feet on her workspace, thinking idly that it ought to be renamed her foot space. There was still no individual to follow up on, but Kendra knew it was only a matter of time before they had a lead. Usually the subject slipped up and left a gap. Someone would notice and make a remark, the remark would turn into something more, and if the mistake wasn't corrected, eventually someone on her team would spot it. An email, a blog, a telephone call, everything was being monitored, leaving the subject with very little room to move. She had all the offices over the region using everything they had to try to intercept every line of communication into, out of, and throughout the city. The system wasn't perfect, but it wouldn't be long before something was picked up.

Recaller Cat Reynolds knocked once and slipped through the door, closing it behind her. She headed silently to the chair opposite Kendra in the cramped office and looked expectantly at her TRD. *Ah*, thought Kendra, *this is progress at least. Good for you, Cat.*

"Yes, Recaller Reynolds?"

"A hospital report has just come through, Detective, from one of our senior plants. It matches the definitions and seems to tick the boxes. The doctor knows the person quite well and was able to make the connection." The Recaller stopped herself and handed the report to Kendra, who felt a surge of approval for her improvement and commitment to discipline.

She glanced at the report, an excited judder running through her body. Realizing that this was worth concentrating on, she re-read it.

'Subject: John Davis. Long-standing patient of Dr. N. Macava, (psychiatrist/part-time consultant). Psychoanalysis/ psychotherapy now ceased, contact continues. Patient recently experienced memory loss or confusion unrelated to matters previously encountered, possible tentative belief in multiple timelines, and expressed opinion that changes between such memory lapses/confusion due to multiple perception of timelines were focused primarily on him. Memory lapses possibly caused him to crash his vehicle.

'Patient was brought to hospital for observation with no injuries, although patient describes crash as extremely violent and resulting in extensive physical injuries. Patient exhibits most of the signs listed on the Directive.'

Kendra considered the report. The most worrying line was 'belief in multiple timelines'. It was as she feared, then. The subject, Davis, had begun to develop an awareness of his abilities and had managed to save himself from the crash that would otherwise have killed him. It was the nature of subjects to become destructive as they recognized their isolation from the rest of the world, although this one appeared to have been accidentally destructive. He was still in the recognition stages, so there was still time to stop him advancing any further.

"Recaller Reynolds, have you had time to survey the radiation reports and the hospital admission rates for the last few days for the Gillworth areas?"

"Yes, Detective. Both are abnormally high."

"Have you submitted a report based on that assessment in conjunction with this report?"

"I have, Detective."

"And what is your recommendation?"

"The subject is a danger to himself and to others," she replied crisply. "The radiation levels following the transitions have not been dramatically increased, but the frequency of the transitions is becoming such that the consequential increase in radiation is likely to reach unacceptable levels. The subject remains relatively ignorant of the extent of his abilities and has yet to learn to control them. This is the best time to stop him, and I see no other option than to proceed with an operation to do so."

"I agree. Nice work, Cat." Kendra paused. A concern that was almost maternal had lodged itself in her chest. She did not want to expose Cat to danger, and the subject was further along than she would have liked. This one appeared to be reactionary. If he was able to reverse his injuries and the circumstances under which they had been inflicted while presumably suffering extreme pain from those injuries, then he represented a significant danger to anyone who tried to harm him. Then again, this was important to Reynolds. She had been working hard on the case. She had to leave it to the Recaller to decide.

"Cat, listen, this could be dangerous. It needs to be clean and smooth, and I work best alone. I'll probably need all my experience and training to bring this one in, and I don't want to put you in danger. If I asked you not to come, would you stay?"

Working alone was a concept both common and encouraged within the organization, and one for which Kendra had been grateful before. The organization had vast resources and possessed the ability and the right to track and locate any given individual matching the subjects' description, people known colloquially as Shifters. The sweeper teams were an exception to that rule, but they worked for environmental agencies and were really nothing to do with the organization. They were used when needed and directed to do whatever was required at the time. They were told that the organization was MI5, or some other impressive-sounding government agency. In reality, the main body of the organization was made up of Recallers, people who could see and feel the transitions but who remained unaffected by them to a greater or lesser extent. The more useful ones became select teams—the Transition Recall Detectives of each region—while the others were put to work in analysis and monitoring operations. Due to the relatively low numbers of recruits and the delicacy of the operations, TRDs tended to operate alone. Potential new Recallers could be approached by the more senior operatives of the organization. Subjects suspected of being Shifters, however, were the jurisdiction of Detectives only, being much rarer and infinitely more dangerous. Traditionally, subjects were no more than civilians, not hard for TRDs to get the drop on and do whatever was necessary. In cases like this, where the subject was potentially so dangerous, a single shot to the head was the only guaranteed way to end it.

Nevertheless, thought Kendra, it was a shame there couldn't be a team of TR Detectives, a group of them to ensure the operation's success. Surely the organization had the resources for that? She reflected on it for a moment. There was a lot about the organization that she didn't understand. That was exactly how it was supposed to be.

She would use the Recaller teams to locate Davis, and then she would take over. There was no need to endanger her team, and especially not her favorite young Recaller. She was hoping to recommend Cat for Transition Recall Detective training later on. She had the talent and the drive, and following this operation Kendra would know if she also had the strength. She wondered briefly if she should involve the civilian police, the armed response units. *Not yet, perhaps. Let's see how we get on alone first.*

Using the civilian police force was annoyingly irksome in any case. Trying to get them to co-operate and actually do what they were asked without question was extremely tough. It wasn't only because she was a woman, though she had noted in the past that her gender didn't help. It was mainly because nobody liked to be overruled, especially when the people doing the overruling were with a tight-lipped organization. Delays and unreliability were the by-products of avoiding the inevitable questions and requests, and they were not indulgences she could afford in this operation. Besides, if she failed to complete the mission alone, she doubted she could do much better even with an army behind her.

Reynolds had not yet responded to the question as to whether she would stay behind if asked. She stared at Kendra. "Not if you *asked* me, Detective," she said flatly. The option was there to order her to stay away. Reynolds was not such a maverick that she would come along in defiance of a direct order. However, that just made it harder for Kendra to forbid her.

"Very well, I won't order you. Just be aware that you must obey every order without question. Do you understand?"

"Of course, Detective." Cat was clearly relieved. Kendra nodded, resigned to Cat's choice. She desperately hoped she could keep her alive.

CHAPTER

The ground was hard and cold under Kendra's face and there were stones biting into her cheek. She lay still, breathing shallowly to avoid inhaling the dust of the road. Slowly she raised her head, wincing as she eased her arms out from under her body. She struggled to her feet, vaguely aware that she didn't seem to be seriously injured. Sudden agony lanced through her left shoulder like lightning, causing her to gasp in pain. Her eyes widened as she stared at the wreckage before her.

Bathed in the orange lights of the motorway, the car looked as though it had been torn apart. Its front end had crumpled like paper and debris was strewn across the road like bits of a toy car flung by a furious child. There was nothing left of the driver's seat. The front and back ends of the car had slammed together with such force that the interior looked like it had imploded. The roof had sheared off and was lying some yards away from where Kendra stood taking in the scene in disbelief.

Of young Recaller Reynolds there was no sign. Kendra knew she was dead even before she made her way around the side of the wreck to where the driver's door should have been. Blood and gore stained the twisted doorframe. She didn't need to look inside to see the mess that had once been Cat

Reynolds. The door had crumpled in, preventing Kendra from opening the grisly tomb even if she had wanted to.

Stunned, she walked to the grass verge. Bizarrely, the motorway was still flowing, the wreckage confined to the hard shoulder. *How could that be?* she wondered. *Why isn't anyone stopping?* Perhaps they couldn't see it clearly. After all, it was night-time on a Friday and the lighting wasn't great. Still, someone should have noticed ....

With further consideration, the answer became clear. This was a reckless transition, one with no forward planning and no careful execution. It had simply destroyed the car without any thought as to how or why. Kendra's memories of the crash were half formed and made little sense. She knew they hadn't crashed into anything, this destruction had simply happened. The Shifter had expected whoever was after him to be travelling alone and had concentrated his efforts on the driver's side. Kendra's lack of serious injury after such massive destruction was testament to the fact that a passenger hadn't been part of the plan. She had simply been in the way.

Cars were braking too hard as they went past, Kendra was sure someone was going to cause an accident. She fought the urge to laugh hysterically—what a profound observation. A single car pulled onto the hard shoulder just ahead of the crash site and a man came jogging down to where she stood. His face was a mask of shock as he took in her appearance. She had a few cuts and bruises from where she had been thrown from the car when her door was torn off, but nothing near what she should have had in terms of injuries. The man was in his thirties, overweight and sweaty. He looked into her eyes and asked her a little too loudly whether she was okay.

"I'm fine. The police are on their way. I'm handling it." She said it as coldly and dismissively as she could, hoping to make him go away. Turning away from him, she walked over the grassy hill at the side of the motorway and pulled her phone from her pocket, hoping it hadn't been badly damaged. The phone was battered, but it still worked.

After making the call, she sat and waited for her helicopter. She hoped it would arrive before the police did. No one had stopped their cars since the fat man, but it wouldn't be long before some busybody phoned the police or a police patrol car happened by. She looked up at the sky, rubbing at her shoulder as she searched for the chopper.

If there had been doubt in her mind, it was gone now. Congealed in ice was the resolution to kill this subject. He had progressed further than she had imagined if he was targeting threats. She had always suspected that subjects might have a certain amount of precognition or mild psychic awareness beyond that of most people, although she had never seen it demonstrated. She had never known a subject to be able to track a person across such distances before. Perhaps he was already in full control of his power. The fact that she had been out to kill him was neither here nor there. She now felt a keen sense of purpose, cold and deadly, that she had not experienced for a long time. Not only had he taken her by surprise, but he had murdered her young aspirant, whose only fault had been to accompany Kendra. She could have stopped Cat coming—she *should* have stopped her—and now she was dead.

Which meant that the Shifter *had* to die.

Having left the hospital reasonably early in the morning, after the free breakfast of scrambled eggs apparently made from rubber, John parked his car in the car park at the back of the shopping center in town. Being a Saturday, it still charged by the hour, but he wasn't overly concerned about that. He couldn't quite remember if he had locked the car as he left it, but he was beginning to think that it really didn't matter. If he could stop the thing from being hideously destroyed simply by wanting it to be okay, then he doubted it could be stolen. A part of him couldn't get used to the new car. It didn't feel like his and he still hadn't got a grip on what was happening, whether in his head or not.

He walked unsteadily, not because of the injuries he had sustained—or not sustained—but due to a sense of euphoria he had never felt before. He felt powerful, unbelievably important, so much so that the people around him seemed completely insignificant. Part of him was saying he was being ridiculous, that none of it made any sense, but this rebellious side was being shouted down by the rest of him. He hadn't come up with an alternative explanation yet and doubted he could. He caught sight of himself in the reflection of a shop window and laughed aloud. His hair was a mess and he looked manic, a stupid grin all over his face.

He had a huge list of people to phone. His brother would be amazed, but probably not surprised. He had always taken the view that something had to happen at some point to change the way things were. He was a kind of romantic and yearned for something exciting to happen in the ordered and sensible world they lived in. A strange outlook on life for an aspiring politician, but his brother was anything but ordinary. They had always been close, had always shared everything. With a jolt the thought hit John that perhaps this was happening to his brother too. Could he be a part of this with John?

"One at a time," he told himself. "Start with someone who wouldn't believe you. Maybe then they can tell you you're crazy." He smiled. There was a chance he was mad, that much he knew, but he was reasonably sure he wasn't. He was looking forward to debating that particular issue with someone.

He found a bench to sit on outside a liquor store, ignoring the startled looks from the people inside the shop. He realized he was probably a bizarre sight, looking like he had just rolled out of bed and grinning like a lunatic.

Scrolling through his phone's contact list, he was surprised to see that Chris's mobile number had disappeared. He frowned and looked up at the sky, trying to recall what the number was. It was getting later in the day, the grey clouds fading into a darker skyline. Had he managed to damage his phone in the crash?

But there wasn't a crash.

John's attention snapped back to the phone, frantically searching for any trace of the missing number. His eyes were wild and he scrolled up and down, from B to D and back. There was no Chris in his phone's memory.

John composed himself by breathing deeply and trying to relax his hunched shoulders. He knew Chris's home number, a throwback from the days before he had a mobile phone. Chris's family had lived in the same house for over a decade and the number had stayed the same.

John flinched as the word 'decade' crossed his mind. It made him feel decidedly old. Putting aside such unsavory thoughts, he typed Chris's home number into his phone and held it to his ear. A woman answered in a voice he didn't recognize. He froze.

"Hello? Is anyone there?"

John broke out of his paralysis and quietly asked if he could speak to Chris. Despite his certainty of what was coming, he was unable to steel himself for the response.

"Oh, sorry, I think you've got the wrong number. There's no one called Chris here." The woman sounded perversely happy about it, as though she was being nothing but helpful.

John's throat tightened. He tried to speak but couldn't think of anything to say. He sat staring at his own reflection in the shop window, his mouth opening and closing in disbelief. The phone fell from his numb fingers, clattering to the wooden bench next to him. He absently thought how lucky it was it hadn't fallen on the ground. The number was right, he knew it by heart. It was the same number they had always had, there was no chance it was wrong.

Had it happened again and done something to Chris? Where the hell had he gone? If he had been moved along with his whole family for some reason, why wouldn't John have the number, especially if John was the one causing the changes?

Cold fingers closed around his heart as he considered the possibility that Chris hadn't been moved at all. These changes so far had been abrupt, sudden and uncompromising—out of control. If Chris had been the focus this time, and he was now gone, the likelihood was that he wouldn't be coming back.

John struggled to breathe as he pressed his head against his trembling hands, trying desperately to understand. There was still a possibility, however remote, that Chris was alive somewhere and that the change had only moved him. He clung to that fragile hope as he gathered his swirling thoughts. If he was the one responsible for the changes then maybe he could change it back, but it no longer seemed likely that he was. He had assumed he was the cause of the changes because they were beneficial to him—although there was no benefit in this. He ignored the cold logic and tried to focus. He shut his eyes tight and concentrated on Chris. If he could do it unconsciously, then he would make it work consciously.

His breathing grew ever more ragged as the futility of what he was doing became clear. He could hear his frustrated sobbing and was vaguely aware of what he must look like with his hands pressed to his head, struggling to breathe. He didn't care. His mind kept churning over the thought that he was wrong, that he had no control over the changes. It no longer stood to reason that he was the cause of them after all. Nevertheless, if Chris was dead, John was the reason. Chris could only have been targeted because of his connection to John, who up until now had been the focus of all the changes. But targeted by whom? Who was behind this, and what possible reason would they have for removing Chris? The thought burned inside him. He was unable to comprehend anything but the wrenching feeling of loss that threatened to consume him entirely. It was impossible, it was murder ....

John's thoughts were a maelstrom of anger as he rose slowly from the bench. He could barely concentrate, his mind filled with memories of his boyhood friend alive and happy, making snide comments and laughing raucously at some inane

STEVEN D. JACKSON

remark ... a lifetime of memories. Were they all that was left of Chris now? Had the same thing happened to Chris that had happened to his flat, his car, and his injuries? Gone as though they had never existed?

Abruptly John's strength failed and he sat back down on the bench, clutching at his head with hands that felt barely connected to his body. Guilt tore at his soul, warring with reason as he tried to believe that Chris wasn't dead. He had to keep his head and figure out what to do. The first thing was to check Chris's house, although he was almost certain he knew what he would find. If Chris was gone—dead—and if John's recent experiences were anything to go by, no one would even remember that Chris had ever lived.

As the moments passed, the anger began to subside. He could feel it settling in his heart and slowly freezing into ice. If someone else was behind these horrific events, he would find who it was, and when he did he would make them suffer. He would avenge his friend somehow. The euphoria of a few minutes ago now seemed like a cruel joke. If he wasn't the one causing the changes as he had assumed, then the fact that he appeared to be their focus suggested someone was targeting him. That meant the people closest to him were in danger too. He suddenly realized how close he had come to contacting his brother. The thought made him feel sick.

A terrible sense of dread settled in his stomach and he grabbed the abandoned phone, stabbing at the buttons, scrolling to his brother's name. A surge of relief rolled over him like a cool breeze. There was his brother's name, untouched and whole. There was no way he would risk calling him now, especially not until he had taken a look at Chris's house. The only question he now had was if he wasn't the one doing this, how could he explain what was happening?

Macava. The name flashed into his head unbidden. The doctor knew more than he was letting on, that much was obvious. The cryptic questions, the weird answers, the coincidence that he just happened to be in the hospital at the time of John's crash, it all added up, and yet there was still something missing. Macava was a clever man, but John would rip the answers out of him if he had to.

Rising from the bench, he headed back to his car, the plan formulating as he walked.

The woods were already dark when Kendra finally made her way to the hospital. Being a normal hospital, she reasoned, there ought to be little in the way of security. If she had taken the proper time to prepare she would have found such details out, but knowing this didn't help. The fact was that she had to get into the place covertly, without the benefit of cover or even a properly formed plan. She had spent most of the day explaining Cat's death and making reports to her superiors. She hadn't mentioned her intention to go after the Shifter tonight, concerned she would be ordered to back down and hand the case to someone else.

Kendra gritted her teeth and stared at the building, watching the lights in the windows for any sign of activity. Things might not be entirely wound down, she supposed, although it was already quite late. Nine o'clock at the earliest, she guessed, although her watch had stopped working shortly after the crash. The day had passed relatively quickly, but it still felt like a lifetime ago that she had been talking to Cat about the mission.

The subject would be taken down tonight. She would make sure of it.

Kendra's fingers absently tugged at the shoulder holster of her 9mm Glock pistol. She had tried to get used to its weight hanging by her side, but it always made her feel uneasy. It was all too clear to her how having such a weapon could drive certain people to take risks they otherwise wouldn't. It was no way to maintain a disciplined state of mind. On the other hand, when something needed doing, it needed doing in the quickest and simplest way possible.

Tonight the gun would be put to good use. She maintained it meticulously and she was a fair shot, although recently she had not had much cause to fire at anything except a stationary target. Concealed in the darkness, she smiled grimly, no trace of humor in her expression. She planned to find a stationary target this evening, and she would let the consequences be damned. The organization could clear it up. She had vengeance to deliver.

Kendra crept through the underbrush to the back of the hospital, to a service door she remembered from her brief review of the building plans before setting off. At this time of night there would be little use for the service entrance, so it was her best chance of slipping in unnoticed. She could hear male voices off to her right, low and unhurried, speaking quietly in an undertone, and as she reached the building she detected a faint smell of cigarette smoke in the air. That might complicate matters. She couldn't exactly break down the door with two people standing a few yards away.

The Detective faded back into the shadows by the nearest corner of the building as silently as she could, which after so many years of practice was pretty silent. Just as she began to run through various ways of dealing with the smokers, one of them jerked his head in the opposite direction. She strained her ears to make out what they were saying.

"Did you hear that?"

"What?"

"There's something over there."

The two men moved off in the direction of the sound they had heard. Not giving them another thought, Kendra whipped around the corner and slid to the service door. With practiced hands, she took her lock picks from their compartment in a pouch on her belt, and within a few seconds she felt the tumblers of the heavy locks turning. With an audible click the door was unlocked. Not a glamorous entrance, she thought, but a seamless one. She smiled, pleased with herself as she slipped into the building.

Gillworth Hospital was vast, so vast that it had been constructed way out on the outskirts of town, nestled in the woodland of the Surrey countryside. John had never been inside before his car accident, and only had vague memories of it from his visit the day before. He cursed himself as he emerged from the dense forest and headed for the back of the building. He had no idea of the layout of the place, or where he would find Macava.

He had spent the last hour piecing together his plan in a rundown wooden shack about fifteen minutes' walk through the woods from the hospital. It wasn't much of a plan, he had to admit, but it was all he could come up with when his tortured mind could barely cope with being toyed with by some unknown force. Especially when a large part of him still feared he was doing this to himself.

He had known about the shack since he had been a student at the university, which also bordered the woods. It was possible on a nice day to walk the length of the woods on the overgrown paths, and he had done that on a good few occasions as a student. The shack was a basic wooden cabin big enough for a couple of people. It was meant to be for birdwatchers, but no one ever used it. The paths weren't known to tourists, and precious few students bothered wandering the woods anymore. As a result the paths through the forest were overgrown, not exactly easy to traverse. The shack was still there, though, and was perfect for his purposes. It had a roof and walls, an old box and one chair. He had boarded up the windows with the wood he had picked up in the hardware shop along with two extremely large kitchen knives, a hammer and some nails, and duct tape. He had gained a few strange glances as he marched into the shop and bought his items in silence with the look of a downcast yet bitterly determined handyman about him.

He had made the trip to the hardware shop immediately after checking out Chris's address earlier that day, having spent the previous night in a restless sleep. It was clear he wasn't living there. The wrong car was in the drive, and neither the bewildered woman at the door nor the neighbors had ever heard of him. John spent a few minutes sitting in silence on the pavement, not thinking about anything. Eventually it had come to him in a flash of clarity—Macava must be made to answer for this.

Now the cabin in the woods was ready, the light had faded sufficiently, and Macava should still be in the building. It was time to make his move, and so John had set out, forcing himself to put aside his grief and anguish and focus on his anger.

Unfortunately, the plan went wrong almost as soon as he emerged from the woods. Two men were standing at the back of the hospital beside the industrial bins, and they heard the snapping of a particularly loud twig as John stepped out of the shadows. He jumped back into the darkness as quickly as he dared, keeping his eyes on the two men as they approached. He maneuvered around and away from them, finding himself opposite a small door. It was only a few yards away, but unfortunately bathed in brightness from the overhead lights. There were deep shadows to the left where the building turned a corner, and John decided to take his chance.

As luck would have it, the door was unlocked. He was in and had the door closed before the two men returned from peering into the woods. Now all he had to do was find Macava and hope to God he wouldn't struggle.

CHAPTER

EIGHT

Kendra threw the file across the office and watched it land in a satisfying heap on the other side of the room. Her breathing raced, her frustration beginning to get the better of her. She glanced contemptuously at the unconscious woman slumped in the seat to her right. Perhaps she should have tried talking to her before hitting her with the butt of her gun, but everything she needed should have been in the file.

Part of her felt guilty for hitting the woman from behind, but stealth was everything. She had managed to disable the security camera network on the way in by making a few changes to the circuit breakers in one of the control panels in the lower levels. She didn't want to be caught on camera dealing with the subject, but it was now apparent he wasn't here anyway. He had discharged himself earlier on, having suffered nothing more than a bruised shoulder. She scowled, trying not to think of the liquid mess that had once been her aspiring Recaller.

The one useful thing she had discovered was a staff photo of Dr. Nicholas Macava. Perhaps she could start with him. It was a flimsy lead, but at least it was something.

She would have preferred to find a photo of Davis in his file so she would know exactly who she was looking for. What descriptions she had found allowed her to form a mental picture of him. She was glad he wasn't any younger. At twenty-four she could handle shooting him without too much guilt. He was old enough to know that messing around with other people's lives was unacceptable. That coupled with his attempt to murder her made it a certainty.

John Davis would die.

———————

John stood outside the door, listening for any sound from the other side. Macava hadn't been hard to find. The doctor had placed signs around the hospital saying exactly which room to come to for the psychological consultancy service he was offering. Macava had set up his service on the top floor of the expansive hospital complex.

Macava was alone. Through the door John could hear the doctor turning the pages of a book. It has to be now, he told himself, trying desperately to rehearse the conversation in his mind. He had to get the doctor out and into the woods as soon as humanly possible or he would fail. John fingered the handle of the kitchen knife, trying to decide whether to go in all guns blazing or try another tack. He reasoned that if he went in calm he could get angry, but if he went in angry he could hardly regain his composure, so he slipped the knife into his jacket pocket and stepped into the room as calmly as he could, taking in his surroundings quickly. His hands were shaking and he could feel his heart beating wildly inside his chest. He could barely believe he was doing this, but he was committed. There was no going back now.

The doctor himself was sitting in a leather armchair in the corner of the room by the window, next to a small table with a lamp. It struck John that the corner made a fair job of looking like a proper psychiatrist's room, but only if you pretended you couldn't see the rest of it. The patient's chair was facing the doctor, so clearly that was the idea. It was actually quite clever. More deception, more manipulation. The whole thing was sickening.

The doctor glanced up, surprised, as John crossed the room with purposeful strides. "John? What brings you here at"—he checked his watch—"an hour like this? No one is supposed to get in except accidents and …." He trailed off, perhaps noting the cold look on John's face, or maybe the shaking of his hands.

John decided to go for a careful ruse rather than instant confrontation. "Something's happened," he began lamely. "It … it's my friend Chris. I think I mentioned him before." John warmed to his theme, using the conviction he put into arguing hopeless cases at work. "Well, he's in trouble and … and I think you might be able to help. You need to come with me."

To add emphasis to this declaration John turned quickly and headed back out of the room. The doctor had stayed seated, an expression of confusion on his face. John was afraid confusion might turn to suspicion and he would lose his only advantage. Whipping around, he shouted at the doctor to hurry, concealing his satisfaction at the galvanizing effect this had on Macava. The startled man placed his hands on either side of the armchair and hauled himself to his feet with what struck John as an alarming amount of effort. Macava suddenly seemed very old indeed. Could he honestly go through with this?

———————

Kendra walked slowly back to the woodland trail, her thoughts bleak. She had failed again, and someone else had died. Cat Reynolds—another innocent person she could have saved. The thought tore at her conscience, taking her back to the past, the terrible wrenching guilt over her failure to save someone's life. She stared sightlessly at the trees as she neared them, letting her vision wander as her thoughts retraced well-trodden ground. She paused briefly, lost in her memories.

The attic was abandoned, run down and falling apart. Floorboards were missing, the roof exposed to the elements. The chill she felt had nothing to do with the cold air rushing in from the darkness outside. A plate of food, days old from the look of it, sat rotting in the corner. The rancid smell of decay was almost unbearable. No sound but the thumping of her heart, the creaking of the overhead beams, the gentle swing of the rope. The horrific vision of the body swaying in the breeze—

Sounds from behind Kendra startled her out of the reverie, forcing her back to reality. Instinctively she spun on the spot and crouched, drawing her gun from its holster in one fluid movement. She could see nothing but the industrial bin before her, but she could hear the sound of footsteps coming closer. Her heart was beating wildly and her thoughts were a jumble. She had let her guard down and was in no condition to deal with whatever was coming.

She cursed herself for allowing her thoughts to wander, feeling she owed it to Cat Reynolds to stay on her guard. If she was discovered, they would soon realize who had attacked the receptionist, and she could not afford to be caught. It sounded as though the footsteps were not pursuing. They seemed rather to be scuffling, even struggling. She could hear male voices not far off but couldn't determine what they were saying.

Kendra moved carefully up to the bin just as one voice shouted a single word and the footsteps became frantic. Reaching the bin, she slowly peered around the side, half expecting to see flashlights pointing in her direction. Her eyes widened in shock at what she saw instead, her mind instantly putting the pieces together and screaming that it was too easy, too coincidental. Her hands moved of their own volition as she brought the weapon to bear and squeezed the trigger.

The doctor had given up asking questions after a few minutes of walking through the corridors. John gave nothing but breathless answers bordering on the hysterical, in as good an imitation of a man in blind panic as he could manage. He wanted Macava to walk himself out of the hospital. That would save him a lot of effort.

It wasn't until they reached the ground floor, almost at the service door, that the doctor stopped moving. John turned, seeing from the look on the doctor's face that suspicion had finally got the better of him. Macava would need some answers before he moved on.

"John, where are we going?"

"I told you, my friend had an accident and we need to get to him ...."

Macava regarded him with narrowed eyes and took a step back. "What are we really doing here, John?"

Dropping the pretense, John leaped toward the doctor, blind rage taking over as he grabbed the older man's sweater with both hands. He spun Macava around toward the short corridor leading to the service door, roughly shoving him in its direction. Macava stumbled, his arms reaching out to steady himself on the smooth, sterile walls. His eyes were wide with alarm and his mouth was open, but no sound came out. John took a threatening step toward him, drawing the knife from his pocket as he did so. His blood pounded and adrenaline flooded his system, his thoughts whirling madly in his head. He was blind to everything except this man; the man who had lied to him and betrayed him, and who had something to do with Chris's death.

"You and I are going to have a talk, Nicholas," he said, his voice sounding steadier than he felt. Glad that he was finally able to tell the truth, he continued in a low voice through gritted teeth. "I know that you know what's happening to me, and if you aren't the one doing it then I'm as sure as hell that you know who is."

He took another step, the doctor retreating before him while staring in horror at the knife glittering in the brilliant light of the hospital corridor. For all his bravado, John could barely stand the look of terror on the man's face, and in that instant he almost threw the weapon away. The impulse to run from the building and never look back was overwhelming, but he steeled himself and bit down on his lip. This had to be done. On the memory of his childhood friend, he had to go through with this.

His hand was shaking, the internal struggle must have been written all over his face. The doctor's form was distorting in his vision and he realized that tears were forming in his eyes. The adrenaline continued to pound, but he felt his conviction waning. John lowered the knife, wiping the tears from his eyes with his free hand and shaking his head. He fixed Macava with a steely gaze and tried to calm his breathing.

"I don't want to hurt you, Nicholas, but you owe me this. I am going to find out what you know and you can either resist or make it easier for both of us. Don't make me do something I'll regret, because I swear I don't know what I'm capable of anymore."

Everything he said was true. Macava could obviously tell, and the way his eyes flicked to the ground as he swallowed told John he was right. Macava knew something and felt guilty about it. The doctor turned and headed toward the service door, John walking close behind him, glad that no more deception was needed. The threat of the knife coupled with his own unhinged mental state ought to be enough to convince his captive, he reasoned as they stepped toward the door. Halting the doctor, John withdrew the duct tape from his jacket and wound it around Macava's hands.

They headed through the service door into the cool night outside. There was no one around and John hurried the doctor toward the woods, casting a quick glance at the bin over to the right to make sure no one was hiding in the shadows. Macava was speaking quietly. He missed the first few words and hurried to get closer.

"... not a bad person, John, you just need help. I wasn't there to help you when you needed it and I'm sorry, but I am going to help you get better now. Everything is going to be—"

John couldn't bear this. "Don't!" he bellowed, reaching

with his free hand to grab the doctor's shoulder. He wanted to make it clear that this wasn't about him, that he knew there was more going on and that the doctor was involved. As Macava turned John was surprised to note that he looked smug. Simultaneously he realized he was off balance, not thinking straight, and was totally unprepared for the blow that landed squarely in his solar plexus. The attack was feeble, not even enough to knock the wind out of him, but the deception brought John's anger raging to the forefront again.

He lashed out with his free hand, missing the doctor by inches. He glared at Macava, the dismayed look on the man's face diminishing his anger. John tried to compose himself but couldn't prevent the emotional outburst that escaped him. "My best friend is dead! You owe me the truth—"

There was a flash from the shadows in front of him, followed instantly by a loud crack that split the night apart. Pain speared through his left shoulder and he reeled backward, gasping. Macava was shouting something, more cracking sounds were splitting his ears, and he couldn't think. Someone was emerging from the service door, shouting and pointing, and John reacted on primal instinct.

Grabbing Macava with his right hand and wondering vaguely what had happened to the knife, he ran blindly toward the woods, pulling the suddenly pliant doctor with him. Running feet sounded behind them somewhere, but they didn't follow as John and Macava crashed through the trees. Within a minute they were deep along the barely navigable pathway. No sound came from the hospital behind them, and there was barely enough illumination from the feeble moon to light their way. John's mind was a torrent of half-formed images. A feeling of warmth coated his back under his left shoulder and he thought he must be bleeding. He was exhausted and struggling to walk, but the cabin wasn't far. His fevered mind kept repeating that he must not let Macava escape.

STEVEN D. JACKSON

The barman wiped the dull wood of the bar, using a rag that looked stained and old. No effort went into the wiping and the man's expression was vacant. Brice watched disinterestedly from his table a few feet away, having nothing else to look at.

The pub was dimly lit at the best of times, but today the light up in the corner above Brice's head was broken. Someone had bashed it with a pool cue from the looks of it, and then snapped the cue in half. God only knew how the guy had managed that, but propped up against the wall near the abandoned pool table was the proof—two halves of a cue leaned dejectedly in the corner. Brice empathized with it.

The smell of stale beer pervaded the pub's musty air and Brice could hear nothing but the wiping of the rag on the wood. No one else was in the place, but then there rarely was anyone around, and that was precisely why Brice chose to come here. Sometimes a few people would stop by, but this was a Saturday night. Saturday was the night to go out with friends into the city or have people to the house, hardly the time to sit in a dingy barroom and breathe that old-beer smell. The solitude suited Brice. He liked having somewhere he could be on his own but where he didn't have to feel like he was alone. He couldn't stand the thought of sitting at home every night eating microwave meals and staring at the TV.

Another week had ended and he hadn't been able to speak to Sarah Kendra. The opportunities just hadn't come up. He scowled and took another long drink from the glass in front of him. The beer was getting warm. He considered getting another one but honestly couldn't be bothered. Reflecting on the last week, he admitted to himself that opportunities had been there. Of course they had. He worked within a few feet of the TRD, and she had shown him on more than one occasion that she liked him. She confided in him, trusted him. Was it such a stretch of the imagination to think she might say yes if he asked her for a drink one night? He could say it casually, like one colleague to another after a long day, and if she said no he could laugh it off and saunter away unaffected. She might even respect him more for that.

His stomach rumbled, bringing him back to reality. Of course she would say no, and he would be mortified. He glanced at his stomach, which slumped over the top of his jeans like an obscene growth. He hated it. He couldn't get rid of it, either. He had tried diet and exercise before, but nothing ever made much difference, and although he knew he had to give it time, the lack of visible results was so disheartening that he always gave up within a week. And so he was a disgusting, sweaty, fat man in his forties, and it was his own fault.

Brice tried to wrench his thoughts away from this self-destructive path, knowing it led only to misery and drunkenness, followed by misery and a hangover the next day. It wouldn't finish with the weight, either. He would go on to his height, his popularity, his hairline ….

He shook his head and grabbed the glass, determined to focus on the good aspects, trying to believe there were good aspects. Sarah did like him. That much was obvious. Probably not romantically, but she liked him in a professional way. He had done his damnedest to keep her using him, had taken as many additional IT-based learning courses from home as he possibly could to keep up with the technology out there. He knew he was still the best on his team, although admittedly his colleagues had more varied assignments, more excitement, more interesting lives ….

No, he corrected himself, they were not specialized. He was specialized. He was TR Detective Kendra's chosen technology guy, she had said so herself. He would make her proud on this one. He had already sent her to the subject she was looking for. Brice bit his lip, wondering if he had done the right thing. He knew the subject wasn't what Kendra thought he was, the reports simply didn't add up. Of course, they did now that he had made sure they did, but he hoped his little amendments wouldn't ever come to light.

The guy was twenty-four, much younger than Brice, who had seen photos of him on internet networking sites. He looked innocent enough, looked like a person who enjoyed life and was fairly successful. Brice hated him with a passion born out of fear and anguish that he could barely admit to himself. His hatred was a guilty hatred, but he hated the guy all the more for making him feel that way.

This guy might not be what Kendra thought he was, but he was obviously someone who would interest her immensely. That fear fretted at Brice's subconscious mind like a fever. He had waited so long, missed his chance so many times, and he might be about to lose his chance forever because of this … this *boy*. Still, augmenting the radiation signatures and increasing the estimation of danger should have sorted the problem. He could rely on Sarah to put the parts together and come up with the only available option. She would make the call, justify the action, and by now Brice had no doubt that the subject was dead. He had expended considerable effort to make sure that she would have no choice but to kill him, he just had to accept that he had done only what was necessary.

A shaft of orange light hit him in the face, momentarily blinding him. He blinked, raised a hand to shield his eyes, and stared at the open door through which the light from the lamp post was shining. A group of youngsters, early twenties at most, came spilling into the pub, talking loudly and excitedly. They were well on their way to being drunk, just like many others would be at this time of the evening. Brice wondered briefly what it would feel like to be in a group like that. Then he looked down at his glass, cursing the youngsters for making him jealous.

One of the newcomers, a tall, dark-haired lad, turned and glanced in Brice's direction. Brice saw his features curl into a poorly concealed smile as he turned back to the bar. He nudged the boy next to him. This lad looked a little more refined. Making an effort to appear casual, he slowly turned and gave the room a sweeping survey. His gaze didn't linger on Brice, but completed the circuit unbroken. It was well done, Brice had to admit. The lad turned back to the bar and whispered something Brice couldn't hear. The two lads laughed and nudged one another.

After a few moments, during which Brice stared determinedly at the table and watched the group out of his peripheral vision, the first youth turned and wandered over to him. Brice tensed, waiting for the worst, his body beginning to pump adrenaline into his system. He hoped his fear didn't show on his face and he stared down at his glass, wondering what would happen.

"Excuse me, mate," the lad began. He had a Northern Irish accent, but had obviously spent a lot of time in England, and he adopted a note of sincerity that barely concealed the mocking tone underneath. "Do you have a cigarette?"

Brice shook his head without looking up. He muttered something and flicked his eyes to see what the youth's reaction was. The boy jauntily strolled back to his friends, calling over his shoulder, "No problem, thanks anyway."

Brice didn't watch him walk back, but he knew they were sniggering at him. This had been happening all his life, and by now he was used to it. He could hear the laughter getting louder and just wanted to get back home. "That's enough, boys," the barman said quietly, obviously hoping Brice wouldn't hear. The laughter quieted and was replaced by whispers. Brice was torn between gratitude for the barman's intervention and irritation that he had sat and done nothing again like some pathetic victim.

He resolved to change, reform himself into someone worthy of respect. He would start by becoming Kendra's right-hand man, he would make himself her main supporter, and she would be grateful. Perhaps in time they could be more than just colleagues, then he would be respectable and this wouldn't happen again. Now that Davis was gone, nothing could stand in his way.

Not especially cheered, Brice drained the last of his beer

and stood up, keeping his eyes down. Edging around the table, he waved vaguely at the barman and wandered out into the darkening night, ignoring the sounds of suppressed laughter from the youngsters at the bar.

NINE

CHAPTER

"**Y**ou're hurt, John. Whatever madness you were planning, you need to stop and think now. You can't carry on with a bullet wound in your shoulder."

John smiled humorlessly and lifted his head to look at the doctor. Was this another attempt at deception? Somehow the almost inaudible tremor in the doctor's ordinarily composed voice gave him a twinge of malicious satisfaction. At that moment he wanted nothing more than to cause Macava the kind of pain he was enduring, the kind of pain that had nothing to do with the ragged hole in his shoulder. He supposed he would be lucky if no bones had been broken in there.

"If you knew me at all, *Doctor* Macava, you would know that appealing to my sensible side at a time like this is going to get you nowhere."

John shook his head and dropped his gaze to the wooden floor. His footprints in the dust were haphazard, a testament to his struggle to get the doctor into the room and tied to a chair while nursing his shoulder. Strangely, the doctor had not resisted. Out of guilt or maybe pity, he had allowed himself to be moved along down the winding track through the woods and into the cabin. John's blood had pounded in his head all the way, or perhaps it was the sound of a distant helicopter, he couldn't tell. The trek was a long one, or at least it had seemed that way, and John had stumbled a number of times, forced to use Macava for support. He hadn't moved since positioning himself on the wooden box against the wall opposite his captive.

John stared at the dark dots of blood mixed into a gruesome paste with the dust on the floor. He was trying to recall what had happened over the last hour or two, but he was finding it hard to concentrate through the throbbing of his shoulder. The desperate feeling that the plan, feeble as it was in the first place, had gone so very wrong wasn't helping him cope. He wasn't supposed to be injured and bleeding, and his captive wasn't supposed to be acting so helpful. John knew that Macava could have escaped with contemptuous ease, and that thought made him feel even more miserable. He had lost his only weapon in the run from the hospital and wondered why Macava hadn't tried to fight back.

The true tragedy was that the less Macava tried to escape, the more John was bound to this course of action. He couldn't possibly give up now. He was disgusted with himself not only for the kidnapping and the fact that he couldn't even get that right, but that he had chosen to take his anger out on a much older man. What had he hoped to do exactly? Beat a confession out of the doctor? He would be lucky now if he didn't collapse from blood loss, leaving him completely at the doctor's mercy. He laughed to himself. He was the worst villain he had ever heard of.

Macava was watching him warily. John could feel the doctor's eyes burning into his head even as he looked at the floor. Summoning his most defiant expression, he returned the gaze, hoping he didn't look too pale and sweaty. What he saw did not mollify him. Macava's expression softened and he gave John a look of unbridled pity.

"John, I'm so sorry."

John laughed derisively and shook his head. Disturbingly, the action unbalanced him and he had to grasp the box for support. "Do you even know what you're sorry for? I doubt it."

His voice was a whisper, his throat choked with emotion as the words tumbled out from somewhere inside him. His lack of control gave way to apathy. What did any of it matter now? "You lied to me, betrayed me, killed my friend. People are hunting me. I don't even know what's real anymore. You did that, Nicholas."

Tears stung his eyes. He squeezed them shut and wiped fiercely at his face with his free hand. He felt his despair twist into anger, whipping up and out of him like a vengeful serpent. He screamed, "How could you do that to me?" his body shaking with the force of his conviction. His thoughts were a jumble and he belatedly realized that he was asking the wrong questions. Breathing deeply, he composed himself, settling back down on the box. "Tell me what this is about, Nicholas. You owe me that, at least. Make it the truth, or I'll have to think of a way to get to the truth."

The last part was said almost to himself. It was not simple bravado. John had betrayed his slipping morality by muttering those final words without intending to voice them at all. His head rolled on his shoulders and he pushed himself back against the wall, propping himself there as he stared at the doctor. The thought occurred to him that if he died the doctor would be stuck tied to his chair. They were too far away from civilization for anyone to hear him shouting. Was he about to murder a doctor by negligence? The idea suddenly struck him as absurd and he giggled lightly.

Macava's voice pierced the gloom surrounding John, low and reasonable. "I can only tell you what I know, John. As with everything in life, you can only know what is yet known. To look for anything more will bring you only misery—"

Perhaps remembering that he was tied up in a cabin rather than dispensing wisdom from a leather armchair, the doctor cut himself off. When he started again, his voice was composed, persuasive, and John found himself unable to doubt what he was hearing. His hearing seemed augmented somehow, as though the voice was projecting directly into his head. He blinked his eyes, trying to focus on what the man was saying.

"I am a psychiatrist, John, but I also work as a consultant and sometimes as a counselor. I have access to a vast number of patients, and people in my position are privy to the thoughts and feelings of others. There are people in this world who are required to monitor the thoughts and feelings of others. We all take an oath, of course, dealing with confidentiality and all that, but there are certain things that override the oath."

Macava glanced away. Something in the mildly defensive way he was talking made John suspect that the doctor didn't really believe what he was saying. He closed his eyes, becoming more and more aware of the throbbing pain in his arm. It wasn't sharp any more, just a dull background ache. He tried to concentrate, his thoughts becoming increasingly more abstract.

"There is a body—a company, I suppose. All properly authorized, as far as I know, although not being a lawyer I can't be sure, but as they have access to what they have access to, you assume they are legitimate. Anyway, this organization monitors the complaints that people in my profession come across from the general population."

John stirred on his box, fixing his wavering focus on the doctor and trying to form a reply. His voice felt clogged, but he managed to croak a single word. "Why?"

If the doctor was aware of John's rapidly deteriorating state, he gave no sign. "Who can say? Does a farmer tell a sheep why it has to get back in its pen? No. People do as they are told, John. It's the way of the world, as you well know. All I know is that when you started talking about losing time and feeling like reality was moving about, it ticked the boxes on their little directive. I had to see you to be sure, but I couldn't justify not making the report to them in the end."

John's interest was piqued. Even through the haze he was driven by a need to know more. His exhaustion was extreme, but he was determined to see this through. "What report? Who to?" His voice sounded distant, hollow, but Macava didn't seem to notice.

"Ordinarily they go off to a company address in London which I am certain is a front, but a few days back I got a new directive requiring reports to be made directly to a man named Darren Brice. I sent off the report saying what you had told me, that's all."

Macava sighed deeply and his voice cracked. "Look, John, I really am sorry for what has happened to you. I know you are a good person, and I told them that in the report. I don't know why they are interested in you or even who they are, but if they are the ones who shot at you, then I can see I made a mistake. I had no idea, I swear to you. As far as I knew, it was for your own good." He paused, shaking his head. He stared at the floor for a moment before closing his eyes, adding quietly, "You deserve your revenge. On them, on me if you feel you must have it, but I hope you'll give me the chance to help you, and maybe in time you will be able to forgive me." The doctor fell silent, not looking at John, lost for the moment in his own thoughts.

John felt more wretched than ever. His head pounded and his arm hung limply at his side. He could feel his back sticking sickeningly to the wooden wall as his blood congealed. He shifted his weight, trying to reach across his body to move the useless arm, his balance twisting alarmingly as he did so. Falling back against the wall he began to panic, his breath coming in short, agitated gasps. He couldn't focus his vision, but his mind was clearer. Perhaps Macava wasn't the key player in this nightmare. Yes he had lied, and yes it was a betrayal, but the doctor hadn't done anything except make a report. Yet how had John repaid him? By attacking him and kidnapping him and dragging him through the woods to a shack where he was most likely going to die.

A single thought lanced through the haze like lightning. *You can't let him die here.*

With a tremendous effort John forced himself to one side,

sliding off the box onto the floor. Nausea flooded through him as dizziness set the room spinning. He didn't think he could get to his feet, but he was able to drag himself across the dusty wooden floor with his good arm. His shoulder felt warm again. The wound must have reopened. He hadn't even noticed it had stopped bleeding before. The thought crossed his mind that perhaps he was making a terrible mistake. Grimly he pushed the thought aside and tried to get his knees under him, reaching out with his free arm for a purchase on the smooth wooden floor.

He caught a glimpse of Macava's horrified face as he crawled closer and groped for the knife he had left in the cabin earlier. The irony of the situation hit him as he touched the handle. He had brought the knife to scare and interrogate, and here he was using it to set the captive free and save his life. Macava was making sounds which could have been speech, but John's focus was directed solely at the bonds around the doctor's legs. His vision swam before his eyes, a strange ringing in his ears blocked out all other sound but the vague echoes of the doctor's shouting. His shoulder was heavy, impossibly heavy, his head wouldn't move and he couldn't see. The floor was cold and hard beneath him. The ringing was getting fainter and the sounds of Macava's voice were growing dimmer. Finally, he heard no more.

———

"Nicholas Macava?"

A woman's voice cut through John's dreamless slumber, bringing him reluctantly back into the world. A male voice answered, one he knew well, although he had not heard it adopt such an authoritative manner before.

"Yes, I am *Doctor* Macava."

"*Doctor* Macava, my apologies." The woman sounded anything but contrite. Her tone was almost mocking. "I have reason to believe that you might be in contact with a man named John Davis. Is that not so?"

John's eyes snapped open. He was lying in a bed, staring at a dull green curtain. His head whipped around, his eyes taking in his surroundings, desperately trying to comprehend what had happened. The curtain surrounded the bed completely and a ventilation machine stood next to John, making rhythmic pumping sounds. It reminded him of Darth Vader and he shook his head, trying to clear his thoughts.

He was obviously in the hospital again, waking up for the third day in a row to the smell of disinfectant. All that remained was to find out whether his memories of the night before were real or not. He sank back on the pillow, raising his free hand to his eyes and rubbing them in frustration. He was sure he was going mad.

The voices continued, becoming more heated but maintaining their veneer of polite civility. "And why would a psychiatrist be in the hospital on a Sunday when he isn't doing consultancy work, Dr. Macava? Perhaps you could explain."

"If you would like to conduct a detailed examination of my timetable, Detective, I am sure we can arrange a more suitable time and place. This happens to be a hospital ward, and these happen to be extremely delicate patients."

"It's a burns ward, Doctor, hardly injuries you are qualified to deal with."

"My qualifications or lack thereof do not prevent me from walking around other departments in my place of work, *Detective*, although I might be inclined to suggest that mine at least entitle me to be here uninvited. Unlike yours, whatever they are."

There was a pause.

"You were hiding in here to avoid me, Doctor. You know that the organization I work for relies heavily on the medical profession, and you know it has great influence. You would do well to keep on my good side."

Macava did not reply.

"Now that I've found you it hardly matters. Where is Davis and what else do you know about his movements?"

"You saw me yesterday, Detective. He was in the process of kidnapping me. Do you honestly believe I would help the man? He ran off into the woods and I came back here. I was too shaken up to drive home, so I spent the night in my office upstairs. I doubt very much whether Mr. Davis will return here, now that you have the place staked out and will no doubt be watching me. I thought I would be safe here."

The woman's voice became a sneer. "I have no interest in watching you, Doctor. You managed to get yourself caught and interrogated already. I doubt he will come back here. Nevertheless I trust that you will keep a look-out for Davis and report it immediately if you hear anything from him."

"Why do you want him so badly, Detective? What is he to your organization?"

The woman did not reply. John could hear footsteps making their way out of the ward. He held his breath, waiting. Less than a minute later Macava stepped behind the curtain and gave him a broad grin. "Don't worry, John, it all happened."

John smiled. "Yeah, like that's supposed to comfort me."

"If the world was comfortable we wouldn't need armchairs, John. Remember that."

"Do you just make those things up on the spot?"

"Generally speaking, yes. They sound good, though, don't they?"

John laughed as Macava came closer and peered at the bandage covering his shoulder. "I think I did a pretty good job considering I'm not a surgeon," he remarked, glancing sideways at John.

John felt a leap of panic. "Nicholas, you didn't try to patch me up yourself, did you? Jesus, how long has it been since you did anything remotely—'?"

Macava cut him off with a chuckle and a wave of the hand. "Don't worry, don't worry, I jest only. I have a very good friend who owed me a favor or two, and he agreed to come over last night and sort you out. Don't ask me who he is because I won't tell you."

John grinned back, relieved beyond measure that Macava hadn't had his shaky old hands in among his shoulder blades. "Nicholas, about yesterday ...."

Macava's expression grew serious and he sat down in the chair opposite. "Before you get started, John, let me say that I owe you an apology. I know that whatever you are going through is crippling you, and it stands to reason that the symptoms you have experienced are not psychological in origin if a detective who works for a secret organization is tracking you and trying to kill you because of them. Whatever is happening is happening in reality, and it's no good pretending that I didn't know anything about it."

John stared at the doctor, wondering what was coming. Macava sighed deeply and started again. "There are none so blind as those who will not see."

John wasn't impressed. The cliché was more worn-out than he was.

"On some level, of course, I knew that the reporting wasn't simply a governmental survey or whatever they were passing it off as. It was something much more important, but I just never gave it much thought because I wanted to keep my NHS patients. If you want to work with a public organization you have to obey the rules. Do the hours and file your reports. It's incredibly dull, but if you want to do your bit for people you have to do it. There are so many tick boxes and targets that you don't give a lot of thought to the other, more unusual, rules. Like making reports to an organization with a special interest in memory lapses."

Macava sighed, shaking his head and glancing out of the window. John waited, feeling more than a little skeptical that anyone, let alone a doctor, would choose to ignore what was obviously a suspicious group of people. Something rang true in what the doctor said, though. John had always known how important it was to Macava to 'do the right thing' regarding his NHS patients. It was almost as though he felt guilty for not being a full-time public servant. It made sense that he would want to keep the boxes ticked if it was for the greater good.

Macava took a deep breath, lowering his gaze to the sterile floor before continuing in a quiet voice. "Besides which, I had never met anyone with the symptoms you displayed. You came to me for help, and I reacted by leading that awful woman right to you. I have no doubt she would have killed you if the hospital employees hadn't heard the shot and run after her. I suspect not being seen was more important than getting you, because she fled as soon as the alarm went up. Poor Alice in reception had been bashed over the head as far as I can tell, so no wonder they were crazy enough to chase after an armed woman. Everyone likes Alice." Macava paused. "So you see, John, I understand the anger you felt. I understand why you came for me, and you mustn't blame yourself. I would have done the same."

John laughed lightly. "This time yesterday, Nicholas, I wouldn't have believed that. But from what I saw of the cunning side of you, and after you tried to hit me and escape even with tied hands at the age of God knows what, I've had to change my opinions. You're a devious man and not above a bit of violence yourself."

The doctor looked proud of himself and smiled smugly. "Let's not forget who saved your life, my ungrateful friend."

John gave him a wry look. "Only after I saved yours. You would have starved to death in that cabin if I hadn't cut you free."

Macava nodded sagely. "True. Hadn't thought of that. Anyway, John, I want you to tell me the whole story again. This time I want to see if I can come up with any ideas as to what on earth is happening here."

John sighed and looked down at his hands, collecting his thoughts as he prepared to recite the whole tale. He needed to get this right. They had to work out what was really going on, and fast. If last night was anything to go by, the stakes were now very high.

CHAPTER

The helicopter ride the night before had been painful. Kendra had sat in silence, gazing out of the window, her eyes searching the woodland below with a growing sense of disillusionment. She had failed properly this time. She had been given a second chance and she had blown it. Why? Because she had been lost in bad memories. Subjects had escaped her before, but this was different.

She barely remembered touching down back at headquarters and making her way through the deserted building to her office. She had stayed there the whole night, looking through files and eventually sleeping in one of the rooms upstairs before setting out early in the morning to see if the doctor had returned to the hospital. Now she could barely recall the useless conversation with Macava. Whether he had been protecting the subject or not she couldn't be sure, but something about him had made her angry. She had ended up storming out, irritated beyond measure and still no closer to finding Davis.

Now she sat on a desk in the Recallers' room, staring around the deserted open-plan office littered with files and desks, wheeled chairs and coffee cups. "All this," she muttered, roughly pushing her long hair behind her ears, "all this and I couldn't catch him."

She had seen Davis in the open, had him in her line of fire, but her wild thoughts hadn't let her concentrate enough to hit him where it counted. Of course, at the time she hadn't known for sure it was him, but the fact that he was the right age and in the process of fleeing the hospital with Macava had made it clear. Something, however, didn't add up. She had hit him in the shoulder. It would have been painful, yes, and left unattended he would probably have bled to death, but if he was strong enough to selectively destroy a car and kill the driver without causing disruption to the motorway itself, surely he could cope with altering the severity of his wound?

"Perhaps," she muttered into the silence, "perhaps he has healed himself. That might be why he wasn't at the hospital." It was a feeble theory and brought her no closer to resolving anything. She slid off the desk and began to pace, her eyebrows furrowed in concentration. She counted the known transitions on her fingers as she walked.

Weather, something else, whatever put him in the hospital, my vehicle—

She stopped mid-pace. The third one was the one that didn't fit. Hurrying back to her office, she dug out the report by Dr. Macava. Davis had been brought in following a minor car accident from which he had suffered a bruised shoulder. "Shoulder again," she mused, wondering whether that was significant. The main point was that he had been taken to the hospital, so whatever the original injury was, it must have been severe enough to warrant his admission to Accident and Emergency. Then, despite being severely injured, he had managed to fix himself. Surely he would attempt to correct a bullet to the shoulder. Why had she not felt any attempts to tamper with her memories? Instead, he had simply run away.

She put the file back down on her desk, knocking over a stack of other files in the process. She didn't care. What if there was another explanation, something she was missing? Come to think of it, why had Macava been running with him last night? Macava was Davis's psychiatrist—or maybe not any more, it didn't make any difference. Whatever he was, he was

Davis's doctor and someone he trusted. Macava would know everything about him. Macava would have been keeping tabs on him. Macava was close to him.

Realization came to her like the sun penetrating the veil of night. What if Davis was a Recaller? One strong enough to see through unusually powerful transitions, even when standing in the same building. That kind of Recaller would be a serious threat to the subject she was hunting, unless he was kept close, kept in line, and kept away from the organization …. She stood up from the desk, horrified that she had been right next to the doctor, inches away from the very person keeping close to Davis, keeping him in line, keeping him away from her. The doctor's hostility made sense now, and although some parts of the theory still didn't fit, Kendra was fairly sure. Macava had to be the subject.

It all added up. Macava could have engineered it so that the Recaller would come to him for help, would trust him. That was why so much of what had happened was centered on John Davis. Could Macava have arranged for Kendra to survive the crash so she would attack Davis in a state of emotion, driving her to shoot but not kill? Davis would think that the organization was trying to kill him. Macava could then point Davis in the right direction, hoping he would bring down the organization or be killed in the process, depriving them of a new Recaller.

The doctor was right. A Recaller of Davis's magnitude would be very useful to the organization. He just hadn't counted on Kendra working it out. Well, if Davis was on his way, she would be waiting for him. She would make it easy for him to find them, and she would make sure he arrived on her terms. Macava would be eliminated. She just needed to pick her moment. For now she would make sure she was on the right track and check out her assumptions and anything she had on Macava, but she was fairly sure she was right.

She smiled into the deserted office. Tomorrow she would make the calls, pass off the failure as a last minute realization of the truth, and begin on the next phase of the plan. The final phase.

———————

On balance, John felt that bringing Jenna into his plan couldn't be seen as a betrayal of trust. He knew that whoever or whatever was out to hurt him, whoever had killed his best friend, could potentially attack anyone involved with him. Macava was already involved, and Chris had been eliminated for doing far less than Macava. John sat outside the café, shifting uncomfortably on the metal chair and trying to keep the table from rocking too wildly as he moved. His hot chocolate tilted treacherously in the cup every time he changed position, but the chair had apparently been crafted with the sole purpose of making the user extremely uncomfortable. This coupled with the fact that he was trying to rationalize some seriously immoral actions he was about to take—had already taken— made for a decidedly distracted state of mind.

Trying not to think about it, John unzipped his coat and hung it on the back of the chair, glad of the day's refreshing chill. He was still confused as to what time of year it was. The brilliant sunshine and cool air suggested a step back in time of about two months. Glancing around for the discarded newspapers that always floated around cafés, John collected one and took note of the date. It was Sunday and it was September. He had already accepted that the day he had driven home in the driving rain, a Wednesday in November as far as he was concerned, had been changed. The rhyme or reason for it he had yet to discover, but he would, and when he did someone was going to answer for it.

Taking a sip of the hot chocolate, he reflected on what Macava had said when he had finished telling the doctor the whole story. Macava had been dumbfounded, scarcely able to accept what he had heard, but having seen what he had seen and having been shot at by a mysterious woman who turned

113

out to be a detective from some unknown organization, he had found himself with little choice but to believe.

The doctor's input was invaluable to John. He had been instructed to make his reports to a man named Darren Brice, by a telephone number that was clearly redirected but was from the Southampton area. Brice was their only key to finding the organization, but first they had to find Brice. Luckily, according to Macava, Brice had not come across as particularly bright so he might not be too good at covering his tracks, especially if he didn't know his tracks ought to be covered.

John had a very useful friend, the kind of friend everyone should have; competent with computers and software to the point that it was actually quite scary, the kind of friend who could be used as a consultant for any computer-based query. Unfortunately, that friend was either dead or had never existed, and since losing Chris, John had vowed to make sure that none of his other friends followed him. He had two other friends who were good with technology, or at least better than him, but he wouldn't risk having them ripped out of his life as though they had never been there. He needed someone else.

Had he been wrong to contact Jenna instead of his friends? He was hoping she wouldn't be targeted so quickly because she didn't know him so well. Perhaps she wasn't being watched.

He smiled humorlessly and shook his head. If he was honest with himself, he had chosen her because he wouldn't risk anyone else, and if something happened to her he wouldn't be too burned up about it. He swallowed guiltily. He had to get on with it. What choice did he have?

Footsteps clattered up behind him and a breathless Jenna appeared next to him, mumbling an apology for being late and sitting on the cold metal chair opposite him. She was in a smart black jacket and jeans, and John was surprised to note that she actually looked pretty good. He wondered if he would ever stop being surprised that Jenna was good looking. It was

STEVEN D. JACKSON

because of her shyness that he automatically thought of her as mousey.

It wasn't until she had bought herself a coffee and mentioned the weather a few times that Jenna finally asked why he had called her out of the blue. "Erm, well, the last time I saw you I was in the hospital," John began, sheepishly remembering the way she had stormed out after he had ignored her, "and I don't think I was particularly nice to you."

Jenna beamed, obviously heartened by the start to the conversation. "Oh no, don't worry, you were ill, it's okay," she said all in one string. "I shouldn't have been so annoyed. It's just that I was there worrying about you and you pretty much ignored me and I didn't think it could be because of the illness or the accident or whatever. I just assumed you were being rude. Then when I got home I realized how stupid that was." She laughed nervously. "I thought you'd never speak to me again, and now here you are phoning me to apologize. I should apologize too."

John smiled and shook his head. "Don't worry, you don't need to apologize—"

She cut him off with a sharp look that seemed to him completely out of character. "Yes I do."

John's good humor soured a little and his smile faded as he wondered whether maybe Jenna had a couple of screws loose. Some kind of self-recrimination complex. Considering her timid character it wasn't entirely impossible. Perhaps he ought to rethink the plan a little.

"Okay. Look, Jen, there's another reason I brought you out here. There's something I need to tell you and I need to see if you think I'm just nuts or not. The thing is there's something happening to me ...."

Jenna listened to the story with a puzzled look on her face, but she was visibly alarmed at the part concerning Chris. "Oh, my God. What do you mean, he disappeared?" She frowned, as though trying to puzzle her way through what he was saying.

Then her eyes became a little wild. "You never mentioned a Chris before."

"No, I know, that's the point. You wouldn't remember because in this reality he never existed. Although he used to. He was my best friend, and only I remember him."

Jenna was staring at him with what looked like horror, but he couldn't tell if it was out of pity for the loss of his friend or the loss of his sanity. He decided to carry on. He told her about when he had kidnapped Macava, barely able to believe it had happened at all.

"I went a bit mental, actually. I had a knife and everything." John laughed in spite of himself, not considering how it would look to laugh at such a statement.

Jenna was appalled. "A knife? You threatened a doctor with a knife?" She spoke in a kind of hysterical undertone, as though to say it aloud might raise an alarm.

"Yeah, well I had to make it look serious, and I almost got him out into the woods when I got shot." He undid his shirt slightly and pulled it back so she could see the new bandage.

Jenna looked almost angry. She was shaking her head and staring into her coffee, and when she spoke it was almost as though she was talking to herself. "I missed it all, I didn't know. Jesus, you could have been killed." She looked up at him accusingly, but John was too lost in his thoughts to care as he continued his narrative.

When he got to the end of the story John paused, weighing his options. He knew it was time to make a decision. Taking a breath, he carried on. "So now Nicholas and I are going to find this organization and work out what is actually going on. It'll be dangerous, I expect, because they might know we're coming and they're probably still out to kill me. The thing is, Nicholas is old and I don't think I can do it on my own. Plus I'm not very good with computers, and I don't have anyone else to ask. I'll be honest with you, Jen. The fact that you are not exactly a known accomplice of mine makes you a better choice than anyone else. They won't be expecting me to team up with you, so you might be safer than anyone else. It'll be dangerous, though, so you have to decide."

Jenna leaned back in her chair, regarding him seriously. "What is it you want me to do, John? I'm happy to help, but I'm not the kind of person who can deal with breaking into places and things like that. Plus I really don't know how much of this I can believe. I wonder if maybe," she hesitated, groping for the words, "maybe this is all in your mind?"

John smiled and nodded. "I wish it was, Jen, really I do. All I really need you to do is help me track down this Brice person. He's the contact Nicholas was given, and you're better than me at computer stuff."

Jenna was silent for a while. Then she slowly nodded, although she appeared uncertain. "Okay, John, I'll help you find him. If it makes you happy, I'll do it. I'll come over after work tomorrow and I'll take the next couple of days off."

John was appalled. "Tomorrow? Jen, don't you see how serious this is? We could be dead by then."

She stared at him, her expression one of disbelief. "Look, you just asked me to jump into this insanity with you, and you aren't even sure what's happening anyway! You asked me to drop everything and maybe even risk my life on your say so and I've agreed, so the least you can do is give me a bit of time to think it through. I'll come tomorrow. Don't try to tell me you think we'll all be dead by then, because if it was that serious we wouldn't be sitting in a café chatting about it."

John gritted his teeth, biting back a response. What on earth was there to think about? Still, she was right. He needed her help, so he had to give her the time she asked for, irritating though it was. He let out a breath and smiled at her, nodding affably and agreeing to her request.

She smiled broadly and began to say something else, but John wasn't listening. His mind was racing ahead, trying to think where they needed to start and how long it would take. He was so distracted that he didn't notice the smile fade from Jenna's face.

Darren Brice slammed the door of his microwave oven and stabbed at the power button on the front. The door made a satisfying bang but failed to lessen his frustration. Sarah Kendra was the best in the business as far as he was concerned. She was talented, beautiful, and intelligent, so how had she managed to fail? He had picked up what had happened during the course of the day, from the beating up of the receptionist to the strange sight of Davis running off with one of their pet doctors. Stomping ponderously to his cupboard, he pulled out a glass, lost in thought.

Kendra had read the report. She would have known there was only one option. Following the car accident that had killed her favorite Recaller, she should have been utterly merciless. She should have marched straight up to Davis and put a bullet through his head. Something had gone wrong, something Brice hadn't foreseen. He cursed under his breath as he pulled the orange juice from the fridge. His problem was that he didn't think far enough ahead. He lived in the present and found it hard to concentrate on things further away than a day or two. It always struck him as pointless anyway, because how could anyone know what would happen? How could anyone know if their plans would count for anything at all in the next few hours, let alone days? Brice was in a better position to know that than most. Then again, his view wasn't shared by those he worked with. Kendra made plans far into the future. He knew that from her remarks, although she had never really told him what they were. That was probably for the best.

The fact that Kendra had failed meant that Brice had to think very carefully about what to do. What was the logical next step for Davis? He now knew someone was after him and he would have found out pretty quickly what the doctor knew, so he would be aware there was an organization full of people willing to shoot him. The doctor was now protecting him, which meant he had told Davis everything, though he didn't know much.

Except your name.

The electronic bell of the microwave pinged, cutting through the silence and making Brice jump. The damn thing was a liability. When there was no other sound in the flat but his own movements, it was unnecessarily loud. He supposed it had been built with deaf people in mind, or busy people. It was a shame you couldn't shape technology the way you wanted it.

This thought struck him suddenly as absurd. Of course technology could be shaped. If there was one thing he was good at, it was that. And this Davis guy was relatively young, he would think of the internet as a first step to finding out more about the name the doctor had given him. He was also clever. *But not as clever as me.*

All Brice had to do was make sure the information was there to be found, and then be there when Davis showed up. The microwave meal was forgotten in the time it took to him waddle into his bedroom and power up the computer. He hummed softly. This was going to be far too easy. Laying the trail would be relatively simple. The difficulty would come when he actually met Davis. How to take him out was the question Brice needed to answer.

Not only that, but if Kendra wanted Davis and he was shot by Brice, she wouldn't be best pleased. It was therefore vital that Brice never actually hear her say that she wanted Davis alive. The last thing she had said to him was that they needed him dead and that Brice should get the evidence to justify this decision. Since he hadn't been told otherwise he was free to assume that Davis had to die and could easily justify killing him. He would need to sneak into work tomorrow and sign out a weapon. No one would suspect him, and then he could call in sick and head to the site of his planned ambush.

His mother's house was in the New Forest, not too far from Southampton where the organization made its headquarters and where Brice had his poxy flat. She had died some time ago, but he had never sold the house. Sometimes he went there to be alone with his memories of her, looking at the ornaments still in place and the pictures still on the walls. The reverence he felt for the house prevented him from living in it. It was rundown and more like an old fashioned log cabin than a house, but it was a palace by comparison with his flat and had a good few acres of land around it. It was isolated, and while not exactly in the Forest itself, was still a long way from the public road and farther still from any neighbors. It would do nicely.

Brice grinned to himself, ignoring the grumbling of his ample stomach and the smell of the microwave meal as he began to create a path for John Davis to follow.

Jenna and Macava turned up about seven o'clock the next evening, before John was ready for them. Despite his desperation he still wanted to do things right and had planned to get some food and drinks ready. He had, however, spent the day worrying, writing down everything that had happened to him, everything he had surmised, everything he had been told, and everyone who was involved. He was trying to come up with a diagram to reflect the circumstances just in case he had missed something. Now more than ever he was afraid he was leading the others into a dangerous situation, one they might not come out of very well—if at all.

Macava arrived looking cheerful and optimistic and wandered around the spacious flat, commenting on the size of it and how clean it was. The one thing John had managed to do that day was run his Hoover around the place, but it was definitely not clean. Nicholas was simply being, as always, exceedingly polite.

"Not to worry, John," he said, "the sooner we find out everything there is to know about this organization, the sooner we can get rid of it completely. Then you can set about fixing your flat." He chuckled and resumed his pacing of the lounge, looking at the pictures of John and his brother on the windowsill. He picked up one in particular, of the two of them sitting on an old bench in a military base, both looking as dashing as they could manage. In it, the brothers looked remarkably similar. Although George was taller and darker than John, he did have the same set to his facial features, and when the two of them wore the same expression it was easy to see they were brothers. John kept the picture on the windowsill for that reason. It was testament to their brotherhood. John liked it a lot.

He was so pleased that Macava had picked out his favorite photo that he almost didn't notice the cryptic nature of the remark. The doctor appeared to be on a mission to bring the organization down, whereas John wanted to find out what they wanted him for. Destroying the place wouldn't give him his answers, but he didn't want to question Macava just yet, not while their aims were essentially the same.

Jenna looked decidedly sullen when she turned up, which was quite a change from the enthusiasm of the previous day. Still, it was enough for John that she was on board, and he was happy both his guests had arrived in good time. He had volunteered to head out for some drinks and nibbles to keep them going, acutely aware of the utter lack of anything edible in the flat except cheese and bread. He hurried out to the corner store and gazed around the shelves, trying to find something suitable for everyone. The selection of beer was shocking, ranging from cheap watered-down stuff to slightly more expensive watered-down stuff, and the wine looked pretty nasty too. He had never thought about it before, had always simply wandered in, looked at the prices, and happily bought the maximum alcohol content for the cheapest price. Now, though, he had a psychiatrist and a girl to entertain, and he was utterly perplexed.

He eventually settled for two bottles of red wine of a fairly passable appearance—despite being on a two for one offer—

and made his way to the checkout. As ever, he was the only one in the shop except for the large, round man who had sold him alcoholic beverages for some considerable time and who had never seen him be so picky before. The man smiled an extremely lascivious smile and said in his most suggestive voice, "Ah, entertaining perhaps?"

John smiled weakly. Trying to avoid the horrible thought of what the man might be picturing in his sweaty head, he fished in his pocket for his wallet. The price was surprisingly low, and only then did John realize he had forgotten the nibbles. Sighing inwardly, he hurried back through the darkness to the flat, the bottles clinking together in the plastic bag as he walked. Now came the difficult part.

CHAPTER ELEVEN

t was dark enough now to justify heading up to the building. Apparently Dr. Macava saw his patients in a special annex off the side of his house. The house was huge, at least seven or eight bedrooms, so it had probably been built with the idea of having an annex wing in mind. Kendra crept soundlessly across the dark grass, making for the office door at the side of the building. As she expected, no one appeared to be home. She knew the doctor lived alone, so there was no reason to expect anyone else to be there. Not that it mattered. His living arrangements would be irrelevant soon enough. She would see to that.

For now she would settle for a bit more information on her quarry. This office was likely to contain a lot of useful information, and she intended to go through it carefully while Macava was elsewhere. She had no doubt that the psychiatrist was with Davis, probably grooming him for some kind of assault on the organization. The one thing she was sure of was that Macava did not have enough information on them yet to make an effective assault. Anything he tried would be felt and targeted with their full force. He would no doubt use Davis to help him unless she got to Davis first, which, she had to admit, she probably would not. Brice had provided her with the doctor's address, but had been unable to get much on Davis.

While that stood to reason, particularly if Macava was assisting Davis, something about it just didn't sit right with Kendra. Brice was the best in his field, and this was the first time he had failed to come up with something useful. Since she no longer believed that Davis was the subject, she hadn't pressed the issue. However, as she didn't want to let Brice go off the boil, she hadn't told him of her newest discovery. She wanted him working on the assumption that anyone she requested information on could be the one. The last thing she needed was him forming opinions of his own.

She reached the door, which was locked. She considered using her lock-picks, but looking at the old and faded doorframe, she thought a few solid kicks might do it. She stared almost longingly at the door, trying to justify her reckless impulse to kick it down. Taking a step back, she lined herself up and glanced around at the street before returning her attention to the exact spot right next to the door's feeble lock where a powerful blow would splinter the wood. She caught herself before she went any further, retrieving the lock-picks and getting to work. It really wouldn't help her cause to tip the doctor off if he came back to a splintered, broken door.

A few minutes later the door swung inward on rusted hinges, giving her access to the dark room beyond. She closed the door, glad she hadn't kicked it off its hinges in full view of the street. She had to get a grip on herself. She wasn't normally this cavalier. Closing the curtains, she flipped the lights on and glanced around the room. It was cozy, with a fireplace at the end opposite the door with a comfortable armchair beside it. A low coffee table sat before the armchair and separated what she assumed was the patient's armchair from that of the doctor. The patient would have no view of the door or the clock, presumably to give the impression of an unhurried and calm atmosphere. There was a lamp on a stand next to both the doctor and the patient, and pictures of various landscapes in heavy oak frames hung on the walls. It was a nicely decorated room, as homely and unthreatening as a room could be.

On Kendra's side of the room stood filing cabinets and a desk with a simple chair. She moved to the cabinets and pulled out the drawer for D, immediately finding John Davis's file. Her eyes moved from paragraph to paragraph of medical history and allergies, to the 'personal background' section, compiled from a number of entries dating back two or three years. Clearly Davis had been having sessions with Macava for a long time. No wonder he was close to him, she thought, and no wonder he had turned violent when he discovered Macava had been making reports about him. That would explain why Macava hadn't used a transition to hurt John when he came for him. The doctor cared about this patient. By now she supposed Macava would have done something to heal the bullet wound John had suffered, so he would be in even more debt to the man he knew so little about yet who knew virtually everything about him.

Kendra read some of the background information, feeling her resolve falter a little in the face of the sad picture being built up.

'... John is plagued by his obsessive nature. The difficulty is that there does not appear to be a specific reason for him to be so afraid of the world, so it can be difficult for him to believe that he can be 'cured', as he puts it; he considers that he is either inherently damaged or else his fears must be justified. Unfortunately, since I cannot agree that he is inherently damaged, showing him that his fears are not justified is unusually complicated. I am confident that eventually we will find a way to increase his confidence in himself so that he can look the future in the face and move on with his life. However, until we reach that point, he will forever be tormented by the idea that he is unable to cope, that the future is chaos, and that people cannot be relied upon. His fear is compounded by the worry that his ability to form relationships with other people might be stunted, which is one of the reasons why he came to me to begin with ....'

'... John has missed his last few appointments and I am beginning to worry that the emotional breakdown he suffered at the last meeting has compounded his difficulties. If he does not attend the next one I will call him. He is not dealing with this as well as I had hoped ....'

'... His tendency to think deeply about everything he encounters causes him a lot of difficulties; he often cannot accept things at face value, even something as simple as an emotion or an idea. This is especially true if he believes his own jaded view of the world has already affected his experience of the idea. My one consolation is that he recognizes that his obsessiveness about the reliability of people, the world, and reality itself is affecting his experiences. I see this as a positive development ....'

'... John fixates on what might be and how to get there, but feels powerless to help himself reach his goals. He needs to learn to pull himself back from his obsessions and regain control, to be confident in his ability to cope with the future and in the trustworthiness of others ....'

Kendra flipped forward to the last few entries, her eyes narrowed in thought. The writing had been on the wall for some time with this one. He had demonstrated an obvious mistrust of reality itself, along with everyone in it. How tragic that he had been right all along. In her experience nothing was reliable. The only difference was that John was only worried about the future. He couldn't have known that the past could be rewritten too.

She made a mental note to get more reports earlier on. If this kind of obsession was the precursor to a Recaller's ability manifesting, then she should really be looking out for them.

Finally she replaced the file. She now faced a dilemma. John Davis would not take kindly to her murdering Macava. She might not be able to persuade him to join the organization afterwards and he might do something reactionary, like going to the press. If that happened, she would have to take him down. She recoiled at the prospect. Shooting the poor guy when she had no real reason to would be inhumane, but at the same time she had to remember her priorities. *No,* she reminded herself, *your priorities are keeping everyone safe. Macava dies because he is a threat and there is no choice. Davis lives unless you have no choice. You have a choice at this point, so he lives.*

She nodded, and turned to survey the rest of the room. She needed to find Macava quickly. The clue to his whereabouts would be somewhere in this house, unless he did her a favor and came right to her.

———————

Something wasn't right. Darren Brice had to be one of the easiest people to find in the entire world. It had taken Jenna about two minutes to find his unprotected Facebook page, and then a few more to find a personal blog website with photos and a home address. John had shouted and whooped when she found the pages, intoxicated with their success, the fact that they were on their way, and that the plan was working. Until, that is, he felt a strange misgiving which he mentioned to the others. Macava reacted by saying they shouldn't over-think it, if it was there then they should go with it, but Jenna agreed with John. Their success had been far, far too easy.

Macava sat deep in thought, rubbing his hand across his forehead and going back over the arguments again. "I have to confess that when I spoke to the man on the phone he didn't seem at all clever to me. I had the distinct impression that he was, you know, a pen pusher. A nobody who collated reports for people like that Kendra woman we saw at the hospital. I really find it hard to credit he would even consider people might be looking for him, so what possible reason would he have for protecting his web blog thing, whatever it is? Surely it's no wonder that the information is so accessible?"

John raised his head from the arm of the leather sofa upon which he had been reclining. It wasn't nearly as comfortable as his old sofa, but to moan about it would be like complaining you had an uncomfortable Jaguar instead of a cozy Metro. In any case, the sofa changing was a good thing. The old one would probably have collapsed under the strain of two people sitting on it.

"Nicholas, as far as I knew up until, oh, let's say Wednesday last week, I didn't think anyone was after me either, but you type my name into Google and you'll find two entries. One listing me as a solicitor under the law society thing, which doesn't have any details except my name and my firm, and the other is my Facebook page where you can only see my name and my profile photo. I put all the security stuff I could think of on it, or rather I got someone to do that for me. The point is there are people out there collecting and stealing people's data and the last thing you want is for someone to get hold of stuff like that. Plus there's the fact that you don't want your boss seeing your full profile because it has pictures of drunken parties and stuff on it. I don't use things like Twitter for the same reason, it's just not safe."

Macava nodded. "So someone who works for this kind of organization would probably know about security and be as paranoid as you two seem to be?"

"Exactly. So something weird is happening here."

"Yes, but this man isn't all that bright, as I said, so his plan probably isn't that foolproof, is it? He must have expected us to follow his little false trail, so he wouldn't expect us to dig very deep."

Jenna came back to the lounge, a look of smugness on her face. John shifted lazily on the sofa, turning to face her as she entered the room. "Any luck?"

"Yes, thank you," she said tartly, assuming an aloof

SHIFTER

expression but with a telltale smirk curling at the corners of her mouth. "Okay, here's what I did—you ready for this?" She smiled again.

John had no idea how good she was with computers. He supposed it was just luck that he had met her just when he needed someone with computer expertise. Trying very hard not to pull that fragile hope to pieces by shining some realism on it, he turned his attention back to Jenna.

"So, you know that computers all have IP addresses, and that the internet basically runs off those and the TCP ...," she trailed off, seeing the blank looks on both men's faces. "Internet Protocol and Transmission Control Protocol? No? Okay, well, basically I tracked the computer that put that blog site up and traced some other things it had done, some other places it had visited, and I managed to work out where it lives. There was a hell of a lot of work involved with this, you two. Stop looking at me like that."

"Like what?" John asked innocently.

"Like I'm speaking another language or lying or something."

John laughed. He had no idea what she had been doing except that she had somehow managed to find the computer. "So where is it?"

"It's registered to an address in Southampton, not too far from the New Forest. He obviously doesn't have much of an imagination, either that or he's lazy. The fake address is only about twenty minutes away from the real one."

John was more than just impressed, he was overjoyed. They had smashed the guy's plan to bits and it was all thanks to her. He peeled himself off the sofa. Bouncing across the room, he enfolded Jenna in a comradely embrace. "Nice one, Jen, we've got the guy now."

Jenna laughed weakly and brought her arms around to clap him self-consciously on the back. Her breath was shaky and he could feel her heart beating fast. He pulled away, concerned. "Everything okay?"

She looked at the floor, nodding vigorously. John realized

it was just nerves. She wasn't quite ready for anything like a hug just yet. Still, he thought as he turned away and went back to his nest on the sofa, she was making great progress. He had never thought he would be able to have a proper joke with her, and tonight she had been great. He looked forward to getting to know her better.

"So when do we move out?" Macava said in a terrible attempt at an American accent.

This struck Jenna as absolutely hilarious and she collapsed in fits of laughter. John watched her, grinning in spite of himself. The comment had been lame, almost groan-worthy. It had certainly not been that funny. Macava had done it to break the tension, and for that John was grateful. He turned back to the doctor. "I say we go tomorrow, get some supplies and head down in the early evening. We should stay over in one of those cheap hotels and go and see Brice the next morning. If he set up those fake websites to lead us to that fake house of his, he won't be expecting us to turn up where he actually is, and he certainly won't expect it during the daytime. I think he'll expect us to make our move on the fake house in the evening, so he'll head over there to ambush us just before it gets dark. We get to him in the real house before he goes out."

Macava nodded, mulling over the plan. John watched him apprehensively, hoping he would agree. The plan was logical, and if Brice was really waiting for them, he would probably expect an attack at night. Macava looked at him, his brow furrowed. "I am a little concerned, John, that this man presents himself as a fool when quite clearly he has the presence of mind to set up fake websites when he suspects an attack. He was smart enough to figure out that the only link you had to the organization was him, through me, and he took intelligent counter measures. I can't help but wonder whether there is even more to this than we think."

"You mean a double bluff?" John was doubtful. This was a fruitless path to go down. They could twist themselves inside out trying to guess whether Brice would have guessed they

STEVEN D. JACKSON

would guess what he was up to. "Nicholas," he said, sinking down on the sofa and clasping his hands, "you spent a long time telling me not to over-think, so logically we have to choose whether to go with the bluff or the double bluff. In the end it comes down to a fifty-fifty which house to go to."

"No, John, because if the first house is a fake as we think it is, if we then go to the second house and *that's* the trap ...."

They talked about the problem for what felt like hours without coming to any conclusion. The truth remained that the internet trail could either have been designed to lure them to an ambush at the first house, or to make them think they had figured out and avoided an ambush at the first only to fall into one at the second.

John rubbed his hands over his face. This was beginning to make his head hurt. "It stands to reason in my mind that he isn't planning on us working out that the internet trail leads to a trap."

Jenna nodded. "Unless that is exactly what he knew we would think."

Sighing deeply, John stared up at the ceiling. If he didn't make a plan soon they would talk around this issue until they all died of old age. He closed his eyes and spoke as he reasoned it through.

"We go to the false house that we know is a trap, but we get there before he sets it. He'll turn up to set the trap and we'll catch him when he arrives. If he doesn't show up, we'll know we were meant to go to the real house after all. That way we'll know his actual place is the trap. We win both ways."

The other two were silent for a minute, thinking through the logic and passing no comment. Finally Macava stood up, stretching and saying through a yawn, "I don't think we'll ever really know until we try the plan, but we need to be prepared for the fact that we might be falling into the trap even by thinking we are outwitting this man. We need to be on our guard, but I think the plan is as sound as we can make it. I'm going home. I'll see you both tomorrow about one o'clock.

We can get the supplies and book ourselves into some hotel for the evening. It will take about an hour and a half or two hours to get down there, so I think that will leave us plenty of time."

Jenna glanced unhappily at John. She had firmly resisted the idea of using any weaponry or offensive tactics, and the suggestion of buying 'supplies' of that kind had made her very uncomfortable. John gazed back as impassively as he could. The decision had been made and he wasn't prepared to discuss it any further. They would be foolish in the extreme not to go prepared for resistance. Jenna sighed, made her farewells, and headed off with the doctor, leaving John alone to obsess over the logic puzzle and whether or not he was about to get two people, as well as himself, killed.

Kendra had been through every sheet of paper in Macava's office that looked even remotely important. She had gone over every surface, picked up every file, yet nothing she saw gave her anything useful. When she moved on to the rest of the house it was another story. There were personal possessions everywhere, keepsakes of a well-spent life.

From numerous picture frames around the spacious building, various people smiled out at her, one of them a woman at various stages of life, ranging from very young to what seemed to be late twenties or early thirties. She was a stern looking woman, not unattractive, but not beautiful in any traditional sense. Kendra lingered for a while trying to work out who she and the others were before returning her attention to the search for documents. Since Macava was alone now she assumed that the woman had been his wife and briefly wondered what had happened to her.

However, the doctor's personal life was of no importance. The man was dangerous, manipulative, and ruthless. He was responsible for at least one death, and she wondered whether his apparent success was real or something he had engineered himself. Perhaps he was even responsible for whatever had become of his wife. She soon found herself snarling at the happy faces in the pictures, feeling that the doctor did not deserve such lavish surroundings and hating the fact that others had perished to provide them. When she kicked over a coffee table in frustration her guilt was swept away by a wave of righteous rage, and she began ripping drawers open and searching through bookshelves with an abandon that gave vent to her feelings.

Finally, in the doctor's bedroom, she found a useful file of paperwork. Bank statements and credit card details all neatly kept in a leather-bound folder. She didn't really need these things. She could have gotten someone to track down the numbers and alert her when they were used. Nevertheless she took the folder and made her way through the ransacked house to the door by which she had entered. She couldn't waste any more time. She knew she wouldn't get a second chance to catch him at home, but another Recaller would have to take over the vigil while she concentrated on leads elsewhere.

Tomorrow she would begin the trace on his credit cards. If Macava used them she would know. She thought he would, eventually, whenever he had to stop running. When he did, he would send a signal straight to her. Kendra sauntered purposefully through the office door, flipping off the light switch and closing the door out of sheer force of habit. She allowed herself a half smile as she headed into the night.

The trap was closing.

TWELVE

CHAPTER

The digits on his mobile phone told him it was one in the morning. John groaned and flopped back onto the pillow, squeezing his eyes tightly shut as if he could force his brain back to sleep. The bed was warm and his hand was cold as it held the phone an inch off the bedside table. He let it drop and tucked his hand back in, trying to think what on earth had woken him.

The banging came again, more insistent than before. Someone was knocking very loudly on his door.

Groping sleepily for something to wear and managing to grab an old crumpled shirt which was conveniently lying next to his bed, John staggered toward the light switch, tugging on the shirt as he went. He didn't bother buttoning it and just let it flap loosely around him as he wandered through the lounge, rubbing sleep from his eyes. Just as he reached the door the knocking came again. Someone was pounding on the other side like they were planning to knock it down.

"Who is it?" His voice was slurred, but his brain was waking up fast. There was no way he was opening that door without good reason.

"It's Nicholas! John, please let me in."

Macava sounded desperate, his muffled voice managing to carry a note of hysteria even through the wooden door.

Clicking the deadbolt to one side, John opened the door and admitted the doctor, letting it latch as he turned back to Nicholas. Then he thought better of it and dead-bolted it again. Macava had the look of a hunted man, his eyes were hollow and his face was pale. John hurried toward him and guided him to the sofa. The doctor was in a terrible state. John perched over him, trying to look into his eyes.

"Nicholas, what the hell's happened? Are you alright? You look awful."

Macava was regaining control and he cast a wry eye in John's direction. "I could say the same for you, John. Do you always greet your guests half naked?"

"Huh?" John blinked at his unexpected guest, thinking it was the most outlandish thing to say after such a panicked entrance. He was aware that he was wearing only a pair of boxer shorts and an open shirt, not the most sincere of outfits for a late night emergency, but why was the doctor commenting on John's lack of attire at a time like this?

He frowned at the doctor and made his way to the kitchen, buttoning the shirt and muttering to himself. If this was some kind of joke, then he wasn't the least bit amused, but since he was awake he might as well make a cup of tea. He left the kettle boiling and headed back to his bedroom for a pair of jeans, still not knowing what to make of Macava's sudden and perplexing appearance. As he made his way back to the kitchen, the doctor started talking again.

"My house has been taken apart, John. I don't know who did it, but when I got back the place was in a dreadful state. Papers everywhere, furniture knocked over. It's obviously not a robbery because nothing is missing." He paused, probably realizing he was preaching to the converted on that point. John would never have considered it a robbery. "They went in through the office door. I've shut it all back up, but that door won't close properly now. I think they forced it with picks. I can lock the main house from the inside, but all my files are wide open for anyone to read, not that there's anything of any interest to anyone unless

135

they're looking for someone in particular. They got to me, John. They know I'm helping you. I don't think you should stay here tonight. I think we should leave now."

John placed the doctor's tea on the coffee table and took a seat in the armchair, trying to clear his sleep-fogged thoughts and take in what was being said. "No way, Nicholas. I'm not leaving here at one in the morning. They had all day to come for me and they didn't. I'm not running now, not when we are about to bring the fight to them. Besides, I don't have anywhere else to go. And Jenna isn't here, and she's coming with us."

"You aren't thinking properly, John. They tried to kill you before. Now they've tried to get me. What makes you think they—"

John cut him off by leaning forward suddenly, almost spilling his tea. He was faintly aware that he would have burned himself if he hadn't gotten dressed. "You said your files are wide open?"

"Yes, the office door was open—"

"Is mine in there?" John was suddenly nervous. He didn't know for sure what was in that file, but he had a fairly good idea. Whoever was after him had been able to see, quite literally, inside his head. He hated the thought that a stranger had been reading about his personal demons. Panic began to creep through him.

Macava looked down at his cup. "Yes, John, it is. I didn't even … I'm sorry." He said it quietly, without looking up. He was silent for a few moments before glancing at John to see how he was taking this news.

John stood up, absently placing a hand over his mouth and rubbing his chin as his thoughts raced. It didn't really matter, did it? All those sessions in the past were just that, the past. It wouldn't do to get upset about them now, but his attempts at rationalization couldn't hold back the rising sense of desperation he felt creeping into him. He closed his eyes briefly and turned to face the doctor, determined to put a brave face on it.

"It's okay. It's okay, Nicholas, they're old files anyway. I guess this might even help us a bit, especially if they think I'm nuts." John forced a laugh. The effort of keeping his voice jovial and casual was getting too much. He wanted to go sit somewhere quiet and think, or better yet, to go back to bed and never come out.

Macava stood up and moved toward him, but he barely noted the doctor's approach. He stared fixedly at the floor, feeling hands on his shoulders. He was dimly aware that Macava was trying to look into his eyes. His voice when he spoke was low and soft. "I don't want you to worry about this, okay, John? It was only a file. It was out of date and it was only my recording of my own thoughts. It doesn't give anyone anything more over you than they already had. It doesn't mean we are going to fail. Don't let this make you lose heart, alright? Just don't think about it. It isn't important. What is important is what we are doing tomorrow, not what someone thinks they know about you. Now, we aren't running tonight, I think you are right about that. I want you to go back to bed and relax. I will sleep here on the sofa."

John nodded numbly. Mentioning the file and its contents had made him go back over everything the file must contain. He was now reliving thoughts and feelings he hadn't experienced for a long time. His confidence in himself, the plan, everything they had been discussing, fell to nothing. He was vaguely conscious of the doctor leading him back to his bedroom. He managed to mumble a thank you to the man he had trusted for so many years before he closed the door and moved mechanically toward the bed.

John pulled off the shirt and jeans and collapsed, feeling like the last few minutes hadn't happened at all. He reached over to the lamp and switched off the light, wanting the darkness to swallow him.

John woke to the sounds of sizzling and pans clattering. As they progressed gradually through his sleep-clogged brain, he became slowly aware that someone was cooking something in his kitchen. It was odd to think of the kitchen actually being used for cooking, especially since John's culinary skills began and ended with a can opener.

Dragging himself from the bed and remembering to get dressed this time, John headed into the lounge to see what Macava was up to. He was fervently glad to see that the doctor was also dressed. He dreaded to think what the alternative would have done to his appetite. John sat on the sofa and waited for the man to notice him, staring vaguely out of the window and listening to the doctor singing softly to himself. He was of two minds about the plan today. It had all sounded so viable before, but now he felt like it was full of gaping holes.

"Ah, good morning, John," called Macava from the kitchen. Stirring himself from his negative musings, John stood up and wandered through the doorway, stopping short at the sight before him.

Rarely, if ever, had his kitchen seen such frenetic activity, either in this incarnation or the first. Macava had used almost every item of crockery in the place to produce what appeared to be a huge array of breakfast items. "Er, Nicholas, exactly how many people are we feeding today?" John was wondering if he ought to start fearing for the man's sanity.

Macava turned to face him, both hands wrapped in an oven glove and holding a frying pan overloaded with scrambled eggs. Grinning broadly, the doctor bustled past John and placed the eggs on the sideboard, removing his hands from the glove and turning back with a look of triumph. "I thought since we were going into battle we could do with something decent to eat. Young Miss—er, what's Jenna's surname?"

"Stanton."

"Yes, young Miss Stanton will be here, so that's three. I

slipped out while you were asleep and got some decent supplies. Honestly, John, I thought you went to buy food last night. Don't you ever eat?"

The doctor peered critically at John's frame. He had never been a big eater and he was a bit on the thin side. John straightened his back and tried to appear healthy, the effect being more akin to that of a flustered peacock. At that moment there came a knock on the front door. Glancing quickly at the clock situated above the fridge, John noted it was only 10:00 a.m.

"Hiya," came Jenna's distracted greeting as she hurried through the front door and into the lounge. "I wanted to get here early so we could talk about getting supplies. I was thinking, I know we discussed this yesterday, but I really don't think we need anything, do we? I mean, we are going to Southampton and staying in a hotel, but we won't be, you know, attacking anyone, will we...?" Jenna was talking very fast, her hands held in front of her as if to slow the madness of what she was suggesting.

John covered his surprise at her flustered entrance and his irritation at her mentioning this again. He held her gaze as levelly as he could, not wanting to give her any false hopes. "Look, Jen, like we said yesterday, we don't know what it might come to. This man we need to talk to, he might know we're coming and he might not. We need things we can use in any situation that might come up. We might have to interrogate him, fight him, or defend ourselves from him, so we need those kinds of supplies. It's okay. I sort of did the same thing when I kidnapped Nicholas." He laughed sheepishly, absently rubbing his shoulder where the bullet had hit him.

It was strange, he thought, the wound wasn't in the least bit painful any more. It ought to be extremely sore, but it hadn't bothered him at all since yesterday. He was given no time to ponder his rapid recovery. Jenna had discovered the extremely enticing smell coming from the kitchen and was moving in its direction. Before she could take two more steps, though, Macava came bounding out, laden with plates.

"Since John has nothing resembling a decent table in this place," he said jauntily, "I suspect we shall have to eat on our laps, but never mind, it's the food that counts."

Jenna turned a slightly perplexed gaze on John, shrugging her shoulders and accepting the plate of food gratefully.

Soon after the breakfast of sausage, eggs, bacon, beans, and various other foods had been finished and cleaned up, the subject turned to the rather more serious matter at hand. Very quickly they ran into problems and the mood soured considerably.

"I still think we ought to rethink all this," Jenna insisted. "We can't actually be thinking about kidnapping a man and questioning him, can we? What are you planning to do, torture him?"

John sighed. They had been through this already and his patience was running out. "Jen, if the guy tells us what we need to know then it won't come to that. But to be honest, if we have to, then yes, we will."

"Well, what gives you the right to—?"

"Because my best friend is dead!" John rose angrily to his feet. He could feel his grip on his temper loosening and he didn't care. At that moment he felt only rage and a deep, burning desire to do as much damage as he possibly could to anyone who had been complicit in Chris's death. He turned away from them, his eyes watering. He swiped at the tears in irritation.

The room was silent. Jenna was staring at him open-mouthed, her eyes taking on a pitying look before she too looked away. "I'm sorry, I really am. I forgot the reasons we're doing all this."

John stared at the floor, feeling mastery of his emotions slowly return. When his breathing was back under control he headed back to the sofa, not looking at either of them. "I think we've been over everything now, haven't we? Can we just get going? I'd feel loads better if we just got moving."

Macava stirred. "I agree. There's no point going over it all again. Let's just head into town and pick up the things we need. We can take my car."

Once in town they headed off to get the various supplies, each going to different shops in search of the items on their list. It had taken a while to come up with the list, as no one was sure exactly what they might need. From John's point of view all they really needed was some duct tape—he had left his back at the shack near the hospital—another big knife, and a sledgehammer in case they needed to break down doors or something. Jenna added that because they were staying away for a while they should have backpacks for clothes and a tent in case they had to run away. She was clearly thinking they would end up on the run in the New Forest. Following on from that, the ideas turned more toward comfort than necessity. John, out of impatience, divided the items up and told them to add whatever they thought they needed as they went along.

He was waiting in the car park with his bag of essentials when it occurred to him that if this all went wrong he could end up dead or in prison. He had been running on adrenaline for so long that the reality of it had somehow passed him by. He stood in the sunshine looking around at all the normal people around him. Did they have any idea that their lives could be twisted and changed, manipulated in a way they could neither prevent nor remember? No. They were totally unaware, and while John knew that the cliché demanded he envy them their blissful ignorance, it was actually very refreshing to be the one who knew the game, even if he didn't know the players or the rules.

Ignorance was not bliss at all, he reflected, but being aware of other people's ignorance was terrifying and gratifying in equal measure. There was a certain comfort in that thought, the concept that he knew what was really happening, because it struck him that if he was caught and killed, or ended up in prison, he would at least have known the truth.

A strange feeling of liberty crept over him. What if he had been given a purpose above and beyond everyone else's, and what if he had *carte blanche* to pursue it? Macava's voice cut through this thought from a few yards away.

"We're back! I think we have everything now." Hurrying to the car the doctor hoisted his bag of clanking objects into the boot and took Jenna's from her. "Okay, let's get moving!" Macava smiled brightly and practically skipped around to the driver's door.

John watched him with curiosity. The man was so much happier this morning, so alive somehow. John realized that this trip was more than a dark journey of revenge and discovery for his former doctor. It was an adventure, a mystery to be solved. He suddenly felt a great, wrenching pity for Macava, who he thought must be a very lonely man. He had never taken much of an interest in his psychiatrist's life. Perhaps he should try to get to know him a bit better. He felt he owed Macava that, at least.

It was early evening by the time they arrived at the roadside hotel, having stopped for dinner on the way. John paid for their meal out of guilt, knowing that he was leading them into danger and feeling that the least he could do was get them something to eat. It had occurred to him during the meal that although he had chosen Jenna precisely because he didn't know her very well, as time went on the fear of losing her was growing. Despite her initial shyness she had been there for him throughout this ordeal, and he was enjoying getting to know her.

The lights were startlingly bright inside the hotel reception area, the uninteresting yellow and brown decor making the place look as though it was glowing. It all struck John as distinctly odd, and he was extremely glad they were only here for a few nights.

Before we end up in prison or dead ....

He quelled the treacherous voice inside his head and hauled his bag and Jenna's behind him as he followed Macava into the building.

"Hello, my dear," Macava said to the girl behind the desk.

142

She was heavily made up, with her hair piled up on top of her head and leaning at an improbable angle as she sat smiling widely at them. "Could we have two rooms please, one twin and a single?"

The girl nodded happily and started tapping on her keyboard. She appeared quite ecstatic at the whole idea, but John supposed she had just been trained to smile idiotically the whole time she was in the presence of a customer. He smirked to himself, imagining the Human Resources training she had probably endured in order to maximize customer happiness by having a plastic smile permanently glued to her face. She probably hated this place, her job, and them. Chuckling, John turned to Jenna, intending to comment.

Jenna had moved in close and was about to whisper something to him. John had to jerk his head back to keep from bashing her head with his. Jenna didn't seem to notice, or if she did, she didn't care. "Hey, why is he getting a twin?"

Macava turned and grinned. "Because, my dear girl, I do not have the cash to pay for three singles when a twin for me and John would be far cheaper. Unless you want to chip in?"

John was horrified. "No, Nicholas, you don't have to pay for—" Suddenly he realized the fatal flaw in his plan. He didn't have the cash to pay for nights in hotels, certainly not for more than one night and definitely not for more than one person. "Ah. Yeah. Sorry about that, I don't know why I didn't even think about money. Do you … is it okay?" He felt decidedly sheepish.

Macava smiled indulgently, adopting the consoling tone a grandfather might use to his hopelessly useless but greatly adored grandson. "Never mind, John, I'm perfectly happy to get this. It's only right that I get to spend a bit of cash on this little trip. I can't take it with me, can I?" He chuckled to himself as he turned back to the smiling mannequin behind the desk and handed over his credit card.

THIRTEEN

CHAPTER

As John and Macava chose their beds and began unpacking their toothbrushes and clothes for the following day, there came a knock on the door. Jenna had finished unpacking her own stuff and had come to see how they were getting on. "Yeah, pretty much done," said John in answer to her question, looking around the room and feeling slightly awkward for some reason.

Jenna stepped inside and glanced around the room, looking as though she wasn't really looking at all. "Hey, do you fancy heading out to that pub? It's still kind of early." She said it casually, but John got the feeling she had been rehearsing saying it casually for some time.

John nodded. He was glad to have a reason not to sit around waiting to go to bed. Macava declined with a glance at John, saying he would prefer to sit and read his book before getting a decent night's sleep. "Just don't wake me up, you crazy kids," he warned playfully, raising one eyebrow and pointing at each of them. John forced a laugh, still feeling inexplicably awkward. He bade the doctor goodnight, took the key, and headed with Jenna to the busy pub over the road.

It was about eight o'clock by the time they got their drinks. John had gratefully gulped down the first and was most of the way through his second when Jenna asked a serious question.

"John, why were you seeing Nicholas in the first place?" She said it lightly, keeping her eyes on him as she spoke. She obviously knew that the subject was delicate, but she wouldn't be happy with a brush-off answer.

John didn't reply at first but sat staring sidelong at his beer, running his fingers up and down the glass while he watched the bubbles rise. "A couple of reasons," he began, toying with the idea of telling her everything. "To start with, it was to get a grip on my obsessive behavior. I was a kid then, and used to get worked up about things that I couldn't understand. I'd get frustrated and upset. After a while Nicholas got me through that and I was okay with it. Then it was more that I was worried about my future and things. It was like a massive frustration at being, you know, helpless and out of control." He took a deep gulp of his drink, thinking he would definitely need another in the next couple of minutes. "Well, not out of control, but not in control."

Jenna took a slow sip of her drink. She was on her third already. John had never been a particularly fast drinker. He supposed she had found the courage to ask him these things through the alcohol. "Does it upset you to remember all that?" She said it quietly, peering at him with a strange intensity that made him feel vaguely uncomfortable.

"To be honest, I try not to worry about it anymore. It doesn't affect me now, or at least it doesn't upset me now. I'm, you know, more confident and trusting." He gave her a sidelong smile. She didn't smile back. He looked down at his drink, feeling uncomfortable to admit he had been so helpless once upon a time. He sighed. "It's like being burnt, I suppose. Eventually you just live with the scars, because life carries on. I'm happy now, so I'd rather not focus on when I wasn't."

Jenna nodded reluctantly and looked away toward the crowd of people at the bar. "Some people would prefer to have the scars removed," she murmured, looking wistfully at the crowd which was slowly degenerating into drunken silliness.

"Ah, well. Never mind. How about you, why are you so

quiet all the time?" John hadn't meant to sound rude, but his grip on civility was loosening and he said it as soon as it popped into his head. Wincing inside, he made a mental note to try more tact the next time he criticized someone's personality.

Jenna was surprised. She leaned back in her chair, a look of mock outrage plastered on her face. "I am not quiet all the time. I've been talking to you loads recently. It's hardly my fault you never paid me any attention before, is it? And by the way, I'm not so sure I appreciate being yanked out of work on a whim and made to come along on an adventure with you when the only reason you asked me is because I'm the least likely of your friends to get killed!"

John laughed, nodding and holding his hands up in surrender. "Yeah, I guess that is kind of a harsh reason to invite someone on a deadly trip of doom. Does that mean we're friends then?"

Jenna stopped laughing. "Huh?"

"You said you were the least likely of my friends to get killed. So that makes you a friend, doesn't it?"

She smiled and pushed her chair back, heading to the bar without a backward glance and returning with two pints of beer.

"You drink beer?" Now it was John's turn to be surprised.

"Actually," she said, slurring her words, "I don't drink at all. This is the first time I've had alcohol in a very, very long time. Things get out of control when I drink." She grinned and laughed a manic laugh.

"So you thought that being on a dangerous mission was a good time to mix your drinks on a shocking scale?" John said dryly. "That's beer and, what, vodka and coke, is it? One after the other. I haven't done that since I was sixteen, and I was extremely sorry for it the next day. I swear your head is going to kill you tomorrow." He suddenly remembered what they were doing tomorrow and his mouth dropped open in alarm. "Jen, we mustn't be hung-over tomorrow, we have to get up early! This will have to be the last one. Actually, thinking about it we should probably head back now."

She wasn't amused and leaned back in the chair. Crossing her legs defiantly, she gripped her pint. "I'm enjoying myself, John. I haven't done that for a long time, and I'm not stopping now."

He let it slide. It was he and Macava who needed to be on top of their game tomorrow. Jenna would probably be okay finishing her drink.

The pub was closing by the time they left, the last of the drunken patrons fading into the darkness, various shouted goodbyes following their footsteps into the night. He and Jenna walked in silence back to the roadside hotel, Jenna's arm locked through his as she huddled against a non-existent night breeze. John could see the front of the hotel coming into sight and thought it was more like an American style motel. The rooms were all on the ground floor and they opened directly onto the car park for easy access back to the road. He watched as the front of the building came steadily closer, aware of the tension growing between him and Jenna as they made their way to their rooms.

They stood outside the door to Jenna's room, not speaking. Jenna had her head down and was looking at the floor while John gazed over her into the quiet night beyond, wondering what to do. Her muttered voice was barely audible. "I had a really nice time tonight."

"Me too." His response was automatic and his voice sounded flat and hollow even to his own ears.

She raised her head to look at him, still clutching his arm. She was so close he could feel her body heat. The moment stretched as he looked into her eyes. His heart was beating harder than normal. He could feel it against his ribs.

You don't know her. It's not worth it. You have work to do tomorrow. You need to focus. You'll only disappoint her. She'll end up getting hurt. Don't trust her.

His mind was hysterically hurling reasons why he shouldn't

do what the situation was moving toward him doing. He could barely focus. The familiar, inexplicable fear grew inside him, the anxiety that made him avoid this situation whenever possible. He was disappointed that he still felt like this around people. His mood slipped into melancholy.

He swallowed hard and took a deep breath, easing Jenna's hand out from under his arm while smiling an empty smile into her face. She wore a look of confusion, a look he had seen many times before on many other faces. It was a look of uncomprehending bafflement because this should have ended only one way. He had given no indication that he was anything other than happy and comfortable and there was no reason for things not to progress. He hated himself for what he was about to do, but this was not the time to test his mental resolve. He gritted his teeth. The moment stretched.

"So, I'll see you in the morning then. Get some sleep, okay? We're going to need it." His tone sounded falsely cheery, even to him. He turned away, barely hearing her softly spoken reply as she turned and unlocked her door. He could feel the glance she gave him as she stepped inside and hoped it wasn't a look of pity. He was disgusted with himself. The last thing he wanted was pity. He had that in buckets.

Macava was still awake as he let himself in. The older man turned his head away from the feeble streetlight as John crept inside. "Didn't expect you back tonight." His voice was groggy with weariness.

"I thought it best to get some sleep, Nicholas." John's tone was defensive, he couldn't help it.

Macava was silent, knowing exactly what that meant. John was grateful that the doctor understood him, but at the same time resented giving himself away so obviously. John resolved to talk frankly to Jenna about it the next day, to explain the problems he and Macava had tried to iron out of his psyche but of which he wasn't entirely free. He needed to let her know it wasn't her fault. He wondered if he could ever stop believing it was his.

Macava was making an annoying noise as he slept. The fact that the noise was beginning to annoy him made John aware that he was, regretfully, waking up. Memories of last night flashed before his eyes. He felt pretty bad for Jenna and disappointed in himself, but overall he was glad he hadn't done anything stupid or handled it badly. This meant he could patch things up with a little bit of honesty, and he had already laid the groundwork for that last night.

That is, if Jenna actually remembered anything from last night, he thought wryly. The alcohol she had managed to down would probably make whatever she did remember quite fuzzy. He smiled knowingly, remembering the countless times he had woken up with the awful sensation of having done something terrible the night before and dreading the moment when he would have to check his phone. The outbox was always a horrible place to look. He was one of those people who for some reason always wanted to phone and text everyone he was thinking about when he was drunk. Heartened by the fact that he was awake and not hung-over, John rolled out of the narrow bed and headed into the little bathroom behind him.

He was halfway through brushing his teeth when Macava called sleepily through the door. "So what happened last night?"

John grinned as he brushed. The effect gave him a manic look. "You planning to get me on your couch again?" he called back, remembering belatedly that Macava didn't actually have a couch. "Hey, how come you don't have a couch, Nicholas? Shrinks usually have couches." He frowned, wondering if the toothpaste would go crusty on his lips if he didn't stop brushing soon.

"Would you have preferred a couch?" the doctor muttered, his shuffling sounds telling John he was getting dressed. John decided to carry on brushing to avoid walking in on a half-dressed Nicholas.

"Not especially." John re-entered the room and slumped back down on his bed, starting to pack his things into his bag. The doctor wandered into the bathroom and started his own morning routine. By the time he was finished John was packed and ready to go, and within a short space of time they were both surveying the room, making sure nothing had been forgotten. John had already recovered the last rogue sock from a corner of the room.

Before they headed outside Macava turned to John and held him with a steady gaze. "You don't have to tell me anything you don't want to, John, but you know you can trust me. I want you to know that I am still here for you if you are having difficulties. If what happened last night was more of—"

John cut him off, turning his head away and refusing to meet his eyes. "It was, but I don't really want to talk about it, Nicholas. It's something I want to deal with myself and it won't help me to keep, you know, crying to you about it." Macava nodded sagely, still not looking away. A thought suddenly struck John. "Why did you …," he paused, trying to decide how to frame his thoughts without garbling his words completely. "Why did you agree to come with me? I kidnapped you, held you hostage, and almost got you killed. Why did you really come?"

Macava's smile didn't reach his eyes. He turned and walked a few paces before giving John a considered look. "The benefit of being the shrink, John, is that you can understand everyone and hope never to be understood. So it is with me. Perhaps one day you and I can discuss me and my secrets, but for now suffice it to say that I came because I have a vested interest in making sure you're okay. I feel I owe you something, and on top of that I suppose I'm just a crazy old man."

This time his grin was real. John was mollified, but not completely. Something else was on Macava's mind and John wondered what it could be. He headed to the door, musing that the doctor had been a little defensive about his motives, so maybe John had unwittingly touched a nerve. He opened the door and held it open for the doctor, the two of them fiddling with the bags as they lugged them through the door. It wasn't until he was halfway out of the door and glanced up into the sunlit morning that John's heart froze in panic.

———————

Kendra leaned back against the side of the black Vectra and looked up at the sky. It was very early morning and the sun wasn't yet fully up. The sky was dark blue, tinting her surroundings the same color. The effect was peculiar, but she had always liked the blue-hued twilight, finding it calming and peaceful. This morning, however, there was little that was calm or peaceful about her thoughts. As the sun crept higher into the sky and the morning began to brighten, she reflected on what she was doing here and what the price of the stakeout might be.

That fool Macava had used his credit card to rent two rooms at the roadside hotel, obviously not thinking that the cards would be traceable the instant they were used. An oversight which she intended to exploit to the full. The Shifter wouldn't have seen or felt her coming as she and her team had left in the dead of night and arrived at a very early hour. They had set up their vigil in the car park, having worked out the exact location of the rooms which were, surprisingly, side by side. If Macava really was on a mission to bring down the organization, then he was going about it in a very sloppy manner.

Slowly, Kendra loosened her gun in its holster, acutely aware of the trouble she would be in otherwise if the gun was sticky with dew or cold when she had to draw it. Chances were the Shifter would be more than capable of doing something horrific if she messed this up. She had to make sure she got it right. "One shot to the head," she muttered, "one shot, no warning. One shot to the head." She recited the mantra as she prepared for the task ahead. There was no room for mistakes.

As the morning wore on she could feel herself tensing. The moment was drawing nearer. She looked around at the four other cars—all Vectras, all black—and at the Recallers she had brought with her. None of them were particularly strong as Recallers. They worked mainly as muscle in this kind of operation. They had their uses, but they were not particularly stimulating company, especially when their orders were to stay quiet and act only if Kendra failed to bring the Shifter down with her first shot. There had been a lot of half-hearted complaining at headquarters, a lot of support among the younger and more eager Recallers for an alternative plan, which was to storm into the room in the night and fire blindly until they were sure the subject was dead. The idea was ludicrous as far as Kendra was concerned. The only viable option was the stakeout plan.

And now here they were, sixteen others plus herself, all standing attentively by their cars, hands hovering around their guns and itching for an excuse to fire them. She turned her attention to the doors before her, wondering if she had ever been as eager as her team clearly was.

Kendra had her gun out of its holster and into a firing position before the door of the right-hand room was fully open, her arms slightly bent and her finger resting lightly across the trigger. Her practiced eye was targeting even before she realized it. A figure exited the room. He was facing away from her and hunched over the bag he was dragging. She couldn't tell if it was Macava, but she could see John Davis behind him, holding the door open. Neither of them had looked in her direction yet, and she could feel the tension of the Recallers around her as their hands moved to their weapons.

She saw Macava step to the side as John Davis came through the door, glancing up with a look of utter horror as he saw the seventeen armed people surrounding him. She felt a twinge of pity for Davis as she quickly refocused her aim on the doctor, his dumbfounded face right within her sights as she squeezed the trigger.

———

John stared at the gun in the woman's hand, his mind sluggishly feeding him the rest of the image as he tried to make sense of the blaring alarm he felt. The woman moved almost in slow motion, her aim moving to Macava as the knot in John's stomach tightened even more. He couldn't move, frozen in disbelief. How had these people tracked them? How could he have been so stupid as to think they wouldn't be seen arriving? How could he have let his friends follow him into a death trap?

Darkness descended as a shot rang out. John saw a flash and heard a loud crack as the world around him turned instantly from day to night. Had he been shot? He stood listening to the scrambling footsteps out in the car park, realizing that he was alive and that Macava was still standing next to him. He could hear the older man's labored breathing as the shock of the last second washed over him.

Darkness. Total impenetrable darkness clouded Kendra's vision and she shook her head violently. Her shot had disappeared into the blackness, going wildly into the air. She blinked, trying to focus, desperately looking around for some source of light. There was utter silence around her. She was alone. Finding her voice, she desperately cried out to the Recallers who were supposed to be with her, trying to make sense of what was happening. To the left and behind her she heard a desperate shout. "Run Nicholas!" She whirled, firing blindly in the vague direction of the voice, knowing that the chances of her hitting anyone were minimal. If Davis got hit then she would be sorry, but she couldn't let the Shifter get away like this. He had been right in her sights, and now he was getting away.

CHAPTER

FOURTEEN

John grabbed Macava by the arm and pulled him to the left, shoving the man in front of him and telling him to run, not knowing where they could go or how they could possibly escape. Their car was parked at the far end of the car park. There was no way they could get to it. Maybe they could escape back into the hotel. Surely the woman wouldn't be so brazen as to shoot them in there?

More shots from behind him. He felt something fly past him in the dark and hoped to God the woman would run out of bullets soon. There were flashes of light around him and the sounds of people shouting and running. A light from one of the rooms appeared directly in front of them and John pulled Macava back before it exposed them completely.

———

Kendra took three running steps toward the rooms and suddenly found herself sprawling face down on the tarmac of the car park. Her foot had caught on something in the darkness. She could hear the sound of car doors opening and scrambling feet. Flashlight beams waved wildly around her as men shouted at one another. Lights were coming on in the hotel rooms; the shots had alerted the residents and it wouldn't be long before the police were called. She swore. She had screwed up again and she knew it was over. Lying face down on the unyielding ground, Kendra could feel the burning shame of failure. She shrugged off the hands that were clutching at her arms and rose to her feet, humiliation gnawing painfully at her as she walked back to the cars amid the chaos.

"Detective!" A young man was calling from one of the cars. He came running over, his flashlight shining in Kendra's face. "What happened? Where did they go? How did you know they were going leave at this time of night?"

She stared at the boy, who couldn't be more than nineteen or twenty, wondering if he was stupid or just a useless Recaller. She snarled, "It wasn't night two minutes ago, Recaller, which you should know if you were any good at what you've been trained for." She walked past him, ignoring his bewildered look. Turning back she asked him what time it was. She had effectively lost six hours. She would probably be feeling jet-lagged soon. She was angry and vengeful as she stomped to her car, pausing only briefly to bellow at the Recallers scurrying around the hotel to get back to headquarters immediately. She was not in the least amused that none of them had been able to resist the Shift, and she was trying as hard as she could to blame the fiasco on their lack of support.

Macava had escaped and taken Davis with him. They would be harder to catch next time, but she would think of a way. She just hoped she would be on the case long enough to think of one.

John huddled with Macava against the wall of the building, not daring to hope they wouldn't be found. He was trying to think of an escape plan as increasingly desperate ideas popped into his head. He could think of nothing. They were doomed.

Then, incredibly, a woman's voice rang out, ordering the rest of the people back to their cars. She sounded resigned and angry, as though she thought they had escaped and was none too pleased about it. It suddenly hit John that she must think *they* were responsible for changing day to night and had thus saved themselves. If that was the case, he thought, then great, but who the hell *was* responsible for the change?

———

Brice hurried back to his car, keeping out of Kendra's sight. This little eventuality had been very fortunate for him. Davis had been flushed out of his hiding place and had taken the doctor with him. Soon—very soon, he hoped—they would come to the end of the path he had laid out for them and he would finish Davis off.

He watched Kendra scream furiously at the other Recallers and turned his face away when she glanced in his direction. He was fairly sure that in the pitch darkness she had seen nothing. This case was getting to her in a way he hadn't seen before. She was flustered and fraying around the edges. Only the death of Davis and that doctor would please her now. Yet she had failed to hit her targets, and now he would be the one to catch them and kill them. *He* would be the one rewarded. Then Davis wouldn't be able to ruin everything Brice was working to gain, and he would earn Kendra's undying respect.

He smiled to himself, rubbing his stubbly face with a sweaty hand. It had gone better than he could have hoped and he was one step closer to winning everything.

———

As the cars drove off, leaving the night quiet again, John made a decision. Running to the door they had come through, he grabbed the bags and hurried back, collecting Macava on the way. Pulling the doctor to the car, he threw the bags in the boot and slammed it shut, wanting to be away before Jenna came out of her room. He was hoping that the gunfire had frightened her enough to keep her inside, or at least that she had slept straight through it, because he had decided to go on without her. Macava had his reasons for coming along, although what they really were John wasn't sure, but it was wrong and unfair to involve Jenna. Her only crime was to care about him. He and Macava would go on, do what was needed. Jenna would stay safely behind.

John slammed the seatbelt into its catch and shoved the key in the ignition as quickly as he could, focusing on getting away and ignoring the voice in his head telling him he couldn't run away from his fears forever. He knew the voice was wrong. He was not running from his fears, he was saving Jenna's life.

He was almost sure she would understand that.

As the morning grew brighter the motorway lights began to shut off, heralding the start of a new day. John had immense trouble reconciling this with the fact that he had already lived through this morning once already. By his reckoning the morning was long gone, and he was getting very hungry. His thoughts turned dark as he reflected on the events of the last few hours.

He had been ambushed by the same woman who had been looking for him before. He had once again narrowly escaped with his life, and Nicholas had been with him yet again. John no longer believed that he was responsible for the changes. The woman, on the other hand, must be after him because she believed he *did* have something to do with it. She knew something, and it was her organization he had been trying to track down.

If this Brice character led him to that organization, he would have to face the woman with the armed guard again at some point. The only good thing about that was it would be on his terms, not because he had been caught unawares with only his former doctor for a bodyguard. Something wasn't right, though. Whatever was causing these unfathomable twists in reality was definitely focused on him. That much was clear, even if the changes weren't always for his benefit.

Then for whose?

He glanced at Macava sitting quietly to his left. John swallowed and shook his head, trying to ignore the suspicion growing in his mind. The only common factor was the doctor. He had been in danger the night John had kidnapped him and been shot. He had been in danger this morning when the woman had aimed at his head. The woman, or someone from her organization, had trashed his house.

A cold chill gripped John's heart and worked its way into his stomach. He tried to keep his eyes focused on the road ahead, not daring to look at Macava or speak to him. Could it possibly be that he was the one? Dr. Macava, the man who knew so much about him and who John would trust above so many others. He glanced to his side again. The doctor was staring out of the window at the passing world, oblivious to the suspicions forming in John's head.

"Some morning," John said conversationally, keeping his tone light even as the fear rose inside him. He glanced at Macava again.

The doctor returned the glance before staring once more out of the window. "Some morning indeed," he agreed. "You know, John, I was just thinking. I don't think we should've left young Jenna behind."

"It had to be done, Nicholas, there was no time to collect her."

"I'm not so sure, you know." The doctor's response carried a note of regret, as though he genuinely felt they should have brought her along. John was confused. If Macava really hadn't had anything to do with the strange events they had experienced, then it stood to reason he wouldn't remember the sudden change from day to night. If he thought they had tried to leave at night under cover of darkness, it might explain why he thought they could have brought Jenna along.

John grabbed at the hope, desperate to believe the doctor wasn't behind all this. He allowed the moment to pass, but finally he had to know. He pressed on. "It was the dead of night and we were being shot at. How could we possibly have brought her?"

Macava's response was quick and uncompromising,

accusation creeping into his voice. "We weren't being shot at when we drove off, John, you and I both know that. Did you leave her behind for some other reason?"

The last thing John wanted was to get into a debate about his ulterior motives. "It's not like we weren't under pressure. It wasn't just being shot at that worried me. I didn't want anything to happen to her." He indicated left and turned into Winchester Services. He wanted somewhere to park and sort this out once and for all.

"No. No, of course you didn't. I confess I was shaken myself. One doesn't often experience something like that." The doctor paused, allowing the silence to stretch as they moved into the car park.

"Like what?" John said it bluntly, determined to discover if Macava was aware of the change.

The doctor paused again. "Like daylight becoming night." He spoke softly and turned his head to regard John. "As though someone had turned off the lights."

John didn't meet Macava's eyes. He tugged at the steering wheel and pulled the car into the nearest parking space. Killing the engine, he shifted to glare at the doctor with an intensity that made Macava visibly recoil. "How do you remember that?" He shouted the words, feeling his grip on his temper slipping. "No one remembers the changes except me, so why do you? Is it you? Are you the one doing this?"

His right hand gripped the steering wheel so tightly the knuckles were white. The futility of his feeble plan danced before his eyes, mocking him as if he were a puppet suddenly aware of its strings. Macava stared back coldly, his eyes disapproving.

"There's no need to shout at me, John. If you think I'm low enough to kill your best friend for no reason, then you've already decided the answer to that question."

John was shocked into silence. He had expected either denial or confirmation, not a rebuke. In his temper, he had somehow forgotten about Chris. He stared at Macava, feeling his anger subside as the doctor opened his car door and stepped out. The slamming of the door snapped John back into sense and he quickly scrambled out of the car to chase after the doctor, who was marching into the service station. "Nicholas," he called, "Nicholas, I'm sorry!"

Macava whipped around to glare at him. "You will spend your life being sorry if you don't keep your head on straight and your temper in check! I am your one ally in this game, John. I did not come with you to have my integrity questioned, and I'll be damned if I let you simply apologize and pretend nothing happened."

There was steel in Macava's eyes that John hadn't seen before, and for a moment he was even concerned that the doctor might lash out. He lowered his gaze and shifted his feet uncomfortably, realizing the truth of what Macava had said. He couldn't be the one behind it. "I don't know how to make it up to you, Nicholas. I wasn't thinking straight. I guess my thoughts got jumbled up and I got confused. I ...," he groped for the words, knowing that nothing he could say would do much good. "I forgot about Chris. I wasn't talking about him, I was just thinking about when I got shot and you were there ...."

Macava's expression had softened, though he still looked disapproving, like a stern grandfather berating an unruly child.

John raised his head and looked at Macava contritely. "Will you stick with me, Nicholas? I don't know if I can take Brice down on my own."

Macava snorted and smiled. "I know you can't take him alone. The young, the impetuous, and the reckless need a guiding hand, even if that hand is a bit wrinkled. The trick is learning to appreciate the guidance." Without waiting for a response, Macava turned and headed into the service station, calling over his shoulder to a relieved John, "You can start by buying me breakfast."

SHIFTER

STEVEN D. JACKSON

The sun was almost clear of the lake, its rays reflecting in the depths of the water, making it shimmer with the promise of a new day. Kendra had been watching its progress for some time, but soon she would have to return to her post at headquarters and think up a new strategy. The sunlight became blurred by the tears forming in her eyes and she blinked rapidly to clear them.

She had come here directly from the office following her aborted attempt to finish off the Shifter, Macava. The Recallers had been wary of her, casting her sidelong glances as she consulted the various reports and documents in her office. She knew they were talking about her and knew also that they were wondering if she had lost her touch. It wouldn't be long until she was called by her superiors and required to account for the catastrophic handling of the case so far. She might even be discovered.

She had always liked the peace and solitude of a lake in the early morning, and so she had quickly dismissed the Recallers and left the office. She didn't care if any of them turned up for work today. She could barely remember what their contract said about emergency operations out of hours. Perhaps they were entitled to the next day off or something. She shrugged involuntarily and stared into the lake, trying to focus her thoughts on the future but feeling herself drawn inexorably into the past.

The classroom smelled of chalk, the residue from countless years of lessons taught over and over in this one room. The twenty or thirty twelve-year-old girls sat with their heads down, supposedly learning geography. Sarah stared at the paper in front of her, hating every minute of it. There was no way she would learn anything today. She kept her head down, avoiding the roving gaze of the fearsome Miss Green. If she was caught not doing her work, there would be consequences.

A flicker of movement caught her eye and she glanced up in time to see her best friend twist in her chair. The girl threw a screwed up ball of paper in Sarah's direction. She watched

161

it sail toward her head, too surprised at her friend's behavior to react.

Kendra blinked back more tears as the memory played out in her mind. What harm could the indulgence do her now anyway?

Fractions of a second too late, she reached for the ball, desperately trying to grab it before it caused disaster. She missed, knocking the paper high into the air toward the front of the class. Sarah fell back into her seat, a feeling of dread and horror clutching at her as she watched the paper arc toward Miss Green.

The grass was soft as she ran her hand along it, lost in her thoughts. The sun was warm on her face and she was grateful for its touch. Closing her eyes she lifted her face to the sky and lay back on the ground.

Miss Green roared with anger, her long grey dress swirling about her as she twisted to face the class. Her accusing eyes cast around the room, her spectacles falling from her face as she snarled at the horrified girls before her. Total silence fell. Green prowled the room like a tiger hunting its prey. Sarah's heart leapt into her throat as her teacher's eyes fell to the paper ball on the floor. Her smile was that of the executioner as she picked it up. She unfolded the note, her face a rictus mask as she read. Eyes narrow, Green cast the paper to one side and turned to the girl in the front row. Sarah watched in horror as her best friend was dragged from the room in silence, all protest smothered by fear.

Kendra opened her eyes and rose to her feet. Wallowing in the past wouldn't help now, the pain of the story would never leave her and reliving it would not help. That girl's death was her fault. She should have prevented it but didn't. She wasn't prepared to let anyone else die because of her weakness. Wiping her eyes, she turned to retrace her steps through the forest to her car. She would head back down to Southampton and decide what to do about Macava. She had managed to get the drop on him once and was fairly sure she could do it again.

Pulling out her phone, she noticed that the time was already 9:30 a.m. The other Recallers ought to be in the office by now, if indeed they were obliged to turn up today. She dialed the number for Brice's mobile, in case he wasn't in the office.

"Brice here." The answer was breathless and forced, as though the speaker was in the middle of some frenetic activity.

"Brice, it's Kendra. Listen, I need you to do something—"

"Sorry, Detective, I was on the mission last night and I wasn't planning to come in today. I didn't realize we—"

"No, no, I understand. I didn't think many people would turn up anyway, but I want to speak to you as soon as you get in tomorrow, alright? It's important." She hoped she had put just enough sincerity into the last two words to make him feel needed, although she realized she had been neglecting his services for a while and that it might take some time to rebuild the rapport she relied on so heavily.

"Of course, Detective. I'm just buying petrol at the moment, so"—there were fumbling sounds and noises that sounded like a metallic scraping—"I have to go, but I am hoping that when we talk tomorrow a lot of things will be sorted out."

She chuckled to herself as she hung up the phone, wondering exactly what he was thinking by telling her he was buying petrol. What did that have to do with anything? She trudged through the undergrowth toward her car, shoving the phone back into her pocket when she got no answer from the office reception desk. She hadn't thought Brice was one of the Recallers out last night, but she hadn't been paying much attention to who had accompanied her. Without him it would be more difficult to put any plan into action, but she would be able to formulate a strategy alone easily enough, and it certainly seemed like she would be alone today.

Setting her mind to the mission, she shut out her memories of the past and focused on the present, steeling herself for the next conflict.

John ate his cheeseburger thoughtfully while Macava talked about strategy. The doctor had suggested parking the car some few hundred yards away from the New Forest house and walking the rest of the way to avoid Brice detecting them early. John peered surreptitiously at his companion, wondering exactly how far he could walk. It was true that he could march quite capably through woodland when threatened by an injured lunatic with a knife, but would he be up for a confrontation like this? That was assuming they made it to a confrontation.

"Don't look at me like that, John, I am more than capable of doing this. I daresay I am, relatively speaking, in a better physical state for my age than you are for yours." The doctor's gaze passed critically over John's frame, clearly indicating that he ought to either spend some time in a gym or at least eat a bit more.

John grinned, waving his cheeseburger. "I'm eating. What more do you want?"

Macava let it pass. He was obviously in a much better mood now that he had eaten and they were actually on their way. John wished he could share the man's optimism, but all he felt was a tremendous fear that he might be leading his friend into a death trap.

The plan was decided. They would make their approach as soon as they finished eating. They would park the car off the main road just before the turning to the house, which was hidden from the road by a bank of trees. As his father had often said, the New Forest was more of a New Meadow, so they were lucky there were any trees for cover at all. They would make their way to the back of the house and John would try to find a way in while Macava went around to the front door to provide a distraction. This Brice character was unlikely to know much, if anything, about Macava.

"In any case," Macava added soberly, "I don't come across as much of a threat, so even if he recognizes me he probably won't attack me. I can talk to him and stall for time so you can get in."

John didn't care for that particular thought given that this Darren Brice could be a serious danger, but it made sense. Once they had Brice they would tie him to a chair with the tape and find out whatever they could about the organization behind the woman and the armed guards. Neither of them wanted to think about what would happen if they had to use force on Brice, although John was grimly looking forward to scaring the hell out of the man who had been involved, if only indirectly, in the madness that had overtaken his life in recent days.

He finished his burger and looked up at Macava, who had stopped talking and was staring out of the window at the car park outside. "So, shall we go?"

Macava didn't look at him. He nodded and rose from his seat, finally glancing at John with a grim expression. He sighed, muttering under his breath, "*Jacta alea est.*"

John stared at him, not wanting to spoil the serious mood by showing his ignorance. He spent a while puzzling it out, feeling the moment lengthen as Macava stared out of the window, apparently lost in thought. "What?" he eventually asked.

Macava sighed again, an exasperated smile slowly replacing the grimace. "It's a quotation. 'The die is cast.'" John blinked at him. "We're now crossing the Rubicon? No? I was trying to say that I feel a bit like Caesar, that we're gambling on a throw of the dice. Must you ruin every profound observation I make?"

John smiled and nodded, rising from his chair and adopting a mock-serious expression. "*Sic semper ...,*" he paused, struggling to remember the last word of the Latin phrase that he was sure meant something, "... *fidelis.* How's that?"

Macava stared at him disapprovingly. "That doesn't even make sense."

John laughed. In a serious tone he pointed out that it should be given some consideration before being dismissed out of hand. Macava sighed and shook his head as he headed out, gesturing to John to follow him. "Come on then. Let's get going, Philistine."

John's smile faded as his heart clenched in his chest.

CHAPTER

It would take approximately an hour and a half to get to the Forest, giving John plenty of time to think about what he was going to tell Jenna when he called her. He was fairly certain it would not be a very pleasant conversation. He stared at her number on the screen for a long time before putting the phone away. Macava was a mercifully quiet driver, not given to idle talk while he was at the wheel, which made it easier for John to sit quietly and think. It wouldn't make speaking to Jenna any easier, but it would help him sort out his thoughts.

Finally deciding on what he wanted to say, he once again looked up Jenna's number. With a great effort of willpower, he hit the 'dial' button.

Jenna was less than impressed. "So where are you two?"

"We had to leave, I'm sorry. We had to go in the night. Only it wasn't night when we set out, it was about this time in the morning. We went outside and there were loads of people with guns in the car park. They shot at us and it all went dark, and it was suddenly the middle of the night again and we managed to get away."

Jenna didn't sound surprised. In fact, she sounded irritated. "So why did you leave?"

"We had to leave. We couldn't let you get involved in all this ...." He trailed off, realizing how lame it sounded even to him. It was sad how they were all getting used to the insanity of what had been happening. Nothing would ever be the same for any of them.

Jenna cut in, speaking fast. "But I'm already involved, John, and you damn well know it. Did you not think they might come back here for me? I can't believe you would leave me here when I've been helping you this whole time." She paused, and it sounded like she was choking back tears. "If it's because of last night, I really didn't mean—"

"No, no, it's not because of that, really." He tried to make his voice sound sincere, but he knew she wouldn't be fooled.

She was quiet for a time, and John could tell she was struggling to get hold of herself. "Look, I'm not going to freak out or get upset or anything. I just wish you had taken me with you. I don't know if you ran off because of last night or because of whatever happened, but it's important that you carry on with the plan and get to that organization. Find out what's going on and sort it out, then you'll be happy and I'll be happy. I will just hope you come back at some point. Take care, okay?"

A lump rose in John's throat. He felt meaner than he had for a long time. It was true that they could have taken Jenna with them, but it was also true that she would only be in danger if they had. He didn't want to think too deeply about his motivations, knowing where that would lead, but at the same time he hadn't meant to hurt her. "Okay, I'll give you a call in a while. Hopefully I'll get all this sorted out and I'll come back to work when it's done. I'm really sorry, Jen, I didn't mean to upset you."

She sighed, clearly resigned to the fact that she wasn't going to see the resolution of this adventure. "It's alright, I guess. At least this way I have less chance of getting shot." She tried a feeble laugh and the pitiful sound wrenched at John's heart. "Take care, John."

"See you, Jen."

He hung up. Taking a deep breath, he shoved the phone

into his pocket, glad to have finally cleared the air with her. He was still lost in his thoughts when Macava pulled over and stopped the car. Looking around at the empty expanse of grass and low shrubs for miles around, he nodded and turned to John.

"This is it, my boy, the New Forest and the possibly booby-trapped home of our friend, Mr. Brice. If he isn't in yet then he'll be arriving soon to make his preparations for tonight."

They had come to the conclusion that if the New Forest house was indeed the trap, then it had been chosen because of its isolated location. It was somewhere they knew Brice would be, and somewhere they could interrogate him without fear of discovery. Everything that made it a perfect trap also made it a perfect ambush for them, as long as they got there before Brice did—or at least before he had time to set his trap. Although he would know they had made it as far as the hotel last night, they might still have the element of surprise. Knowing the location of his real address was a bonus. If Brice wasn't at the fake house and didn't turn up later, they could visit him there instead.

John surveyed the grassy surroundings and looked at the sun as he stepped from the car, remembering how cold and wet it had been mere days before. The memory brought last week's confusion into the forefront of his mind. He was determined to get to the bottom of this increasingly frustrating mystery. He and Macava crept slowly over the grass toward the back of the property, keeping in sight the grove of trees surrounding the house and the far-off fence indicating the line of the long driveway. John felt too hot, the sun burning the back of his neck as he made his way over the rough terrain.

Actually executing their plan somehow made it all seem like a terribly bad idea. He couldn't shake the feeling that they should not have tried to outwit Brice at the false house and should instead have made use of their advantage by going to the man's actual home, regardless of the fear of being arrested. Pushing these thoughts aside, John took a covert look at Macava. The doctor, it appeared, was in his element as he crouched lower than necessary and hurried over the grass with his backpack held in place with one hand. John had elected to carry only his knife shoved through his belt since Macava had everything else they might need.

They reached the edge of the trees and peered through them at the white painted edges of the house. It looked more like a cabin, complete with balcony and large windows in the sides. It was big and obviously worth a lot of money, but it had a dilapidated air as though it had been abandoned for some time. John's critical eye picked out flaking paint and rotten wood around the window frames. There was smoke rising from the chimney. Someone was clearly in residence and making no effort to disguise the fact. John's heart rose at the sight. Perhaps they hadn't made a mistake after all.

A car was parked at a jaunty angle in the front, facing away from the house. The boot was open and there appeared to be a long scrape mark in the dusty ground leading to the steps by the front door, as though something heavy had been dragged from the boot. The front steps were still wet where some kind of liquid had been splashed on them. John signaled to Macava to head to the front as planned while he edged around the trees to the back of the house, intending to use the cover for as long as he could. The parallels with his experience at the hospital were not lost on him, and the memory of how that particular disaster had played out lingered just under the surface of his thoughts.

The back door of the house was very old. The sickly green paint had clearly been peeling in the sun for some time and the door looked as though it might fall off its hinges at any moment. There was a small window to the left of the door, and when John peered cautiously through it he saw the retreating figure of a short, fat man moving through the room beyond. He appeared to be heading to the front door, where Macava had presumably knocked to get his attention. Just as the thought crossed John's mind that the plan seemed to be turning out well so far, he froze in fear. He had caught a fleeting glimpse of something metallic in the man's hand as he walked out of sight, something he had seen all too recently in the hands of a woman aiming squarely at his face. He let out a strangled cry and pelted for the side of the building, blind panic taking over as he pumped his arms for speed and cursed his lack of fitness. One thought pounded relentlessly in his head.

Macava was going to die.

Brice had been sitting by the fire, which was over-stacked with logs far beyond what was sensible. He knew it would take a while to reach maximum heat, especially since it was so highly stacked. By the time the heat was important, though, the logs would be burning nicely and the fire would be perfect. Everything was in place. All he had to do now was put the car away and hide.

That Davis would come he didn't doubt. He had seen him running from the hotel and knew the man would be avid for revenge. He had laid the trail carefully. The difficultly was guessing *when* he would come. This was the first day since the incident at the hotel, so tonight made sense. Brice had to make sure that if he was taken Davis would still die, but he didn't honestly believe he would be caught. Davis wasn't the kind of person to have experience with this sort of thing, after all. He was a lawyer, a young lawyer at that, and barely out of school. He could hardly be expected to second-guess a brilliant mind like Brice's.

If the guy was so useless, why was Kendra so interested in him? *No*, he thought, *she isn't interested in him. She's interested in the doctor, Macava, because she thinks he is the Shifter. Davis is just an inconvenient extra.*

Brice stood up, groaning at the strain of lifting himself off the floor. He fingered the gun in his left pocket. At that moment there came a knock at the front door. Brice turned toward it, curious, and clicked off the gun's safety mechanism.

171

As he headed to the door, he checked that the gun was loaded and ready to fire before putting it behind his back. When the door opened and Brice came face-to-face with Macava, he realized how wrong he had been. He had based everything on the assumption that Davis would come alone and at night, not with company during the day.

He blinked, confused. How could he have been so stupid? Blind panic took over as he stared into the eyes of the man who had to be the Shifter, the man who was a dangerous enemy and capable of killing him simply by willing him dead. *Kill him! Kill him now!* his mind screamed as his eyes widened in horror. He felt his arm move from behind his back, bringing the weapon to bear in an unconscious motion. As though in slow motion, Brice saw the old man's eyes move to the gun pointed at his chest, saw his body tense and his eyes flash back to Brice's, eyes filled with fear and desperation. Brice's finger squeezed the trigger as though it was no longer connected to his body.

John reached the corner of the building and struggled to keep his footing in the loose gravel as he rounded the edge. Up ahead he could see Macava standing in front of the door. The gunshot split the air like the crack of whip and John stumbled in shock as a cloud of red mist erupted from Macava's back. Macava took a step back, his hands jerking toward his chest before he faltered, crumpling to the floor like a marionette with its strings cut.

Blood pounded in John's ears as he stared in horror at the prone form of his confidante and friend. A pool of red quickly surrounded the man, coursing down the wooden steps. A figure emerged from the house, the gun still pointing at Macava's chest as though he was intent on firing again. John's anger rose in a torrent and he leaped forward with a vicious scream, closing the distance between them in a second. The man barely had time to look around before John was on him, his right fist smashing into the round, sweaty face with as much force as he could muster.

The fat man yelped and dropped the gun, reeling from John's attack. Pressing his advantage, John closed the distance again, driving his fist into the man's head and reaching down with his other hand to grab him by his collar. He threw him against the wall of the house with all his might. The man crumpled to his knees, raising a hand to shield his face. John stepped back and kicked him hard in the chest, watching the man fall back to lie still against the wooden porch.

Breathing heavily, blood pounding deafeningly in his ears, John stared at the man he had just attacked. Never in his entire life had he hit someone, let alone beat them half to death. He knew he hadn't been in control. Animal instinct had taken over and fury had driven him. This fat little man had shot Nicholas, and he deserved to have his head smashed to pieces against the wooden floor. John felt the urge to carry on, to hurt the man further, to kill him. He could barely contain the rage that threatened to overwhelm him.

Nicholas!

Snapping out of his bloodlust, John turned and hurried to Macava's side. The old man's eyes were open, staring sightlessly at the sky with an expression of disbelief. John slowly dropped to his knees and placed his fingers on Macava's neck, feeling for a pulse. There was nothing. No sign of life remained in the body that had once been Doctor Nicholas Macava. His blood covered the ground in a lake of dark red. John could barely believe the man's body could have held so much blood.

The smell was overpowering, the metallic reek of the blood mixing with a chemical smell that made him light-headed. He ignored it.

John knelt by the side of the man who had been his trusted friend and ally in this madness. His breathing was shallow. He could feel his face getting hot and his eyes watering. He stifled his sobs for a minute, knowing that he had to do one last thing for the man to whom he owed so much. Reaching out with his right hand, his fingertips brushed Macava's eyebrows, pushing down to close his eyes. He knelt for a moment, lost in his memories of the man, tears forming and rolling freely down his face. He knew he had to get a grip and make sure Macava's killer didn't get away with what he had done. Macava's death must not be in vain. John took a few deep breaths, channeling his grief into anger and using the anger to give him strength.

Gritting his teeth, John rose to his feet. His jeans were drenched in blood from the knee down. Ignoring the repulsive feeling, he advanced upon the man who he assumed was Brice. The plan might not have worked, but he had the man at his mercy now, and his mercy was in dangerously short supply.

Brice groaned. His head felt like it had been run over by a train. He blinked to clear his vision, but when he tried to raise a hand to wipe at his eyes, he discovered that his arms were tied securely behind his back. He struggled to move his legs, but they were similarly tied. He looked around, trying to work out where he was. Perhaps he had been drugged? There was certainly a chemical smell coming from somewhere. He could make out shapes that looked like his mother's living room furniture. He could see the fire burning to his left, and when he turned his head to the right he saw a dark shape moving toward him extremely fast.

Pain lanced through his temples, rocking his head to the left and making him cry out in agony. His mouth felt swollen and sore and his cries sounded pitiful even to him. Then a voice came out of nowhere, low and dangerous.

"You are Brice?"

He coughed and spat a lump of congealed blood out of his mouth. "What if I am?"

The voice paused and then replied in a considered tone,

"Then you aren't the one I'm looking for. I will consider letting you go if you tell me where Macava and Davis went."

Brice's heart leaped. Davis had gone without killing him. Although irritated that he hadn't been able to use the failsafe system, Brice was incredibly relieved. But then, he thought, who was this man? "I don't know where they went. I think Davis got me. He traced me through the website I set up and turned up at the door—"

"So you are Brice?"

"Yeah, that's me, but I think—"

He never managed to complete his sentence. The object that had struck him before smashed into his face on the other side, knocking his head to the right and causing flashes of light to appear before his eyes. He was babbling before he knew what he was saying. "Wait, wait, what are you doing?" He was almost hysterical. One of his teeth had come loose. He spat it out and desperately tried to clear his vision.

"My name is John Davis. I think you've been expecting me to turn up, haven't you? And you've killed my friend Nicholas, which I have to say has affected me rather badly."

Something about the cold, calculated way the man spoke terrified Brice. He was obviously deluded. What had happened to Macava? Davis sounded hollow, empty, as though he was quite prepared to—

Lawyer.

The realization hit him suddenly and the pieces fell into place. The trick to get him to confess his name had been a simple one, like the ones the TV courtroom people used. Now all the words were calculated to make him compliant. This Davis was clever, but Brice suspected that he was playing the proverbial 'bad cop' role.

"You don't scare me, Davis," he lisped, trying to put some bravado back into his voice even through swollen lips.

The low chuckle from behind him tore the lie to pieces. Davis wasn't buying it. "I'm not trying to scare you, Mr. Brice. Why would I waste my time trying to scare you when

175

you're already my captive? I want information out of you, and then I want to get you out of my sight. You repulse me. I feel I should kill you. I brought a knife in case I had to threaten you …." The voice trailed off as the man stepped around to face Brice directly. He sat on the table at the other end of the room and Brice could see that his face was drawn and pale. He looked as though he had no energy left. The illusion of the voice was broken completely.

"I'm not going to threaten you," Davis continued, looking into the roaring fire to his right, apparently lost in thought, "but if you don't give me some answers I am going to leave you here on your own, tied to that chair. I assume you have something around that you might use to free yourself, so I wouldn't consider it murder. Then again, if you starved to death before you managed it, it would hardly be my fault." A snarl twisted the young man's face as he glanced back at Brice. "But I doubt that would be for several years, from the look of you."

Something had clearly snapped in this man's mind. Brice was convinced it was no façade. He would leave him here and let him die of dehydration, of that there was no doubt. *Well fine*, thought Brice, *two can play this game*. It was time to get the failsafe working, and the sooner the better. He hadn't expected the smell to be so acrid. If he wasn't careful it would give him away. Summoning his most contrite face, Brice looked beseechingly at Davis. "What do you want to know?"

Davis smiled and slid off the table.

CHAPTER SIXTEEN

John crossed the room to the far wall, pulling a chair in front of Brice. Ignoring the peculiar smell in the air, he sat down on the chair facing his captive. He decided to treat whatever Brice told him with caution. After all, he was clearly a lunatic who was quite capable of killing a defenseless man, so he would have no qualms about lying to an interrogator. Deciding to be honest and open with his questioning, John began with the first thought that occurred to him.

"Who do you work for? Who are those guys with the guns and the woman in charge? What's it all about, and why are they after me?"

Brice glared at him for a moment, defiance flashing across his face before he sighed and looked away. He appeared to have decided to answer, albeit grudgingly. Looking into the flames to his left, he began to speak. To John it seemed as though his mind was somewhere else. He was speaking from somewhere inside himself, and his detachment was palpable as the fire danced in his eyes.

"They don't tell us the name of the place. They recruit you based on what you are, what you can do, because you're different. They refer to it as a company, an organization, a system or network, but if it has a name," he shook his head slowly, "they don't tell us."

"What do you mean, 'what you can do'?"

Brice smiled slightly, still staring into the fire. His voice had a smug edge to it now, as though he was immensely proud of what he was. "We remember. When the rest of the world carries on as though nothing has happened, we remember. We *recall* what it was before, and so they call us Recallers."

John nodded, guided by Brice's gaze to look into the fire himself. So far he had an inkling that what Brice was saying related to the phenomena he himself had experienced, though it didn't explain why anyone would want to hurt him or his friends, or what caused the changes.

Brice continued softly, speaking to himself as much as John. "I remember better than a lot of them, but not as well as some of the others. I was never good enough to be one of the Transition Detectives. Sometimes I miss them completely. Still, they value me. They value me for my skills, not just for being what everyone else is."

John glanced at the man's sweaty face. His expression belied his tone and he looked miserable, as though he didn't really believe what he was saying. "What kind of skills? Why do they value you?"

Brice snorted, looking up at John with a wicked smile on his face. "The kind of skills that brought you here."

John glared back at him. So this was the technical guy, the one they used for luring and trapping. The night he, Macava, and Jenna had sat in the flat thinking about ways to get to this organization, they had considered this possibility. It was almost ironic to have it confirmed now that they had fallen into a trap which they knew was being set. He felt a stab of guilt and looked away, remembering Macava's enthusiasm, Jenna's commitment, his own selfish plan to bring in people he wouldn't mind seeing hurt.

No, he thought, *you couldn't have known it would end like this*. He wished he could believe it as he watched the flames dancing. He noted absently that they were extremely large flames, probably a little too large for safety. And what was that smell? The room reeked of an odor that made him think of old cars. Brice's muttering brought him out of his distraction, bringing him back to the present.

"I've been a great help to them. I've always been there for Sarah. She trusts me and she needs me, and I wanted to do something for her."

John stood up and walked to the window, considering opening it to let some fresh air in. The weird smell was beginning to annoy him. The sun was still shining on the grassland around them, and he thought how perverse it was that the atmosphere within the house was so dark when the world was indifferent to everything they were saying. He addressed Brice without looking around.

"Is she the one who's been tracking me?"

"Sarah? Yeah. She's the senior Transition Recall Detective, the one who has to catch the Shifter. We knew you were involved. I wanted her to catch you. I wanted her to kill you because I thought you were the Shifter. I helped her find you."

"You wanted her to kill me?" John was surprised at his own lack of emotion. He stared out of the window, not knowing how he was supposed to feel at such a moment.

"The subject we were looking for was dangerous. More dangerous than any of the others."

"The subject?"

Brice didn't immediately reply. John turned toward him, a suspicion growing in his mind. The man was being awfully open. He didn't think Brice was lying, but he was certainly being more helpful than John thought he would be. Brice didn't let him finish following his train of thought. He began to explain the situation, and John couldn't help but be drawn into the man's words.

"We call them Shifters. They can change the world around them to fit what they want it to be. Some are better at it than others. They can sometimes do it on a huge scale, and everyone affected by the change carries on as though the changed reality is how reality has always been. No one knows that it was ever any different, except those of us who are Recallers. We remember, and sometimes we can resist. I don't think there has ever been one who could reverse it, but the stronger the Recaller the less able the Shifter is to change them or their minds. If enough of them get together, they can stop a Shift from happening at all. Or if a single Recaller is stronger than an individual Shifter, I suppose they could stop them alone. We aren't usually that strong on our own, though."

John was intrigued. He stared in wide-eyed amazement at Brice, trying to find a hole in the argument. Everything he said explained exactly what John had been going through. The only question was which one of the types Brice described fit John?

"So am I a Recaller or a Shifter?"

Brice looked into the fire and shook his head, his face a mask of bitterness and resentment. "I don't know yet, but I can help you find out."

John was silent. He stared at his feet, trying to find the courage to ask the question he needed to ask without betraying his inner conflicts. He wrinkled his nose against the strange smell still permeating the air. It made it quite hard to concentrate. He had called Jenna after tying Brice up and told her everything. It hadn't been an easy conversation. She had cried openly on the phone and told him to give up on his mission. He had refused, saying that he needed to find out why Nicholas had died. Jenna had sobered at that point, warning him of the danger and saying that Nicholas's murder could be traced back to John. That was irrelevant. All that mattered to John was giving Macava's death meaning and purpose. In order to give it purpose, he had to continue.

"And Nicholas?" he asked softly, still not looking at Brice. He sat down on the chair and put his head in his hands.

"We deduced he must be the Shifter. He was the one Kendra was after. I expect that after the hotel fiasco last night she'll be looking for him again today."

John laughed bitterly. "Well, she needn't bother now, should she?"

Brice glanced at him, a quizzical look on his face. John caught his eye and saw the confusion, his suspicions stirring again. "What do you mean?" Brice asked quietly.

John stared, wondering if he was being goaded. The expression on Brice's face was one of genuine puzzlement, and John could feel the blood pounding in his head as the implications of that confusion hit him. "You ... you shot him dead, less than an hour ago."

Brice's eyes widened in shock. He leaned back in his chair and regarded John skeptically. "I think I would remember that, unless ...."

John waited breathlessly for Brice to finish until it was obvious he wasn't going to. He rose to his feet, grabbed hold of Brice's shoulders, and shook him. "Unless what?"

Brice looked disgusted. "Unless you're the Shifter and you changed what happened so you wouldn't get done for murder."

Incredulous, John backed away. It couldn't be him. He had considered that before he even knew what a Shifter was. None of it made any sense. He left Brice and ran to the front door, pausing in the open doorway as he took in the grounds in front of the house. There was no body. No pool of blood. His mind reeled with the implications and he stumbled back into the house, sinking back onto his chair and staring into the fire.

"He's gone. It's like ...," he shook his head violently, "like it never happened."

Brice looked hard at him and said in a hurried and confidential tone, "We thought Macava was the Shifter for a long time, but normally they can't Shift well if they've been hurt, at least not much beyond fixing their own injuries. If he is the Shifter, he is probably still injured and you need to find him. If you're the Shifter, then you've probably accidentally done something to him. You'll need my help if you want to piece this together, John."

Brice paused, glancing sidelong at the fire. "Go to the closet and pull the door open. It sticks a little. Inside you'll find everything you need."

Numbly John stood up. Could Nicholas still be alive? Was it possible that John had saved him? No, he had seen him die, watched his blood flow out all over the steps. Nicholas couldn't have saved himself from that, surely? It had to be him. He crossed to the closet, staring blankly at fresh scratches on the floorboards in front of it, his thoughts still fixed on Macava. What was in this closet? He didn't know. In fact, he didn't really care. All that mattered was that his friend could be alive. His thoughts were confused, and the nauseating smell wasn't helping.

The door was stiff, but he tugged on it with all his strength and it fell open with incredible force. Something large tumbled heavily out. He fell back from the door and the huge barrel fell with a resounding crash, landing where he had been standing a second before. At that moment all his thoughts became clear. Brice's strange attitude, the way he had fixated on the fire, the awful chemical smell, the way he had kept talking, the way he had lulled John into an unthinking stupor. The fact that Brice was the luring and trapping man, the dreadful chemical smell, the scrape marks in front of the car boot and the closet ….

The acrid stench of petrol filled the room as a torrent of combustible liquid gushed from the barrel onto the wooden floor, rushing like a tidal wave toward the roaring fire. It passed under Brice's legs as it flowed toward its carefully orchestrated destination. John caught a glimpse of Brice's maniacally grinning face as he scrambled back, trying desperately to lift himself off the floor, his fevered thoughts trying to recall if he had been doused in petrol when the door opened.

He had managed to reach the table by the window by the time the petrol reached the fire. He heard the whooshing sound of the liquid igniting and the fire racing back to the barrel, and then the brief silence before the barrel exploded. The sound of the explosion was immense, the pressure of the igniting petrol flung upward and outward, filling the room with a vast, expanding cloud of flame. The blast forced John up and over the table and sent him crashing through the window to land in a smoking heap outside, reasonably cushioned by the grassy earth and incredibly grateful to be alive.

He stood shakily, staring in disbelief at the burning house, the dry wood rapidly yielding to the fire. He could barely believe he had survived and wondered if anything Brice had told him was true. If the man had been planning this from the start, then there was no reason to believe he would have told John anything resembling the truth.

Without another thought John turned and ran toward the car. All his limbs ached and he was badly bruised from his tumble, but except for a few glass cuts he was alright. He would ponder his next move later. For now he had to get away from this place. He was driven by a new desire. He had to find out what had happened to Macava in this version of reality, to find out if he was alive. In addition, he needed to find out what *he* was. John reasoned that both answers would be found in the same place.

He paused briefly, turning to look at the distant building aglow against the shadow of the obscuring trees, wondering if he should go back to see if Brice had survived. A cynical voice in his head whispered that even if he had survived the explosion, there was no way he could still be alive if he was in there now. If he had managed to escape, then it was possible he was alive, but John had no inclination to help the man. Whether in this reality or not, he knew that Brice had shot Macava, and that was enough to damn him in John's eyes. He turned back and hurried to the car, a plan forming in his aching head.

He would go to Brice's real address and find his answers there. The thought repeated itself within his mind as he drove away, glancing periodically in the mirror to watch the receding orange glow of the burning house.

The room was shrouded in darkness. The stillness of the air added to Kendra's sense of the unnatural as she reclined in the simple wooden chair in the corner. She surveyed the area from her vantage point in silence, only picking out vague shapes of furniture and objects in the gloom as her eyes wandered. This was somewhere she had never expected to be. She felt uncomfortably displaced sitting alone in the shadows of her colleague's sanctuary, pondering whether her flair for the dramatic would work for or against her.

She was sure Davis would come here after Brice's attempt on his life. Brice was clever, but he was not careful. Davis was bound to have found something to lead him to this address. She felt a surge of pity for what she had come to view as Davis's tragic figure. He was clearly confused and had little or no idea of his own potential. She shifted her gaze to her foot, which was dangling from her crossed leg, moving back and forth slightly as she waited. Had she been wrong about Macava or had he just been unfortunate? Even subjects of great ability could succumb to an unexpected death. They were, after all, still human. On the other hand, if Macava was not the subject then it stood to reason that Davis was, but Macava was dead and she was prepared to give Davis the benefit of the doubt.

Besides, she reasoned, if Davis was the subject, he was an unwitting one. If she could reach him on a personal level, perhaps she could prevent any further problems. If she had to, she could deal with him at a later stage when she had gained his trust. It would be easier that way, and perhaps he wouldn't have to die.

She had gone back to Macava's house that morning after her visit to the lake, about the same time that Davis had turned up at Brice's house to interrogate him. The place was still a mess, untouched after her ransacking. It had been a strange experience to walk through the house assuming the doctor had gone, only to find his corpse in the bedroom.

STEVEN D. JACKSON

Macava appeared to have died in his sleep. She could see no sign of trauma or struggle except for the devastation she herself had caused earlier. Had he simply walked in through the broken door, gone to bed, and died? It seemed that he had. She knew of no subject able to create illusions or possessing the power of resurrection, and so she was sure Macava was dead. She had left him untouched and returned to the headquarters in Southampton, deciding to let the civilian authorities deal with his body and think up some ludicrous explanation for his death.

While at the half-empty office, she had received word from Brice. He called from Southampton Hospital to tell her the whole story of how Davis had turned up on his doorstep, of his abuse at Davis's hands, of his failsafe mechanism designed to finish them both off. She had sighed in exasperation at that part of the message. He seemed to think he was doing something noble by catching Davis at the expense of his own life, a sacrifice Kendra found impossible to understand. She also couldn't understand, and Brice hadn't been able to explain, why he hadn't simply shot Davis on the doorstep if he had known the man was coming. Brice confessed that this had been his plan, but he hadn't managed it. His recollection of the incident was murky following the shock of Davis's attack.

Kendra wasn't so sure that shock was the cause of Brice's memory problems. He wasn't a strong Recaller, and if it was the result of a transition he most likely wouldn't know. However, Macava had presumably died the night before, so any transition would have been caused by someone else. As it didn't appear to have benefitted anyone, she had decided to proceed on the basis that Brice had simply been knocked out and tied up.

In the darkness of the corner, she smiled. It was hard to feel sorry for Brice, especially as he had rigged his own house to burn down. It had been a stupid plan and he shouldn't have gone into it without approval. He wasn't badly hurt, although how he had managed to get himself out of the house was a mystery to Kendra. She vaguely remembered him mentioning petrol when she called him that morning. Perhaps she should have paid more attention to what he had said.

She had gone to Brice's real address following his latest call, knowing that he was safely in the hospital and not likely to be released just yet. The place was a hideous mess. The man lived in chaos and had little or no concept of housework or hygiene. Dust covered surfaces which looked like they hadn't been touched in years, discarded food containers littered the table, and she was sure she could hear the scratching sounds of vermin.

She had decided she might as well wait for Davis, and it would be more effective if she capitalized on his heightened state of nervousness by staying concealed in the dark where she could get the drop on him. Part of her felt mildly ridiculous, reasoning that she really ought to open the curtains and doors to let some light in, but for all she knew Davis was armed. Given his conduct with Brice, she had no desire to let him get the better of her.

And what if Davis was the subject? She wouldn't kill someone on a guess. She would take him in, test him, and let him think he was being given a choice. Then she could decide what to do on more informed footing.

She scoffed at her own stupidity. How would she possibly get him to undertake the testing? If he had the slightest inkling that she was trying to work out whether she needed to kill him or not he would escape the first chance he got or purposefully screw up the tests. She needed a plan and she needed it fast.

———————

John stood at the front door of the house in the residential street, looking apprehensively at the window to his right. The heavy curtains were drawn. It would be dark inside. Why would Brice have closed his curtains before leaving to set his ambush? It didn't make sense and it worried John. He wracked his brain, trying to think how this house might also be

STEVEN D. JACKSON

rigged to blow up, but then he thought if it was rigged, Brice had probably thought he would break in through a window. Perhaps going through the front door was his best option. The lunatic probably wouldn't have anticipated that.

The girl's plaintive sobbing echoed around the deathly silent classroom as she was dragged from the room. Her classmates looked on in fear.

Neither the girl nor the teacher made it to the door. With a shudder, the space around them seemed to contract. A moment later, they were gone. Sarah stared in horror at the empty air they had occupied seconds before. Before she knew it she was on her feet, taking a breath to scream her friend's name.

The scream died on her lips as the girls in the front row turned to look at her, their expressions displaying surprise and mild concern. They looked at her as though she had lost her mind. Sarah stared back at them, unnerved by the calm around her. Unable to speak, she looked to the desk at the front of the class. A man sat behind it, clutching a book and glaring at her irritably.

She stared at him dumbly. It was impossible. Her gaze shifted to the girl in the front row, her best friend, who was regarding her with a look of delight and amazement. Sarah's heart leapt at the sight of her friend, relief spreading through her for a moment before the shock hit.

Sarah stumbled back, knocking the chair over in her haste and confusion. The man rose from behind the desk, shouting at the class to calm down and get on with their work. Her eyes were wide with fear as he approached her, though the expression he wore was one of concern and kindness. He reached for her hand and she shook him off, edging around the table as he tracked her, confusion clouding his face.

Shaking her head in denial and casting another glance at her friend, Sarah fled from the room. She paused in the doorway and turned to regard the girl in the front row again, her emotions a mess. The girl smiled back at her happily. The sight scared her intensely ....

The school nurse was asking her for the hundredth time what had happened. Once again, Sarah ignored her, staring into the space beyond the nurse's head. She could hear footsteps approaching, and a feeling of dread settled into her stomach. The nurse muttered that she was going to call Sarah's parents, something about a fever. Sarah felt a jolt of panic as the nurse left the office, realizing she was alone. The footsteps reached the office and she looked around.

Her best friend stood in the doorway, smiling that scary smile. She stepped toward her ....

Someone tried the door and she jerked her head up, the sound far louder than she had expected. Shaking off the unpleasant memory, Kendra eased her gun out of its holster. Setting her face in a mask of serious professionalism, she waited for John Davis to walk into her trap.

To John's surprise, the door wasn't locked, firmly cementing his fear. His heart thumped in his chest, demanding that he reconsider and give up the entire plan. He tried to ignore his fears. Too many people had suffered on this journey to justify giving up now. Yet his heart wouldn't be calmed, his breath wouldn't steady, and he could feel the panic rising as the door swung ponderously open.

The light from the street showed John a cluttered and deserted room, a desk with a lamp and an armchair to his right, a table stacked with what looked like pizza boxes and kitchen utensils.

Kitchen utensils.

He still had a knife tucked in his belt.

Without another thought John jumped into the room and slammed the door shut behind him, leaning against it and cursing his stupidity. He forgot his fear in an instant. The knife had been plainly visible to anyone who cared to look as he stood in the street and walked into someone else's house. He would be lucky if the police weren't being called right now by some neighborhood watch enthusiast.

His eyes were still closed, his labored breathing slowly recovering, when a female voice addressed him.

"Don't move. My gun's pointing straight at your face and I'm one hell of a shot at this distance."

Cold and steady, it emanated from the corner farthest from him. John froze, his eyes snapping open as he searched the shadows for the source of the voice. He swallowed, his adjusting eyes gradually making out a shape sitting calmly in a chair across from him. He felt anger rising inside him and a reckless desire to fight back against this half-seen threat. He tried to hold it back, but he could not completely mask the defiance in his retort. "I guess I should be thankful you haven't already killed me. Isn't that how your lot usually works?" He was genuinely alarmed by the sneer in his voice. He hadn't meant to sound so sardonic, but somehow the adrenaline in his system was throwing his caution to the wind.

The woman's reply was low and simple, somehow dampening the mad grip of John's aggression. "It is indeed. And yes, you should."

The words were accompanied by a clicking sound that John assumed was a gun safety. Whether it was being clicked off or on he couldn't tell. To his relief, his sensible side was back in control and he wasn't about to give this assassin any reason to shoot him. From the tone of her voice he was sure she wouldn't hesitate. He waited, wondering what the appropriate response to her last comment was. His mind remained blank as the moment stretched and the imminent threat began to wane. As another second ticked by, the situation suddenly struck him as absurd and he was appalled to feel laughter welling up inside him. If the tension wasn't broken soon he felt certain he would collapse into a fit of giggles. Deciding on a whim to try another approach, he elected to break the tension himself.

"This is all very dramatic." He spoke as calmly as he

could, trying to keep the laughter from bubbling over into his voice. A short, startled laugh from the shadowed assassin was quickly stifled. He saw her rise to her feet, click the gun again, and lower the weapon. When she replied, it was in a similarly over-serious tone.

"You're so right."

John laughed. He simply couldn't help it. He could feel his ribs aching from the force of holding it in and allowed all the tension of the last few minutes to dissipate as he gave vent to the giggles he had been holding back. The fit of amusement passed quickly, bringing him back to the stark reality of being in a darkened room with a trained killer who was holding a gun. He watched as the woman moved to the desk and switched the lamp on. Then she sat down carefully on the sofa to her left, indicating that John should take the chair she had just vacated.

"Sit down, Mr. Davis. We have a lot to discuss."

John didn't miss the implied threat in the statement. He wasn't being given a choice.

CHAPTER

John Davis was not what Kendra had expected. He was an attentive listener with an almost childlike fascination for what she told him. Her throat constricted once or twice during her narrative, overwhelmed by the total innocence he exhibited toward the issues she was describing. His eyes were wide in amazement and she could feel his excitement as he occasionally interrupted to ask a question. She found it almost painful.

You can't kill him, her mind screamed. *He isn't any more deserving of death than Cat was.*

He isn't a child, she silently retorted, *he's an adult and he might be a threat. Keep him interested, keep him talking, get him to go through the tests, and be prepared to do what you have to.*

As she spoke, she thought back to the events of her past. The person in front of her reminded her of her own lost innocence. When had she lost it? She almost felt she had never been innocent. She tried to focus her thoughts on the here and now, hoping to block out the shadows of the years gone by.

Brice had told the truth about the organization. It was as shady as any agency in a spy film, as far as John could tell. The woman was the detective from the hospital. Her name was Sarah Kendra, although evidently the Sarah was not to be used in formal address. From the woman's manner he wondered if anyone ever got to call her Sarah. She was tall and elegant, and John found it hard to focus on what she was saying to the exclusion of her legs, which were long and extremely well-formed. It wouldn't have been so bad if she hadn't kept shifting them, crossing and re-crossing them as she spoke. It was almost as if she was distracted herself. She would frown and pause in mid-sentence, smoothing her hair back although it was already pulled tightly off her face, giving the impression that she wasn't entirely with him. John felt decidedly guilty whenever he took the opportunity as she fidgeted to casually note her new position. He hoped she hadn't noticed his staring. He felt like a teenager gaping open-mouthed at some incredibly attractive teacher in school and hated himself for it. He just couldn't help it.

The TR Detective finished confirming the basics of what Brice had already explained, that they thought Macava was the Shifter and how they had planned to take him down. The shot she had fired at the hospital had been aimed at Macava, but she had missed because of the people chasing her. It all made perfect sense and she spoke with such calm authority that John had no reason to disbelieve her. Brice, it seemed, had not laid his trap with any prior instruction from the organization itself.

"He shouldn't have done what he did, setting some lunatic trap for you, but at least it failed. He didn't even hurt himself particularly badly, and I see that you are none the worse for wear." She gestured dismissively. "No harm done."

Appalled, John stared at her. "No harm done? How can you say that after what he did to Nicholas?" His voice cracked as he tried to maintain his composure.

She looked at him blankly, a frown pinching her eyebrows as she regarded him, her expression quickly growing darker. "What did he do?"

John belatedly remembered that the body had vanished and even Brice had failed to remember shooting Nicholas. He sat back in his chair, rubbing his forehead with his fingers. "He shot Nicholas. I saw him going to answer the door with a gun and I ran around the house, but I only got to the door in time to see Nicholas die. That's when I attacked Brice, and that's why I was so vicious with him. Then it turns out that it didn't happen that way after all, and Nicholas's body was gone. I don't know what happened to it, I don't understand what's happening anymore." He stopped, closing his eyes and wondering if he would ever regain control of his life.

When he opened his eyes he saw that Kendra had looked away from him and was staring into space somewhere to his left. When she spoke it was quietly, as though sensitive to his delicate mood. "Subjects of advanced abilities are capable of some shocking actions. They can manipulate the world around them to a degree I can't even begin to describe. Sometimes they can single out objects or people to affect, sometimes entire groups, and sometimes whole countries. Their abilities can be unpredictable and dangerous, and they can have catastrophic consequences." She glanced down at her feet and paused briefly. "But not always." This was said quietly, as though to herself. "I have never known a subject to be capable of resurrecting himself, though it is possible that one could manipulate the thoughts of those around him to make them believe he was dead. Brice does not remember shooting Macava, but you remember him doing so. No one has seen or heard from Macava since, so it is possible"—she looked at him sternly—"and I say possible, not probable, that he did this himself for his own reasons."

John was confused. Why would Nicholas do that to him? Nicholas trusted him. *No,* he corrected himself, *you trusted Nicholas. Look what happened when you tried to confront him about the possibility that he was behind all this. He reacted badly, perhaps* over*reacted ... and he never actually denied it.*

Kendra was watching him closely, perhaps understanding

the conflict he felt. "I know it's hard to consider this, John, but if Nicholas is the subject, as I believe he is, then it's entirely possible that he wanted you to believe he was dead. He concentrated on you because he suspected that you were a powerful Recaller, capable of resisting all but the most concentrated of direct attacks. He would have recognized the signs from your sessions with him." She paused, looking at him with a guilty expression before mastering her features and continuing. "He would have expected Brice to die, either from his foolish failsafe or by your vengeance, and for you to find your way to me carrying news of his death so that I would stop hunting him."

She looked at him appraisingly. "But he underestimated your abilities. You somehow managed to see through the deception. Whatever the reason, you unraveled the veil Macava pulled over your eyes, which, I have to say, is impressive."

John was replaying the conversations in the wooden house, trying to put his finger on what didn't add up. It all sounded so plausible, made so much sense, but surely something wasn't right ....

Kendra stood and went to the window, pulling open the curtain and allowing the sunlight to stream into the dull room. Staring out at the quiet suburban street, she addressed John again. "Your abilities are strong and I think you would be a valuable asset to the organization. I would like you to consider coming with me, letting me teach you to be a Recaller, perhaps one day even a full Transition Recall Detective. I think we'll need your help to find Nicholas, and perhaps with you on board we could persuade him to come in quietly."

John looked up sharply. She was making him an offer that she must have known he could not refuse in good conscience. Either he went with her and helped the organization, thereby betraying Nicholas but potentially sparing his life, or he refused and allowed her to hunt Nicholas down and kill him. Had this been Nicholas's plan all along? Had he wanted John to find and join the organization? Had his every action been calculated in order to pull and push John to this moment? The sense of betrayal warred with John's conscience. He wouldn't allow Nicholas to come to harm, even if the doctor had betrayed him.

A cold voice inside him sneered that Nicholas deserved everything he got if he was the Shifter and he had killed Chris to manipulate John's anger and grief. The truth was John didn't know anything yet. Neither did Kendra. He had a better chance of finding out with her and would be in a better position to save or destroy Nicholas if he was working with the organization.

He had no choice. Rising from his chair he crossed to the front door of the shabby house and jerked it open. He glanced at Kendra's expressionless face and wondered if anything she had said was true. Deciding that whatever the truth was he would follow her path for a while, he nodded to her. She nodded back and stepped past him, out into the sunlight. The slightest hint of a smile marred the hard set of her features.

The girl's smile faded as Sarah stumbled backward, glancing around in panic to find an escape route. She knew she was hyperventilating, but she couldn't help it. She felt light-headed.

Sarah shook her head to clear it and stared accusingly at her friend. She was too weak, too tired, she needed to sit down. Keeping the distance between them, Sarah sank onto the couch in the nurse's office. Unbidden, tears filled her eyes and she began to cry.

Feeling an arm around her shoulder, Sarah gave in and let the girl hug her. It was all so confusing, so unfair. All she wanted at that moment was to be held, to be told it was all going to be alright.

But her friend did not say what she wanted to hear. She told Sarah she was excited. No one had ever noticed before. No one had ever understood her before. It was special; they were special. She didn't understand how it happened or why, but it didn't matter, it was something magical and exciting.

Sarah pushed away, anger rising as she fought to reject the whispering lies. Whatever had happened was unnatural, wrong. She screamed at her friend to stay away from her, to never speak to her again. She called her a freak.

Running from the nurse's station as fast as she could, Sarah did not look back.

The next day there was no sign of the girl ... or the day after that, or the day after that ....

———————

Brice could feel their eyes boring into the back of his head, raking him with sidelong glances while they whispered. He could tell they were talking about him. How they had managed to find out, or what they had found out, he didn't know. He could just tell that they were acting differently today, and there could only be one explanation for that.

Recaller Stuart Avery came bounding over to him, a relieved grin all over his face. Avery was a tall, well-built man in his late twenties with dark hair, which was always fashionably tousled, and an open grin perpetually glued to his face. He was constantly cheerful, and in spite of being a minor Recaller with a fairly mundane job at the organization, he was an office favorite. Despite being one of the few colleagues who actually gave him the time of day and seemed genuinely friendly toward him, Avery was someone Brice detested. The man was infuriatingly oblivious to the undercurrents of hostility that most people were fairly adept at detecting in an office environment, and as a consequence never picked up on the fact that Brice avoided him whenever possible.

Somewhere inside, Brice knew that he was being stubborn and introverted and that Avery was a likeable character. That knowledge, however, only served to deepen his resentment toward this man who was everything Brice could never be.

"Darren!" Avery called loudly, as though Brice could

possibly have missed his approach. Brice sighed inwardly and turned, presenting his deadpan gaze to the jubilant younger man who was pushing his way past obstructing colleagues to reach him. "I heard you were in an accident. What happened? Are you okay? Everyone's been talking about it." He looked so sincere and sounded so breathless that Brice once again tried to fathom Avery's brain patterns. He had just confirmed that everyone *had* been talking about Brice behind his back, and he didn't even seem to realize it. Idiot.

Resigning himself to the fact that he and Avery were fundamentally different creatures who would never understand one another, Brice made an effort to come up with some form of answer. The earnest young man was looming over him and leaning toward him at the same time, perhaps in a subconscious effort to lessen the height difference. Brice was distinctly uncomfortable and had the impression that everyone was watching him.

"I tried to catch the subject, Avery. Goes with the job. It went wrong, and yes, I was in the hospital but I'm fine." He held up his bandaged arm, wondering again how he had managed to get away with nothing but a few minor burns and scrapes.

Avery was fascinated. He let out a single laugh and peered at the bandage. "Wow, I guess you were lucky then. I heard your whole house burned down."

Avery didn't seem to be looking for affirmation. Flashing Brice a smile full of teeth, he turned and clapped him on the shoulder before sauntering off through the crowd which had surreptitiously edged a little closer during the exchange. Brice smiled to himself. Avery's lack of interest in the gory details was likely to disappoint them. He wondered if the man might be a little dull-witted.

Slumping down at his desk, Brice turned on his computer and waited for it to boot up. He shouldn't really have come in to work today, but he didn't want to miss Davis's entrance into the establishment. He was fairly sure Sarah would waste no time in bringing him here once she found him, especially now that Macava was dead. It was all happening as Brice had feared, and he was extremely angry about it. It wouldn't be long before Sarah decided to train Davis as a Recaller and have him replace her 'irreplaceable' Cat Reynolds. He would quickly outstrip them all, and Brice would once again be the useless one in the corner, friend only to that idiot Avery.

He gazed miserably at the bandage on his arm. He had no idea how he could possibly get at Davis now. It would only be a matter of time before Avery was assigned to take him to the Supervisors to be approved as Kendra's new partner.

Avery ....

Brice straightened, amazed he hadn't thought of it before. All these elaborate schemes and traps were completely unnecessary. Avery would provide him with the perfect solution. He closed his eyes as the plan formulated in the darkness of his mind. It was almost perfect. He felt a minor stab of regret for Avery, but in the grand scheme of things the Recaller's fate was insignificant. He smiled to himself as he opened his eyes and gazed across the room at the back of Stuart Avery's head, which was bobbing animatedly amongst a group of guys all standing about listening to him and doing very little actual work.

Brice genuinely regretted the fact that Avery had to be part of the plan, but as the saying went, nice guys always finished last. At least this way Avery would finish early.

John looked through the miscellaneous papers stacked in Kendra's glove compartment as they headed toward the organization's headquarters. Evidently it was in Southampton, and according to the official letterhead it was known to the outside world as the Office of Transitional Regulation. John had never heard of it. It sounded like something to do with sewage treatment. Quite clever, really.

"We use a different name for different authorities. The

organization doesn't really have a name. As I understand it, that reasoning was a concession to the fact that subjects could change the name if they felt like it, so there was no point in having one." Kendra chuckled as she drove. "Strange logic, if you ask me. I think they just couldn't be bothered to pick a name."

John nodded in a non-committal manner. He thought it sounded like a lie, not the best start to their new collaboration. "So what's the plan when we get there?" He kept his voice light, trying to shake the feeling that he was walking knowingly into the lion's den. He wanted to call Jenna. He needed to tell her about Nicholas. As soon as he got a moment he would call her. He also wondered where he would be staying in Southampton. After all, he only had a few things with him in the bag he had packed two days ago before hunting down Brice. The day he had packed it seemed an age ago now, before the ambush at the hotel, before the shooting and the fire ....

"I'll have someone show you around the facility, and then we need to get started on finding out how strong your abilities are. I have my opinion, but it needs verification."

John looked at her, instantly suspicious. "How?"

"We have a Shifter of modest ability working at headquarters. The condition of his employment is that he doesn't use his ability against us, and with a building full of Recallers he couldn't exactly hide it if he did. His job is testing the ability of new Recallers. You'll like him. He's old and harmless now, anyway."

John instantly thought of Nicholas, but pushed the thought angrily away. He gazed out of the window, watching the world go by and wondering where he would be this time tomorrow. What if it turned out he had no ability at all?

The car park into which Kendra drove was huge. In front of them a sprawling building loomed up toward the evening sky. It had the appearance of an old-fashioned school, with many windows and what looked like spires at the sides. A flight of steps ran up to the huge wooden doors which were standing open, beyond which John could make out the shapes of people moving with purposeful strides. As he followed Kendra inside, he saw a spacious reception area, a large, open-plan office full of people and desks, and staircases leading to the second floor.

John felt horribly out of place in this testament to ordered efficiency. He doubted that anyone would ever have accused him of being ordered or efficient. This place was a revelation to him, and in spite of himself he liked it. He followed Kendra to the reception desk, watching as people scrambled out of the Detective's way. He was amazed by the effect she had on people and couldn't help but be impressed. She had a purposeful gait and wore a stern expression, and when she spoke it was in a voice of steel which John had not heard her use before.

"TR Detective Kendra returning from assignment. Prospective Recaller John Davis also checking in."

Prospective Recaller? John repeated the words in his mind, wondering whether this was for real. The man behind the desk mumbled something and made a mark on his register. He avoided looking at Kendra. She didn't wait for an answer, but turned and led John into the crowded office to their left. Without stopping, she made her way across the room to the other side, where John could see a private office cut off from the rest, sporting a large glass window with shutters on the other side. From the look of it, the private office was a terrible mess.

Looking closely, John saw that nothing in the large office was ordered at all. Files lay heaped on desks and people at computers were calling to one another over other people's heads. Others on telephones were shouting to make themselves heard. It was structured chaos. John rather liked it. Kendra led him to a tall man in an open-necked white shirt. The man turned at her tap and his grin faded slightly.

"Detective, er, ma'am. Is everything okay?"

Kendra smiled, her shoulders dropping in a way that suggested to John she was relaxing her guard.

"Hi, Stuart. I need a favor. Could you show John Davis here"—her emphasis on the name Davis was slight, but John still caught it—"around the facility and then take him to Tom? I need a full test of both Alpha and Beta, if possible. Then report back to me."

She smiled briefly at John before marching away to the separate office, shouting across the room at another Recaller to bring Tom to her. She crossed into the office and pulled the shutters, and John turned back to Stuart, more nervous than he had felt in a long time. Stuart's smile was disarming, however, and John instantly warmed to him. "So, you're Davis? Guess you're pretty lucky to be alive too! Okay, let's get started." Stuart clapped his hands together and put an arm around John's shoulders to guide him out of the office. "I'll show you the cells first. They are *definitely* the coolest part."

John's smile wavered as he was led toward the cells, sudden apprehension lancing through his chest.

EIGHTEEN

CHAPTER

John's thoughts wandered as he followed Stuart. His memories of Macava were resurfacing, reminding him bitterly of the reason he was here on this tour with Stuart in the first place. What had the doctor proved in the end? That no one was trustworthy in this life? Certainly John felt as though he could never easily trust someone again. He found himself going back over the things he and Nicholas had discussed over the years. Had they all been lies too, designed to manipulate him? Or was his present bitterness tainting his memories? Detachment was not easy to achieve at this moment.

Stuart had introduced himself as a 'pilot without a cause'. He was the organization's helicopter pilot and a Recaller too, but then so was everyone who worked here. The helicopter was his pride and joy, he did all the maintenance on it every week, and as far as he knew he was the only one who ever took an interest in it. People very rarely needed it, although he had been called out to Gillworth not long ago to pick up Detective Kendra from a car crash and then from a field on the other side of some woods near a hospital. He had enjoyed that immensely, and John kept very quiet as Stuart happily told the tale.

It was Stuart's job to organize the teams on the ground

and to coordinate transport. He called himself the transport coordinator, but whether that was a grandiose term for a very basic job John didn't want to ask. The guy was happy with it, and after showing John his 'office', which was in fact merely a cordoned off area with a radio and a map in addition to the usual desk and computer, they moved on to the lesser used rooms at the back of the building.

They were now heading down a wide flight of plain concrete steps under the main structure of the building. The atmosphere was that of a prison with grey walls and bright lighting which nonetheless made the place seem dim. Their footfalls echoed around them as they went lower until the steps ended in a long corridor with what appeared to be jail cells on the left. Each cell was empty and held a cot and a sink with a toilet in the corner. They looked designed for long-term internment, John reflected, a cold feeling creeping up his spine.

"So yeah, these are the cells where we put some of the trickier ones. The thing is, if they are Shifters they can probably get themselves out of here easy enough, so we have to give them a shot."

John looked at him sharply, thinking less and less of this organization as he took in the information. Stuart, unaware of his change in attitude, helpfully elaborated on the unspoken question. "Sort of a tranquilizer. An anti-psychotic. It stops them from doing their thing, but it also does what it would do to anyone else and knocks them out. I guess we don't really know if it would stop them if they were conscious." Adopting a conspiratorial tone, Stuart leaned in close and confided, "To be honest, we don't get many in. If we find them, they're normally taken down in the field. We have our own Shifters who are sometimes used to put them in a more manageable place, sometimes in high security madhouses. You know, for criminal crazies? Places like that. Kendra, though, she doesn't trust Shifters to take down their own, and since she took over they get dealt with a little more decisively. She doesn't get that many though ...." He trailed off and frowned as he gazed into the cell.

Disgusted, John looked away. So they hunted them either to kill them, to catch and sedate them, or to put them somewhere drugged up for ... what? The rest of their lives? Or did they make them forget what they were? Stuart was leading him away, back toward the staircase, when they were met by an old man wearing a faded suit. He had wispy white hair and what had to be false teeth. He smiled and extended his hand to John, introducing himself as Tom. Stuart seemed delighted to see Tom and quickly ushered them back up the stairs toward the rooms at the rear of the building which, as he had said previously, were quieter than the others.

Guiding them to the first of the double doors in the corridor, Stuart vigorously shook John's hand and bade him good luck, calling over his shoulder as he hurried off, "Remember, we've all been through it. You'll be fine!"

Perplexed, John watched his receding form. He turned to ask Tom what was happening, but the old man was busy unlocking the large double door. With a creak the doors swung open, revealing a large square room with no windows. The interior was brightly lit by a light hanging from the center of the ceiling and was unfurnished save for two armchairs and a table positioned in the middle of the floor. Around the edges of the room were various items. John could see a football, a telephone, and numerous boxes, all lined up against the walls. Wondering what on earth was going on, he followed Tom into the room, closing the door behind him at the old man's gesture.

Tom seated himself on the first armchair and smiled. "So, let's begin, shall we? The important thing is that you relax. This won't take long, but it needs to be done."

Tom's voice was high and slightly wheezy but not nearly as disturbing as his smile. His teeth were far too white and didn't fit well in his mouth. John could barely keep his eyes off them. In an effort to blot out those dazzling teeth in the

204

wrinkled face, John busied himself with sitting down and pulling his chair forward to the table.

"Okay, but what are we doing here, Tom? I'd quite like to have a word with Sarah, if possible, because I really don't know where I'm going to stay tonight. It's coming up for six o' clock and I haven't booked anywhere or anything."

He paused. Tom was smiling again. It seemed to be his default expression and John really wasn't sure it was all that sincere. He had always hated clowns for that very reason, with their disingenuous smiles and false faces. He shuddered inwardly.

"We're here because *Detective Kendra*"—he emphasized the two words with a slightly disapproving tone, which he somehow managed to achieve without adjusting his smile— "wants to know just how good you really are. I am what you might have heard them refer to as a Shifter, but only of very mild ability. I can't do much, so they keep me around, but it means I hold the privileged position of tester."

John smiled and almost retorted jokingly until he realized that it was genuine pride and not sarcasm in the old man's voice. Tom had apparently come to consider it quite an honor to be used as a tester, even against his own kind. The smile faded from John's face as he wondered what choice, if any, Tom had been given.

Tom was looking at him expectantly. John nodded and sighed, trying to put thoughts of coercion and threats out of his mind. "Okay, so what do we do?"

"Well, if you wouldn't mind going to the wall and collecting the football, I'd be grateful. Just bring it back here to the table."

John stood and went to the wall, looking suspiciously at the football. Gingerly collecting it, he turned and made his way back to the armchair, but before he had taken two steps he felt a light pressure on his head, pressing down gently as though he were underwater. The feeling was strange, barely noticeable, but impossible to miss in the bright quiet of the room. Brushing it off as an irritation he returned to the chair, the feeling fading as quickly as it had come. As he went to place the ball on the table, he stared in surprise at the object in his hands.

He was holding a watermelon. Tom watched him with a guarded expression, obviously waiting to see if John would notice. "It's a watermelon," John said stupidly. He had experienced such changes already on a number of occasions and even had two people explain it to him. He was now in a building full of people who had experienced similar things, yet the entire concept still struck him as lunacy. Shaking his head he tried to regain his composure and focus on what the test was designed to assess.

"It was a football and now it's a watermelon. You asked me to get the football and it changed."

Tom's smile returned and he nodded encouragingly. "Well done, son, that's the first part out of the way. I was focusing on the ball and not on you, but we can try the harder type now. Let's see what happens if we focus on you and not the object."

The tests continued for almost an hour. Tom clearly had some skill as a Shifter because with each attempt John's focus slipped further. The pressure in his head increased as the tests wore on, and Tom's toothy smile reformed less and less each time. When he eventually indicated it was time for the final test John was mentally exhausted, and although he knew nothing had happened to his body he still felt out of breath and nauseous.

Tom ran a hand over his face. Summoning some enthusiasm with what appeared to be a great effort, he gestured for John to stand. He smiled wanly. "Well, at least we know you aren't a Shifter, my lad."

The corner of John's mouth twitched in a half-smile. They had established this fairly early on, when John had almost given himself a hernia trying to change the melon back into a football. The obvious truth was most definitely that he had all the mysterious Shifter power of an apricot. Or possibly a watermelon. He stood reluctantly, not wanting to continue any further. He eyed Tom with brewing resentment. He hadn't yet received any indication of how he was doing.

Tom went to stand behind his armchair and leaned on the back of it. "This last one is the most I am capable of, John. We've tested mental, physical, external, and a bit of internal capacity, and now I want to join everything together. I am going to try to make you move from where you are now to the other side of the room. I am going to try to force you to think that my name is Alan because I was introduced to you as Alan, and I am going to try to make you think you have always been standing there waiting for the last test to begin. It will feel horrible, I'm afraid, because it'll be focused entirely on you. It isn't much, I grant you, but see what you can do with it. Of course, you have a bit of a head start because you wouldn't normally know it was happening. Try to resist both the mental and physical changes. Don't worry if you can't do the physical, a lot of people are confined to just remembering."

John nodded, feeling his heart begin to pound in his chest. He stepped from foot to foot while gazing warily at Tom. Without warning, he felt the slight tingle inside his head. He concentrated his whole mind on what he knew was true, screaming silently against the force he could feel building within his mind, pressing on his consciousness like a fist closing around his brain. His vision shook and blurred, he lost sight of Tom's strained face as he focused his entire being on reality. A terrible sense of vertigo threatened to overwhelm him and he could feel empty space beneath his feet, as though he was stranded in space with nothing above or below him but a vast, yawning eternity. The pressure built to a point where he could barely stand and he almost cried out, reaching for the thought that he must succeed, must survive this test.

Test ....

He grabbed the flash of truth as it snapped past him, wrenching himself back to reality with the knowledge that this was a trial and he was going to pass it. The pressure vanished

207

abruptly. John slowly opened his eyes and fought to control his breathing. He was standing facing where Tom had been, his hands curled into tight fists by his side. The room was as calm and still as it had always been.

John glanced around, wondering where Tom had gone. Had he, in fact, failed? Was this part of the test? He stepped slowly around his armchair, casting his gaze to the floor as he did so. A pair of feet protruded from behind the other chair and John rushed to Tom's side, shoving the chair away so he could kneel beside the old man. He was out cold but breathing, a small trickle of blood running from his nose. John whispered his name and repeated it a little louder, realizing how pointless it was to try to wake someone quietly. Yet it seemed wrong to speak too loudly in this oversized, empty room, even though Tom had been knocked unconscious by the effort of trying to Shift.

Not knowing what else to do, John dragged the older man's limp body into the armchair, propping him up in it like a rag doll and pulling the other chair over to make a makeshift bed. The man's legs were slightly too long to allow him to lie full-stretch, so John put him on his side and bent his legs at the knees. A vague memory about recovery positions from the first-aid course they had done at school when he was about eight bobbed into his head. He stood back and regarded his handiwork, thinking that if the recovery position wasn't exactly right, Tom looked comfortable enough. It would have to do while he went to get help.

Feeling strangely pleased with himself despite apparently knocking out an old man, John went to the door and tried to remember the way back to the office he had been in before. He held the door open for a moment, staring back at the chair supporting Tom's prone form. "What the hell am I getting into?" he muttered, wondering how long it would be before he was offered a choice like Tom's. What would happen if he said no? Casting one last glance over his shoulder, he hurried out in search of Kendra.

"**He**'s dangerous. He tried to kill me."

Brice was insistent and his voice was beginning to irritate Kendra, sounding like a whining drone in her head. How many times did she have to tell him?

"He is just as dangerous as you or I at this point, Brice. Until I have confirmation of his abilities—the tests for which, I should add, he has agreed to—"

"By deception!"

Brice was furious, evidently forgetting protocol and the fact that he was addressing his superior. Kendra let it pass, not caring what Brice thought anymore and wanting to be rid of him.

"He is to be welcomed as a potential recruit. And afterwards, Brice," she paused and glared at him meaningfully, "if he does come to work here, *you* will make him welcome. You have seen the files and worked with me on this. You know he would be a useful asset if my assessment is correct."

Brice stared at her, his eyes a little wild and his breathing ragged. All were signs that he was losing control of his emotions. He was dangerously close to overstepping the mark, and a rebellious part of her wanted to let him cross it. She suppressed it. "Don't make me regret the esteem in which I hold you, Darren."

The sweating man blinked as though confused. Her *coup de grace* was the use of his first name. She smiled slightly to add emphasis, smooth and deadly as always. Perhaps Brice was starting to come apart. She had noticed in recent days that his attention was elsewhere, and evidently he had been planning to blow up his house. If he was coming apart she needed to do some repair work, if she really needed him at all anymore.

He was calming down, his irrational panic attack about Davis passing as quickly as it had come. The man hadn't tried to kill him. It had been Brice's own crazy plan that had got him his burns. Still, now was not the time to remind him of that.

"Thank you, Detective," he said breathlessly, shaking his head as though trying to puzzle his way through his own thought processes. Glancing once more at her, he made to leave only to stop dead in his tracks as John Davis hurried through the door unannounced, closing it behind him.

Davis almost ran into Brice without noticing him, letting out a quick "Oh, sorry, mate," before noticing who he was talking to. Davis stopped short and stared at Brice as though he could barely believe his eyes. Kendra could almost see the warring emotions reflected on his face. They ranged from shock to barely suppressed rage before he mastered himself and adopted a neutral expression. She was quietly impressed.

The moment stretched as the two men stared at one another. Kendra could feel the tension building and wondered if she should intervene, deciding in the end to watch it play out. Eventually Brice moved past Davis and left the office, leaving Kendra and Davis alone in the cluttered room. She sighed and leaned back in her seat, putting her feet up on her workspace and gesturing for Davis to sit down opposite. He didn't move. He didn't even look at her.

"So how did it go? Where's Tom?" she asked as casually as she could, hoping that her concern over him having returned alone would not show on her face.

The young man blinked and looked at her sheepishly. He fiddled with some papers on the desk as he moved to the chair and sat down. "He, ah, he's going to be okay. I got some help for him after he kind of passed out. We did some tests and it turns out that while I can't change footballs into melons, I can take everything else. With the last one it was a bit mad and he threw everything he had at me. I thought my head might implode, but in the end it didn't work. He passed out from the effort so I tucked him up on the armchairs and went to get someone. They sent me to see you."

Kendra nodded as sagely as she could manage, staring out of

210

STEVEN D. JACKSON

the window with a noncommittal expression on her face. This was incredible. He had resisted everything Tom could throw at him to the extent that Tom lost control and passed out. It was a fantastic display of power from someone so new to the game. He was far and away the most remarkable Recaller she had known in some considerable time. But then what about the Shifter? Whoever it was knew Davis's potential and had targeted him from the start, but was it to get him killed or to drive him here? She couldn't think of a reason why the Shifter would want Davis to come here and realize his potential. It made more sense for him to want Davis dead. Indeed, she had almost killed him herself on more than one occasion through events orchestrated by this subject. Perhaps the subject feared Davis would survive a direct attack and discover their identity, and therefore used puppets whenever possible.

Whatever the reason behind the Shifter's actions, she needed to have Davis on board to help her take him down. If that meant feeding him more half truths about it being Macava, the great betrayer, then so be it. For now, however, she needed to get things moving. Reaching across the desk, she picked up her phone and pressed the reception number. "Get me Stuart. My office."

She smiled over at Davis, who was engrossed in a file on the other side of the desk. Kendra's heart gave a sudden jolt. What the hell was he reading? Her panic was broken by Stuart entering the room. Davis glanced up and smiled. He had obviously warmed to Stuart.

"Hiya, mate," said Stuart, smiling down at John. "So how'd it go with Tom?"

Kendra interjected, as much to take control of the conversation as to give a meaningful answer. Stuart, for all his charm, could be counted on to go off on a tangent whenever possible. "Tom's out cold, I'm afraid. John here was a little too much for him. Absolutely no Alpha potential from the sound of it, but plenty of Beta, and that's what we like to see."

Stuart grinned his self-deprecating smile, Kendra's favorite.

211

She often wondered whether it would be worth promoting him so she could have that smile around a bit more often. "So is that me out of a job then? Since I'm such a brilliant Recaller and all."

In spite of herself she laughed. She was about to retort when she remembered her intention not to let the conversation drift too far. John was too fast for her, quipping back with a remark she missed which had the two of them trading increasingly loud and immature comments. She sighed. One Stuart was bad enough. With two in the office she would probably have to keep an eye on them. Not a bad idea in any case, an inner voice whispered rebelliously. Derailing that train of thought before it went any further, she cut through the bravado-drenched conversation and pulled it back to reality.

"Stuart, that's enough. I need you to take John to the Supervisors. They are in London tonight. I've already cleared you, so I want you to go right now, if you have no objection."

The reaction was immediate. Stuart's face lit up, his mouth opening in a wide smile as he turned to look at John. "Yes! We get to take the helicopter!" He was jubilant as he grabbed John and hurried with him out of the office, giving John no chance to ask questions, which was just what Kendra wanted. John would go along with Stuart, and when he got back she could get down to working out their next move. The important thing at this stage was to have the Supervisors know that she was making progress. They would be in direct communication with the other Regions, and she needed to send a good report. She was beginning to feel desperate.

The situation was far from resolved, and it would be her head on the block if it got any worse.

CHAPTER

John followed Stuart up a few flights of stairs to get to the roof. Stuart was mildly concerned to discover that the heavy metal door to the roof was unlocked.

"I always lock it myself," he said, ushering John through and slamming it behind them. "I guess I forgot."

The helicopter was top of the range, like something out of a high budget military movie. It was sleek and black and far bigger than John had imagined. The night was cold and clear and a slight breeze was blowing. Stuart said it was a perfect night for flying. John was finding it hard to look forward to the trip given that no one had told him who the Supervisors were or why he needed to see them. In view of what he had learned today and how much it had twisted his formerly sensible world out of all recognition, he decided to go along this time. Perhaps acceding to the machinations of fate might serve him better than resisting.

The helicopter slowly rose off the helipad. John kept his eyes on the large painted 'H' on the roof, trying to keep it in sight to gauge how high they were. As he leaned over in his seat the helicopter gave a sickening lurch and the world tipped sideways. John fell back and grabbed at the seatbelt that Stuart had assured him would not be needed, shoving it into place with a force born of primal fear. The chopper circled wildly, the world spinning as the helipad drew closer at an alarming rate. Warning beeps sounded and lights flashed all over the controls as Stuart feverishly stabbed at them and pulled at the lever by his side. John pressed his hand against the window and tried to force himself further into his seat in the hope that it might help to brace him on impact.

The sound of the rotor blades was increasing, mixed with the groaning of tortured metal. The spinning roof rushed up to meet them as the chopper's tail smashed into the concrete, slamming the body of the vehicle into the roof with incredible force. Stuart was thrown against the cockpit's toughened glass and collapsed in a heap, sprawled partly over John's legs. The helicopter had landed on its side. The door on John's side was crushed against the concrete with the full weight of the machine pressed against it. John could detect the acrid smell of fuel and his mind filled with thoughts of explosions and fire.

Unclasping his seatbelt, John wriggled out from beneath Stuart's prone body, not stopping to check if he was alive or dead. He clambered past the pilot's seat and clutched at the door release above him. Mercifully, it gave and opened. John pushed it outward and climbed onto the seat. Reaching back down into the cockpit, he took hold of Stuart's arms and heaved him up, trying to keep hold of him with one arm while hoisting both of them out of the door directly above him. He managed to stand with Stuart, but the deadweight of the pilot's body was simply too heavy for him to lift. He tightened his grip around Stuart's chest with his left arm and gritted his teeth as he strained to pull him up just a bit farther. His right hand clamped around the headrest of the seat above him. His muscles burned and his heart thumped against his ribs, threatening to give up if he carried on. Letting out a frustrated cry, he let go of the headrest and fell back, relieving his left arm by taking Stuart's weight on his right. He clearly wasn't strong enough to lift Stuart out of the helicopter, and frustration tore at him like a ravening beast.

STEVEN D. JACKSON

Lowering Stuart's body and grimacing at the grotesque angle the pilot made as he crumpled onto the wedged door, John resigned himself to the fact that the only way to help Stuart was to get out and get help. He turned and pulled himself out of the helicopter, trying hard not to breathe in the fumes which were becoming stronger. He desperately tried not to think how combustible those fumes might be. Jumping down to the helipad and ignoring the jarring of his legs as he landed, John reached up and gave a tug on the remains of the chopper's landing rail. One pull was enough to convince him that he would never be able to tip the wreck over himself. To rescue Stuart he would need help, and he had no idea how long he had until the fuel caught fire, engulfing them both in flames.

He turned and ran blindly toward the door to the building, catching his foot on a heavy piece of debris and crashing to the floor like a statue. The cold, unyielding concrete met his skull with a dull crack and his vision blurred. He tried to look up at the sky as darkness overtook him, wondering whether he was destined to die in a fire after all.

Through the darkness came the sound of a door opening, of footsteps, of indistinct voices calling to him.

Hands tugged at him, jerking him over the rough ground which scraped at the skin of his knees. He struggled weakly, trying to show them he was awake and could move, but they wouldn't let go. He could hear voices shouting at him to move, but somehow they didn't seem to make much sense. Why should he move when the ground was so cold, so soothingly cold, the smell reminding him of the lawn trimmer his Dad had used when he was younger, the smell of petrol and smoke.

The hands wouldn't let go and he angrily tried to raise his head to demand that they release him. A wave of nausea washed over him. Perhaps something was wrong after all. His vision began to return, the figures becoming sharper and the voices becoming distinct. The memory of what was happening and where he was came back to him and he desperately tried to get his feet under him, to pull free of the helping hands and get back to the helicopter. His mouth wouldn't work properly and he could barely mumble the name.

"St-Stuart …."

Reassuring voices told him not to worry, that they had already taken Stuart out of the wreck. John didn't know whether to believe them, but as his reason returned he knew he couldn't do anything for Stuart anyway. He didn't think anything was broken, he didn't even feel hurt, just slightly confused and dazed. He wondered if he was in shock. A metal door slammed shut behind him as he was half carried through the aperture, the strength in his legs gradually returning. He disengaged the helping arms as he started to walk for himself. Thoughts pounded through his mind as he walked. Stuart was the pilot, he did all the maintenance. How had the thing crashed if it wasn't a Shift? But if it had been a Shift, why hadn't John felt the same tingling he had felt in the experiments? Surely someone would have been able to stop it happening, like he had stopped Tom's Shift.

This place with its Gestapo tactics, its uncompromising attitude toward people who were potentially threats, its pre-emptive attacks on unknowing 'subjects'; none of that could save their own pilot from a helicopter crash. It was hypocrisy, all of it. They couldn't save anyone, they couldn't even help themselves. They were as blind and powerless as everyone else, and their 'organization' was built on a fallacy. The memory of the crash fueled his anger at the utter futility of it all. Maybe Macava was dead, maybe he wasn't, maybe Chris was dead, and perhaps he had never even existed. "That's it," he muttered to himself, earning a bemused glance from a girl to his right, "I'm done with all this."

Whether the chopper had exploded or not he couldn't tell. On reflection, John thought that perhaps things didn't just explode the way they did in films. He was fairly sure there had been fuel pumping out of the thing. He was amazed to find himself slightly disappointed. Now he knew that Stuart had been taken to the hospital and everyone seemed to think he would be okay, John couldn't help but feel that it was a shame he hadn't seen an explosion. He wondered what that said about him.

———————

While waiting for Kendra to return to her office, John idly flicked through some random papers which had been thrown on the desk. He tried to ignore the splitting pain in his head from when he had fallen. His breathing still hadn't returned to normal and memories of the crash kept creeping into his mind, but he was determined to speak to the TR Detective and let her know exactly how he was feeling.

A plastic pot of pens was standing amid the sea of papers. John didn't notice it until he dislodged a bit of paper which was far larger than he expected and tipped the pot's contents all over the table. He jumped, trying to catch them, but succeeded only in smashing his knees into the edge of the desk, sending a large pile of papers sliding onto the floor. An ominous crack sounded from the desk, and as John rubbed at his painful knees, which were already suffering from scrapes and bruises, he could see that a panel had snapped and come away.

Forgetting his pain, John dropped to the floor and looked up at the underside of the desk. There was definitely a separate compartment underneath the heavy wood of the topside. Glancing back at the front of the desk, he realized it was a drawer that had been cleverly concealed and made to look like solid wood. He swallowed down guilt as he prodded the splintered wood with his finger, wondering what it was hiding. Standing up, John retrieved the pens and the pot and busied himself with replacing all the things he had knocked over, desperately trying to ignore the temptation to look in the secret drawer. Maybe it was old and no one had used it for years. Maybe it had something weird or exciting in it.

"Maybe it's nothing," John muttered, tearing his gaze from

the cracked drawer and gazing at the other side of the room, hoping there might be a book lying around that he could pretend to be reading if someone came in. His eyes flitted over the uninteresting room, finally coming to rest once more on the drawer. It wouldn't matter if he looked inside. After all, it was probably an old, forgotten drawer that no one ever used.

His fingers brushed the drawer, still undecided. Finally he could resist it no more and pulled at the front panel. The damaged drawer slid open at an unusual angle, looking as though it might snap off altogether. Inside was the uninspiring sight of another file, quite old and apparently well used.

Looking hurriedly over his shoulder, John bent low over the papers the file contained and began to read. They seemed to be comprised of excerpts from other files. From what he had read of the other files on the desk, these appeared to be report sheets about completed missions, presumably compiled to be sent to the Supervisors. These all seemed to be draft versions from what had to be hundreds of different cases spanning nearly fifteen years. Each one was heavily annotated in pen and in the same handwriting as he had seen on other files. He assumed it was Kendra's.

'Subject apprehended and rated too low for containment.' This was crossed out and the note read 'see #204 - already done - say escaped'. Other such comments filled the remainder of the documents, obviously serving as an *aide memoir* for when she came to write up the final reports for submission. Why would they need to be kept hidden, though? Unless the final reports were heavily doctored and these notes contained the evidence.

John stared at the words written in almost illegible scrawl across the papers. In each case there appeared to be a draft of the reason given for the mission's failure. The failure rate must be extremely high in reality. Judging by the drafts, it seemed that as long as there was a plausible reason for the escape of a low level subject, the failure would probably be accepted and forgotten in time. Some of the reports had notes advising the reports be rewritten to show the subject as dead, as opposed to having escaped or being under supervision.

Dead? John's mind recoiled at the thought. Would the mysterious Supervisors be happier with a dead subject rather than an escaped live one? Were these people so cold as to want every remotely threatening subject dead? In spite of his misgivings, his own experiences rang true. This organization could be ruthless and unbelievably cruel. Why the hell had Kendra doctored these reports?

Frowning, he flipped to some of the more recent sheets. Each one followed a similar vein and either referred to former files as a warning not to re-use the same excuse or simply lessened the subject's potential threat to make it seem unimportant. Was this Kendra's way of upping her success rate? Falsifying the reports to make herself look good? He shook his head, marveling at the lengths people were willing to go to for the sake of appearances. Some of these people were dangerous subjects according to the reports, and she was lying for her own benefit? Either she was far less competent than her colleagues thought or she didn't believe in the principles of the organization, which didn't make sense considering her recent conduct. It was just another blow against John's image of the place as some vital, omnipotent body using questionable methods in line with tough regulation for the greater good. This organization was corrupt as any other, which stripped it of any legitimacy in John's eyes and shattered his few remaining illusions entirely.

He tossed the file back into the drawer and slammed it shut, leaning back in his seat and letting out a humorless laugh. The office door opened and Kendra hurried in, leaving it slightly ajar as she crossed to her seat and sank into it. She let out a sigh and placed her head in her hands, clearly not noticing John at all. The sight was slightly pathetic, but John was not in the least bit moved by the performance.

"Any news on Stuart?" he asked languidly, looking at her with pitiless eyes.

She raised her head and leaned back in the chair, her expression making it clear that she had detected his combative mood. She returned his gaze coolly. "He's badly hurt, but he should make a full recovery." She glanced out the window into the darkness beyond. "What happened?"

"I was hoping you could tell me," John snarled, his anger beginning to rise. "After all, you're supposed to know everything, aren't you? Be in control?"

She didn't look at him, her chin rising slightly as she inhaled. "Was it a Shift?" She used the same tone she had used before, still staring at the black window.

His frustration getting the better of him, John leaned forward sharply, knocking a stack of files over with a sweep of his arm as he shouted, "How am I supposed to know? I've been part of this for all of five minutes and you've been doing it for years! You have a building full of your precious Recallers, and you're telling me no one knows if it was a Shift?"

She turned her head toward him, her expression defiant. "What if Macava did it?" Her tone was only mildly aggressive as she began to lose her composure. "What if he knows you're here and wants to stop you? Maybe it's no coincidence that it happened after your tests."

Throwing his hands in the air, John stood and turned his back on her, surveying the rest of the cluttered room. More maybes, more what ifs. She could be lying, for all he knew, and there wasn't a damn thing he could do about it.

She rose and took a step toward him. "Maybe Macava—"

Whipping around, John snapped, "Stop talking about Nicholas!"

Without warning Brice burst into the office, stepping between John and Kendra and glaring at John with unnerving intensity. The fat man closed the distance between them, his face a mask of rage. Confronted by the one person he hated more than any other, John glared back and moved to push Brice roughly away as the shorter man came too close.

Brice's reaction was immediate and surprisingly powerful.

Shrugging off John's indignant shove he barreled into him, forcing John to stumble backward, surprise affecting him equally as much as the shock of the impact. He tripped over a pile of documents. He heard Kendra bark, "Brice, that's enough!" as he tipped back onto the floor and once again bashed his head.

As he lay rubbing his aching skull and trying to replay the bizarre events of the last few seconds, John caught only snatches of the flustered conversation. Still, it was enough.

"What the hell was he doing?"

"It doesn't matter, Brice, just get out of here and—"

"Was he blaming you for Ma—?"

"Brice, just—"

"—already dead and—"

There were a few more shouted commands until finally John heard the door slam shut. The silence was oppressive. He could feel it surrounding him as he pieced together what he had heard. Slowly he untangled himself and straightened up from the floor. He looked Kendra square in the face, feeling empty of emotion. Her expression was distraught. Adding that to the dialogue he had heard, John was convinced he knew why. "Nicholas is dead, isn't he?" It wasn't really a question. He stared at her, waiting. She turned her face from him silently, looking down at her desk. One hand idly fiddled with a file as she stared into the wood.

"You lied to me." He said it without inflection. It was a simple fact, a final betrayal to add to the list. "Where is he?"

"He was found dead at his home. He was asleep when it happened. Whatever you saw, that isn't how it happened."

He nodded wordlessly. Everything she had said at Brice's house was a lie. She had said it to make him come here. The silence stretched. "Then who's the real Shifter?" He asked it to fill the moment. He honestly didn't care.

She shook her head again. She didn't know. "There's still a chance it's Macava. I was hoping you'd help me—"

He laughed derisively, crossing to the office door and

pulling it open. "I'm finished with this. If someone's targeting me, then they'll get me with or without your help. If they don't want me, then the best place for me to be is as far away from you as possible. Frankly, there's nowhere I'd rather be."

He left her office, his last glimpse showing her standing among her papers, head down and shoulders slumped. Ignoring the pang of pity he felt, he marched through the larger office to the reception area. The man at the desk looked up at him, obviously tired, trying to summon a smile.

"I'm leaving. John Davis. I won't be back."

Without waiting for a response he turned on his heel and headed out the heavy front doors. Walking down the steps, he followed his feet, giving no thought to where he was going. He wondered how far he would be allowed to go.

CHAPTER TWENTY

The night air felt heavy, as though storm clouds were gathering. He crouched lower in the bushes as he watched the figure cross the graveyard to the heavy oak doors of the church. Why the man had come here was not his concern. All he knew was that he mustn't let this guy out of his sight. He would need to seek shelter in the church before long, but he couldn't get in through the front doors without being seen by his quarry. Still, the man didn't know him and wouldn't recognize him. On reflection, perhaps it would work to his advantage.

Feeling the first drops of rain on his head, he rose from his concealed position and crossed to the door of the church, intending to be as unobtrusive as a shadow. The man was already in the church, far up near the front by the altar, sitting alone and looking up at the life-size model of the crucified Christ. The nave was dimly lit by electric lights designed to look like flickering candles. He slipped silently inside, positioning himself at the far right, concealed in the deep gloom.

The church wasn't large, but the dim light and the fact that it was empty except for him and the man in the front row made it seem bigger. The pictures on the walls and the various artifacts were obscured by shadows, causing the deep recesses of the ancient building to seem vast, as though the church stretched into eternity on either side of this central point of light. The thick silence was compounded by this sense of enormity, laying heavily on the mind and forcing it to focus in on itself. He tried to concentrate on the man in the front row, reining in this sentimental urge to explore his spiritual side.

The door of the church opened and closed ponderously behind him, causing an echo to reverberate through the gloomy edifice. The man in the front row looked around as light footsteps made their way down the nave.

———————————

John tore his gaze from the disturbingly lifelike portrayal of the crucifixion as the heavy wooden door opened. Footsteps made their way toward him. Jenna had agreed to come as soon as he told her where he was. He hadn't chosen the church for any particular purpose. His feet had simply found their way here through the darkness outside. Somehow it felt apt, and he took a certain comfort in the quiet darkness of the church which he hoped would provide him with some perspective as well as sanctuary.

When Jenna reached him she threw her arms around his neck, her expression one of relief. She stood back, looking him up and down before apparently deciding he was alright. Then she sank down on the pew next to him. "My God, John, when you called I was so worried. I thought something terrible had happened. Why didn't you call me before?" Her words were a breathless torrent, spilling out as though she had so much to say she simply couldn't keep it in.

He wanted to tell her everything. He wanted to tell her the truth, but to do that he would need to start at the beginning. Marshaling his thoughts, he began the tale, trying to keep the guilty tone from his voice.

"Okay. Well, after I called you last," he said, and Jenna looked at the floor and nodded, clearly remembering the last call when he had told her about Nicholas, "that lunatic Brice

224

tried to kill me. He set fire to his own house while we were both still in it."

Jenna's eyes were wide and her gasp was audible in the deadly silence of the empty church.

"After that I headed to his house—you know, the one you found by doing the internet stuff—and I met the woman who had shot at me before." Jenna's eyes narrowed slightly but she made no attempt to interrupt him. "She told me that Nicholas might not be dead and that he might be the one behind it all. She was trying to use me and manipulate me, and I believed it, I suppose. What does that say about me?" He laughed weakly.

Jenna's expression was one of sympathy. She reached over and squeezed his arm. Rain pattered against the stained glass above them as the silence lengthened. "It means you wanted to believe Nicholas was alive," she said softly, "even if it also meant he had to be your enemy."

He shook his head, closing his eyes tightly. "No. It means I was willing to believe the worst about a man who trusted me. A good man. It means I'm an idiot and I never deserved his trust in the first place."

She stifled a sob, clutching at his arm and trying to look into his downcast face. Her voice was a whisper. "It doesn't mean that, John. You're a good person. No one could blame you for hoping Nicholas was alive."

He took a deep breath, mastering his emotions and glancing at her with what he hoped was a reassuring smile. The last thing he wanted was to come apart now. "Anyway, I ended up at their headquarters, where they organize their missions. It's just up the road there in a huge building like a police station. Apparently," he snorted, "I'm one of them. A Recaller, they call it. When these guys make their changes, or whatever they are, I can resist them. I'm pretty good at it too. She was really impressed, but then the helicopter crashed and I nearly got killed—again."

Jenna was silent, but John didn't really notice, too lost in his recollections. "So I decided there was no point being part of their organization if they couldn't even protect themselves. Besides, what they do is wrong, so wrong. They hunt people, Jen. They hunt them and shoot them, or lock them up. Greater good, they said. I knew I couldn't be a part of it. And then I found out that Nicholas really was dead and they'd lied to me, so I left. That's when I called you."

He forced a smile and looked over at her, his smile fading as he noticed her expression. She was staring off into the distance, a look of anger and disgust on her face. It was an expression he hadn't seen on her before, a defiant aggression that looked totally out of place. Yet, at that moment, it fitted her perfectly.

She became aware of his silence and smiled back at him, her expression returning to its former sympathy. "Sorry, John, I was miles away." She forced a laugh. "So they told you Nicholas was found in his bed, and then you left?"

John nodded and was about to recount some of the conversation he had overheard between Brice and Kendra when he froze. His heart skipped a beat. "I didn't ... I didn't mention they'd found him in bed. How did you ... how did ...?" He trailed off, a multitude of unanswered questions sliding into place, half remembered comments, logical deductions clicking together in his mind like a vicious revelation.

The first day it happened it was raining. He had spoken to her about it, and it had stopped. Seconds after speaking to her on the phone about his flat, the place had transformed. The guilty look on her face the day she came to the hospital. The car changing, the crash, his injury, all of it had happened after speaking to her. Her bitterness in the hospital when he had ignored her and talked about Chris. Chris had vanished hours later. His gunshot wound, healed just after Jenna had found out about it. Her comments in the pub about changing things. Healing old wounds. Removing scars. And Nicholas. She had even messed with his death once she found out about it.

He rose shakily to his feet, staring in horror at Jenna's

guilty expression. She looked desperate, as though she was wracking her brain for a rational explanation.

"John, listen, I never intended to hurt anyone. Please, you have to believe me."

He took a step backward, still staring at her and feeling a terrible emptiness clawing at him. "Chris ... Nicholas ... Stuart ...." The names burned in his throat as he said them. They had all died or been badly injured, and sitting in front of him was the one who had caused it all. His mind reeled at the implications. He stumbled blindly past her, and before he knew it he was running down the aisle toward the heavy wooden door, wanting to be as far away from her as possible.

"John, stop! Please!" Her pitiful cry followed him as he reached the door. He turned and looked back at her, his breathing heavy and his hands sweaty as they clutched at the door handle.

"Please listen to me. Please don't leave me." She said it quietly, but her voice carried. It cut deep into his heart with an intensity of fear and loneliness such as he had never heard before. The look on her face was so pathetic, so distraught, that he felt his resolve weakening. He let the handle slip from his fingers and slumped onto the pew to his left, burying his face in his hands as his emotions took hold of him. He barely noticed the stranger who left the church over the agony of his own wrenching sobs.

"It's been a long time since anyone made me feel like that. I've been in control for so long." Kendra spoke quietly to Brice, who was perched on the edge of her desk, looking down at her with pitying eyes. She could tell he was enraptured, delighted to be her confidante, and trying desperately to cover it with a serious countenance. She didn't care right now, she was indulging her misery. John had torn her life to pieces in a few words and she was bitter as hell about it. She continued in a monotone, letting the thoughts out as they came, giving no heed to the warning voice at the back of her mind.

"And then this guy comes along and throws it all up in the air." She laughed sardonically. "I wonder if he's right, Brice, I really do. What the hell is this place and why do we even bother?"

Brice was thrilled to be consulted, she could tell by the way he straightened, his chest puffing out self-importantly as he spoke. "We bother because someone has to stay in control. We bother because it's important to make sure these people can't just play with our lives. We—"

She cut him off with a wave of her hand. If he was about to start spouting nonsense from the handbook then she wasn't interested. "No, we bother because we're frightened," she corrected him bluntly. "We bother because in the face of something you can't fight, in the face of something you can't overcome, you invent a new set of rules for yourself. You build yourself a countermeasure and make yourself believe that you're doing something proactive, whereas all you're really doing is making yourself feel better about the fact that you are utterly powerless."

She shook her head and gazed at the black window. The weather beyond raged against the glass, the storm gathering momentum. She sighed deeply, feeling tired beyond measure. It was getting late but she didn't care. She was questioning her entire career and giving no thought to the hour.

"I've never liked this place, Brice, you know that? Never liked it. But I made sure I progressed, got to where I am, because it was important to make sure someone with a bit of perspective was in control." She paused, looking into the distance for a moment as though she was alone. "I thought I had perspective," she murmured, "thought I was doing the right thing, but I just—I don't know now. Maybe what I have managed to do is ... not good enough."

She thought back to her early days, when she had joined up almost immediately after being approached by a member of the organization. She had seen doctors about her nightmares, the strange experiences at school that had affected her mind, or so her parents thought. The Shifter in her class had ruined her education, had thrown her into a breakdown from which she emerged bitter and angry. She had found comfort in being part of a group that protected others from what she had experienced.

"But you've done amazing work since you've been here. You have the highest success rate of anyone. You caught so many ...."

Brice still wasn't seeing the big picture, but then, to be fair, she hadn't explained. She had sat on her secret for so long that she wondered if she could even recall it completely. After tonight's failure, however, she doubted if it even mattered. Everything would unravel and she would be exposed. She laughed suddenly, realizing that she honestly didn't care anymore.

"Ah, Brice. If only you knew that I didn't come here to catch them." She paused and glanced up at him, smiling sadly at the memories playing in her mind. "I put myself here so that those who didn't need to die didn't die. And to do that, I had to lie. I've lied and twisted and distorted the truth so much that I don't even look like me anymore. The only one who knows who I am is me. Even you don't know, Recaller Brice."

He had fallen silent listening to her quiet confession. She saw no reason not to continue. "Ever since my first assignment, I vowed never to let another innocent person die unless there was no other choice. I doctored reports, changed files, conducted missions alone, all with a plausible excuse for the subject escaping or even dying without trace. The country is full of them, people who've escaped from me."

She scoffed and shook her head. "Everyone thinks I have a great success rate, but look what I've done to get into this position. Look at the work I do now. I've become what I hate, what I set out to stop. I've been chasing after people, trying to kill those I saw as a threat so I'd have a chance to save

229

those who were not. I almost killed John Davis, a man who turned out to be innocent. How many lapses of judgment have I had? Who knows? And worst of all, in the end what have I achieved? Nothing. The organization carries on trying to hunt them, and they only have me to protect them."

She sighed bitterly. "It's only a matter of time before I get found out, and if I can't take this one down, I will be. This one is dangerous, so dangerous they're all watching me. I've spent so long trying to help them get away that I don't even know if I have the skill to catch this one." Her breath caught in her throat, the emotion getting to her. She sighed again, her voice barely above a whisper as she continued. "I've screwed this up so badly. If this one escapes, it could be a disaster for us all. John Davis was probably the most useful asset we had, and I ruined that too."

She glanced at Brice's horrified expression, touched, in a way, that he could have thought so much of her before she destroyed his illusions. She could see he was trying to reason it out, to come to terms with whatever feelings were warring inside him. Finally, he took a deep breath and focused on her, his serious manner almost comical in light of the disdain she felt for him personally, if not professionally.

"Don't worry, we'll get the subject. Davis will lead us to him. They'll make contact soon, I'm sure of it."

That made her laugh. She shifted her feet and crossed them on her working space. Shaking her head slightly, she stared at her boots. "Oh, you're sure of it, are you, Darren?" Her voice was low and quiet, the bitterness of her memories dictating her tone. "The only time I was ever sure of anything was during my first mission. I had tracked someone down, ruthlessly hunted them. I knew who they were. I was at school with them. I couldn't have been more certain I was on the right path, doing the right thing, about to catch the very one who had made me feel so outcast, made me fear for my own sanity."

She scowled at the memory, remembering the pain and

anger that had driven her in those early days. The bitterness faded fast as the memory progressed, to be replaced by the familiar guilt and sadness. Steeling herself against the rising tide of emotion, she forced herself to continue, feeling that she owed the memory her honesty.

"But when I got there," her voice fell again to a whisper, "she was dead. She killed herself. Because of me."

She drew in a shuddering breath, preventing her bottom lip from trembling by sheer force of will. "That's what being sure brought me."

Brice was silent for a moment, his expression uncomprehending. "But you would have killed her anyway ...." He trailed off as she nodded.

"That's the irony of it. Seeing her there, swinging before my eyes, just ... broke a part of me. I couldn't do it. I suddenly saw everything that was wrong with this place. There's no justification for what we do, Brice, no justification. I vowed I would try to help the lesser Shifters escape, concentrate on the ones who were a threat. And now I can't even do that. If those files get reopened, hundreds of them will be rounded up. Hunted, found, killed. All because I failed."

Brice was moved. She could tell by the way he fidgeted and shifted position, his face a mask of indignation as though what had befallen her was unjust and wrong as opposed to a total catastrophe of her own making. She was touched, despite herself.

"You haven't failed, not yet. I'll help you. I'll do what I can. I'll just—"

Whatever he was about to suggest was cut off by a young man bursting into the office, wearing a jubilant smile. He was soaking wet and plastered with wet leaves. He beamed at them from beneath the grime and Kendra felt her breath catch in her throat.

"Detective, John Davis has made contact with the Shifter! She's in a church about a mile away. She confessed it herself and they didn't even notice me watching."

That, Kendra thought, was extremely unlikely. Still, the news was excellent, and she suddenly felt renewed vigor course through her system. She could still pull this back. She could destroy the Shifter and preserve both her reputation and her career. She would not fail this time.

"Brice, get me a tactical layout of the church, including the grounds around it." It felt good to be in full swing again, her cold commands issuing as though on automatic as her mind raced to make the most of the advantage. "I want approaches from the north and west." She pointed at the younger Recaller, who was still grinning stupidly in his sodden clothes. Evidently it was raining something awful outside. "You get five teams armed and ready. Report to me in ten minutes. We're not waiting for morning, we're doing it now."

She swept from the room as the two Recallers scurried off to carry out her orders. For the first time in hours she allowed herself a genuine smile. Perhaps she could succeed after all.

CHAPTER

The rain hammered relentlessly on the church windows, sending echoes through the darkened building. John sat with his head resting on his arms which were crossed over the back of the pew in front. He gazed at the distant figure of the crucifix above the altar, watching as the lightning threw the body into sharp relief for split seconds at a time, the eyes in those instants appearing to bore into his own. The effect was quite humbling, especially when coupled with tremendous crashes of the thunder.

Jenna sat beside him. He only became aware of her voice when she shifted position in the pew beside him, causing the wood to creak and shaking him out of his reverie. "What would you do, John, if you could do anything you wanted? If you could rewrite reality as you saw fit? How could you possibly keep your soul?" She spoke quietly but accusingly, as though justifying herself to him.

He wasn't in the mood to make excuses for her. He was disgusted with her. He wanted so badly to be angry with her, to storm out of the church and leave her behind, but his anger had been extinguished by grief and he felt nothing but a vast conflict now. He knew they had to talk, but he had no inclination to be nice to her.

"What, are you asking me to feel sorry for you? After

everything you've done?" He didn't look at her but kept his eyes fixed on the darkness above the altar.

She was silent for a minute, perhaps gathering her thoughts. "I just want you to understand me, the choices I've had to make, and the things I've been put through because of this." She sounded like she was trying to be assertive while on the verge of crying. The combination just served to annoy him. If she saw herself as some kind of victim then he would make sure she knew how he felt about that.

"No," he said bluntly, leaning back and crossing his arms, "no choices you ever had to make could have forced you to do what you've done. What you've done is unconscionable, it's evil. You don't even—"

"How can you say that to me? You have no idea!" she shouted, her eyes a little wild and her lower lip beginning to tremble. "You with your perfect life and your perfect past, your perfect—"

"You have no idea what I've been through!" he roared, unleashing his frustration and anger. "Don't you dare try to tell me you're the only one who's suffered in the past, the only one who's had to make hard choices!"

He gripped the edge of the pew in front of him, allowing his anger to gush out. "If you actually spent some time looking at the world instead of rewriting it, changing people's lives just because you can't cope, you might actually start to see that dealing with your own issues is better than manipulating everyone else to suit you! You might learn to understand that it's not just you with problems!"

He stood up and walked to the aisle, leaning against the edge of the next pew. He wasn't sure where the outburst had come from, but he was glad he had said it.

Jenna hadn't moved. He could hear her breathing over the rain. It still sounded like she was holding back tears. "I know I'm not, and I'm really am sorry about your problems, but I didn't know. I'm ... I'm not psychic, okay?"

She sounded pathetic and meek. Knowing what she was

STEVEN D. JACKSON

and what she was capable of, he couldn't reconcile this quiet manner with the power she could unleash. The frustration of the thought threatened to overwhelm him. Turning to face her, he threw his hands up and smiled sardonically. "And how the hell am I supposed to know what you are?" He slammed his hand on the back of the pew and leaned against it, regarding her coldly. "Three days ago I would never have believed any of this. Now here I am sitting in a church with a murderer"— he gestured toward her as he looked around the church, wondering what the hell he was doing here—"who can twist and wreck other people's lives without a thought or care to the damage she might be causing."

"It's not like that!" she cried. She leaned forward, her eyes imploring. John turned away, trying to ignore her as she continued. "It just happens. Sometimes I can't control it and things happen that I don't mean—"

He whipped around to face her again, stepping in closer. "It just happens?" He paused a moment before continuing slowly and deliberately as though speaking to a child. "We're talking about people's lives. How can you sit there and tell me it just happens?"

She stared defiantly, a silent tear running down her right cheek. She didn't take her eyes from him as she deliberately wiped it away. "I'm sorry for everything you've been through," she said, her voice trembling. "I'm sorry for what I put you through, but I never intended to hurt anyone." She breathed deeply, and John felt his heart thawing at the sight of her in such pain, but he wouldn't allow himself to say anything.

"It's a curse," she continued, looking down at her feet and speaking almost too quietly for him to hear. "When I'm angry it can sometimes hurt the people I'm angry with. When I'm happy it's the same, but it helps who I'm ...," she seemed to grope for the word, "happy with. Like that day at work when you ... you talked to me, I was confused. Later on I realized you'd made me happy ... so happy, just by talking to me." She closed her eyes tight as she spoke, her face taking on a pained expression, as though reliving this was difficult for her. Quietly she added, "I didn't even mean for the rain to stop."

Her lips trembled and he could tell she was struggling to keep her composure. Her shoulders were shaking as she continued in a voice barely above a whisper. "And then that day in the café, when you asked me to come with you. I knew it was all going to go wrong, but I thought at least I'd be with you, and maybe ... maybe you'd get to like me, so I agreed. I was so scared when we were at your house, but I went along with it because ... because ... Then you left me behind. But I never meant to hurt anyone. I didn't mean to hurt your friend. You just made me so angry I couldn't—my emotions get out of control. That's why I stay away from people. Please, John, please believe me. If you ever believed I'm a good person, then please believe it now. Show me that you believe me ...."

He felt his resolve weakening and came slowly around the pew to sit beside her, looking off into the darkness beyond as he tried to think of a way to say what he needed to say.

"I'd like to," he almost whispered, feeling surprised that he actually meant it, "I want to, I just can't see how I can. After everything you've done ... I don't even know if this is real or if it'll change from one minute to the next. How can I possibly know whether anything you're saying to me will still be true in five minutes' time?"

He glanced at her. Her eyes were closed and she was nodding almost imperceptibly, as though she understood and expected no less. Raising her head she looked him square in the face. Tears were falling freely from the corners of her glistening eyes. "Then just believe me now," she pleaded in a voice on the verge of cracking, "believe me here, in this moment. Tell me now and I'll believe you. Please just ... tell me you believe I'm not a bad person."

In that moment he knew she was sincere. He knew she meant it, but for how long? How long until her emotions took over again and warped everything around her? He realized that it made no difference. In a world where neither the past

236

nor future was certain, they had to live in the moment, and in that moment he believed her.

"Okay," he said, exhaling deeply, "okay, I believe you. Maybe someday I'll be able to forgive you. For now, I'll help you if I can. Maybe … maybe this woman at the organization can help."

She scoffed and looked away, some of her defiant manner returning. "I don't think so. They want me dead, remember?"

"But that's because they don't understand." He was warming to his theme and suddenly thought that going to the organization was a great idea. They could genuinely help. At least that way it would stop them hunting her down. "They use Shifters sometimes, they don't ... they don't kill them all ... don't lock them all up. Maybe we can get them to let you go in, to help them even."

Horrified, she stared at him. "You think that's what I want? To be employed? To make a choice between being killed and working with the people who want me dead? To hunt down people like me? I'm an animal to them, John, hunted and hated." She shook her head and looked away. "I was hoping you might be able to help me, but everything's just gone so wrong. So terribly wrong. Now here I am, no one to help me, even you've turned against me. And it's all my fault."

John paid no attention to the self-indulgent misery she was wallowing in. He pressed ahead with what he thought was her best chance to stay alive. "No, no, they don't know it's you yet. We could both just disappear. I left them. I told them I didn't want to be part of them and they let me go. We can leave, go back to Gillworth, go back to work ...."

"If you honestly think so, then you really are an innocent, John. Maybe I overestimated your intellect." Her voice was suddenly like steel, that strange look coming over her face, the one he had seen before, the defiant, angry Jenna he had thought looked so out of place.

"What's that supposed to mean?"

"What, did you think we were alone in here? Or did you

237

just think it wasn't important that a man just slipped out of the church the moment we started talking about this?"

His blood ran cold. He remembered seeing a man leave just after he had learned the truth about Jenna, but surely that wasn't .... "Come on," he said in disbelief, "you don't think—"

She looked at him pityingly. "I'm in touch with reality, John. Perhaps more than you are. Think about it. Did you really believe they'd just let you leave? Just leave and run off back to where you came from? After they discovered that you're one of the most powerful Recallers they've found for years?" She shook her head sadly. "They had you followed. And you led them right to me."

She was right, he knew she was, and the realization was like a punch in the stomach. He felt sick. "My God ... I have to get back. I can stop them, I can explain."

"They won't be interested. They're going to come for me. I don't know if I can deal with them all."

"No!" he said, determined not to put either of them through any more pain. "No one dies! Don't you see this can't go on? Trust me, I can talk to them, please, they'll listen to me. Just give me the chance. Stay here, alright? They won't expect you to stay here, so I'll be back."

She didn't look convinced, but she nodded and gazed over at the distant altar just as a flash of lightning bathed it in electric blue for an instant. She looked back at him just as the thunder crashed overhead, her expression resigned. She nodded again. He turned and ran for the door, determined to get to the organization before they left to hunt Jenna down. He could talk to them, he could convince them.

He just hoped he could get there in time.

———————

Inside the organization's headquarters was utter and extreme chaos. As John edged closer to the door he could see that a room to the back of the reception area was unlocked, the door standing open. Inside were racks of assorted guns and boxes of what he assumed was ammunition. Two Recallers stood inside the small room, passing the weapons out to the others. The atmosphere of excitement was palpable within the entrance hall as younger Recallers ran backward and forward, shouting to one another and trying to organize themselves.

Perhaps it was already happening, thought John as he made his way closer to the open entrance. It had taken him longer than he thought it would to get here. Time was running out. He began to feel uneasy as he edged into the room, trying to be inconspicuous. Why were they in such chaos?

He slipped around the door and tried to understand the frenetic activity around him. There must be a mission starting, but was it coincidence that this was happening when he had only just discovered for himself who the Shifter was? Jenna had said someone had seen them and maybe heard them, but surely they needed more to go on than a report about John meeting someone in a church? He knew they were probably working on more than one case at the moment. It was likely they were constantly tracking people. After all, they were responsible for the whole of the South East, which comprised a fair few counties. He couldn't shake the feeling, though, that this was a mission to apprehend Jenna.

He looked around the room, trying to find a clear route through the crowd. He had to put a stop to this madness, but the place was a blur of motion and he was already on borrowed time.

A taller man carrying a pile of what looked like belts bumped into him. Stepping back, the man gabbled an insincere apology and scurried around John in the direction of the stairs. He hadn't even cast John a glance as he went by, and suddenly it dawned on John that he would look less out of place if he simply hurried into the office rather than trying to slip through. Assuming a haughty air, he pressed past the group of people bustling around the gun storage room and headed into the main office, keeping his gaze focused above the crowd as though looking for someone. No one paid him any attention as he crossed the room toward Kendra's office, and John was forcibly reminded why he had left the place in such a rage earlier.

So much for calling it an 'organization', he thought as he stepped nimbly into the office. Most of this lot clearly didn't have the skill to organize the capture of a fish in a bowl.

Kendra was standing with her back to the door, fiddling with one of the clips of her gun holster which didn't want to fasten. She had her head canted to one side and John could see the mobile phone jammed between her ear and shoulder as her hands fumbled with the clip. Her demeanor was one of frustration.

"No, sir," she said irritably, her tone jarring with the forced respect she was obviously required to accord the person she was speaking to, "this time there'll be no mistakes. We've eliminated all other possibilities and only this one remains. Yes, sir. That's right. No, no, we are going in now. Full force, there—no, sir, I am mobilizing all of them. We have at least three teams on standby and I am using them all. I know what time it is and I don't see that as a problem. Yes, they are up to standard ... I will ... Full report within the quarter. Yes, sir."

Dropping the clip, Kendra grabbed the phone and raised her head, muttering unsavory suggestions as to what 'sir' could do with his report. John reached behind him and shut the door, letting it close with a click which was almost lost over the sounds of the bustle in the outer office. Shoving her phone into her pocket, Kendra resumed her attack on the clip, turning in a half circle as she did so and coming face-to-face with John. Her face registered surprise, nothing more, and John assumed she was probably too preoccupied with the mission to care why he was there.

"So, you came back," she observed, concentrating on the recalcitrant clip.

"I came to explain a few things." He spoke firmly, determined to do this right. The last thing he wanted was to fall out with her again. He knew this was his one chance to

240

stop the mission and thereby save Jenna from being hunted down and brought in—or worse. His heart was pounding so hard that he could barely concentrate on what he was trying to say. His thoughts were a swirl of half-formed conversation, plans, and pure emotion. It was hard to straighten them out.

"I know you know where the Shifter is, and I've come to tell you that she's a good person. She explained it to me. She can't control it sometimes, and when she does mean to do it, it's for a good reason. She knows what she's done is wrong—" He stopped, his resolve faltering as he remembered his friends who had died because of Jenna's mistakes. The bitter anger began to swell just beneath his composed exterior, and he suddenly wondered if he wanted to stop Kendra after all. Might it be safer for Jenna to be taken somewhere she could be helped? Was he being manipulated again, as he had been all along?

Kendra's expression was stony. She was clearly unmoved but she made no effort to interrupt, looking on with unreadable eyes as he made his garbled plea; a plea in which he no longer fully believed. He knew she wouldn't listen to him. She had been on the hunt for this subject for so long that she would almost certainly shoot on sight. That was why he was here, that was why he had to try to convince her. He had to make Kendra see the hypocrisy of the entire organization for which she blindly worked. His thoughts turned suddenly to the reports he had read, her drafts explaining away her failures. His contempt for her and her pre-occupation with success rates rose, threatening to overwhelm him entirely. No one deserved to be summarily executed.

"She knows it was wrong and she wants help. You can't allow this mission to go ahead, you have to stop it. It isn't needed, she'll come in herself."

Kendra finally stirred. She crossed her arms and regarded him with what appeared to be pity. "Tell me, John, can you think of a single alternative option that could possibly make me reconsider this mission? Other than the one you have proposed, that she comes in herself?"

John looked at her, puzzled. Of all the possible responses she could have given, this wasn't one he had anticipated. "Well …," he thought for a moment, trying to think of another way it could be done, "er—"

She answered for him. "'No' is the answer, John. This was the one possible option that might work out of hundreds of potential options, and you came running here to deliver it like a good boy. She could have run, she could have tried to Shift herself away, she could have tried to change the fate of the messenger coming back to me, but in the end she knew that we would find her. She knew she didn't have much chance of doing anything with us all concentrating on her location, she knew she would be caught, and so she decided to try this. Who knows what she would do if we agreed? Would she, having discovered the organization headquarters, wait for the right moment to attack it when our guard was down? Make it so that the organization never existed? Perhaps you underestimate her, John. We are all Recallers, and with our combined ability we should be largely resistant to her powers. Yet she has proven herself remarkably strong. The devastation could be massive. And here you are trying to make me change my mind when I have her where I want her." She shook her head sadly and looked at the floor, letting a moment pass before adding quietly, "You've been played, John. I'm sorry, but you had better accept it."

John was confused. Jenna had been so convincing, so honest and sincere. There had to be another explanation. He couldn't accept that she had to die, and he wouldn't give up that easily.

"It doesn't matter how dangerous you think she is," he replied, "she didn't mean to do anything. Whatever her motivation for sending me here, the worst it could be was to save her life. I don't think I can blame her for trying to save herself from you and your trigger-happy sociopaths."

He had hoped to force a reaction. Kendra's half-raised eyebrow only served to increase his frustration. "You can't just kill her for being who she is!" he shouted, unable to keep his temper in check in the face of Kendra's cold, emotionless façade. "You can't just murder a human being because you're afraid of them!"

He was breathing heavily, his hands beginning to sweat as he clenched them by his sides. This was not going well, and he could see Jenna's face in his mind's eye, smiling sadly at him. Kendra's soulless attitude terrified him, and he was filled with a sense of futility.

"There is more to this, isn't there, John?" Kendra took a step toward him. "Who is the Shifter and how do you know her?"

"You don't know?" John was appalled that they could have come this far without Kendra actually knowing who the subject was.

"We know where, we have a description. We have someone near the location to advise us of any change. That's all we need, although a name would be nice."

"I'll tell you if you promise to give her the chance to surrender. Even if you have to keep her sedated with that tranquilizer, just promise me you won't shoot her."

Kendra looked at him carefully, moving her glance to the window as someone outside motioned to her. She nodded back to them and returned her piercing gaze to John's pleading eyes. "Tell me the name and I will consider it. That's all I can give you. As I said, we don't need a name for this mission."

The memory of the files he had read in the secret drawer leaped into his head. Perhaps she would find a way to let Jenna escape if she could. If he could just convince her that Jenna wasn't dangerous, maybe she would make up a report like she had for her failures. She might actually consider letting Jenna go. A surge of hope flowed up inside him and he quickly told Kendra the name, beginning in the next breath to explain exactly what Jenna had said in the church.

Kendra wasn't looking at him. She didn't seem to be listening. John trailed off, confused. A second passed and still Kendra did not react. Another passed. John stared at the silent TR Detective. The blood had drained from her face and she was as white as a sheet.

"No," she whispered. "Impossible!"

The smell of decay was overpowering. Dust drifted from the rafters overhead. She walked carefully over the wooden floor, eyes straining in the dark to see the missing boards. A creaking sound filled the stagnant air as she made her way across the room. Her eyes lingered for a moment on the rotting food in the corner, not wanting to look up, to see the rope. The corpse was hanging only a few meters ahead of her, the stench emanating from it was ghastly. She gagged as she moved closer.

Kendra paused at arm's length from the cadaver, finally looking into its face. Recognition of the decaying face was difficult; the body had obviously been here for some time. She had been tracking this one for months, full of zeal and commitment to the cause. She felt sick at the memory of her elation when the location had been narrowed to this place. Had this been the final shift that brought her here? She glanced about the floor. There was no chair, no obvious method of getting into the noose.

A final shift, a suicide transition powerful enough to reveal the Shifter's last hideout. Kendra tried to ignore the thought of it. The horror was almost too much. Or was it the guilt?

Here in this old attic, her old school friend had committed suicide because of her. Because she was angry and afraid and had allowed herself to believe the organization when it told her the subject had to be caught. Sarah's former friend knew they were coming. She knew they would find her. Most likely, she knew what they would do when they found her. Hunted and alone she had fled to this awful place. How long had she

SHIFTER

lived in this attic beneath the dusty wood, in the company of vermin? How many nights had she cried herself to sleep out of fear?

How long until she had made the decision to end it?

Memories of that day in school surfaced unbidden before Sarah's eyes, the smile on the girl's face as she threw the paper ball that resulted in her punishment; the punishment that led her to reveal her ability to any Recallers nearby. Little had she known that her best friend was one, little had she known how badly her best friend would react. She could never have known that her friend would join an organization that utilized their talents to catch and destroy those like her.

Guilt stabbed into Sarah's heart like a blade cast from ice, tears welling in her eyes as she finally reached the corpse of the young woman who had once been her closest friend. Allowing her emotions to take over, she collapsed to her knees, crying openly as she tried to shut out the horror of the image of the woman suspended above her. Covering her face with her hands she uttered the girl's name, a name forever associated with guilt and shame. A name she could never forget.

"Oh, Jenna ...."

CHAPTER

Kendra stumbled away from John, disbelief warring with utter certainty that the Shifter was indeed her childhood friend. Catching hold of the table for support, she clamped her eyes shut and tried to make sense of what John had told her. How could Jenna be alive? How and why had she orchestrated this entire saga? She ran through it logically, finally getting a grip on her erratic thoughts.

Jenna had demonstrated the ability to deceive and alter perception when Macava had been shot. Had she done the very same thing to Kendra on that first assignment? Perhaps she had found a hanging woman and changed Kendra's perception so she would see Jenna there instead. In truth, the features had been so badly decayed it had been impossible to tell for sure. All those years of guilt and atonement, all the deception and lies she had told, all her fears of being caught were the result of someone else's cruel joke. Jenna was alive. The quiet girl from the classroom, the one Kendra had hunted in her first assignment, was alive and well.

Either Jenna was tired of running, or she was out for revenge. Either way, John appeared to be no more than a puppet, used to lead Kendra into a confrontation on Jenna's terms. Her heart hardened. If that was what Jenna was planning, then Kendra wouldn't let her own need for forgiveness get in her way. Jenna was still a dangerous enemy. Perhaps there was some truth to what John said, maybe she did just want to come in and be safe. Well, Kendra would soon find out. Jenna had picked the time and place and had come fully prepared to confront Kendra. The Detective had to respect her erstwhile friend and enemy, especially now that she wanted so desperately to see her again, to relieve the guilt once and for all. Seeing Jenna alive would change everything, but it could also bring her world crashing down.

With an effort of will, she forced herself to remember that Jenna was a real threat, not only to her but to everyone, to everything. Uncontrolled, her abilities could have catastrophic consequences. Jenna had to be confronted and either controlled or destroyed. There was no longer any room for moral ambiguity. If Jenna wasn't stopped, then all Kendra's cases from her first assignment onward would be called into question. Her career would be over and her work undone.

Dimly, Kendra became aware of John standing by the door, watching her intently. Perhaps he thought she was changing her mind about the mission. She smiled inwardly. How little he actually knew of her or the organization to be so sadly misguided. She grabbed her gun from the table and shoved it into the holster which had caused her so much grief while on the phone to the Supervisors. As she passed John, he reached out and grabbed her arm, looking both confused and annoyed.

"Wait, what was all that about? Where are you going?"

His voice held an edge of panic. Reaching down, she removed his hand from her arm, gently but firmly. "This mission is important, John, however little you might like it. She has to be stopped, and I doubt very much she'll come in quietly. She is dangerous. You know what she can do, and no connection to either you or me should be allowed to cloud our judgment."

John jerked away from her, his eyes wild. He looked on the verge of a panic attack. "Connection? To you? What do you ...?" He groped for words, his mouth opening and closing as he struggled to catch the meaning behind her words. She waited for him, watching the emotions playing out. He shook his head violently and glared at her, regaining control of his voice.

"You can't do this. I know what'll happen and so do you, and it isn't right! You ... you have to help her. You've done it before, I saw the files. You have to let me go back to her. You have to let me bring her—"

Kendra felt a flash of fear. Which files did he mean? Surely not *those* files. How had he managed to get hold of those? Her eyes darted to the desk, saw the cracked panel. Panic rose within her. Her breath caught in her throat and a single thought flooded her mind. She needed to stop him. She needed to contain him. He was about to expose everything. John was still babbling at her, his voice desperate. Her fear subsided slightly. He was beyond rational thought and had no idea of the effect his words were having. She suddenly realized that the office door had been open all this time and that their exchange had been seen by a number of the other Recallers. They were standing around, casting concerned glances at them. This was her chance.

Catching the eye of a group standing not far away, she motioned with her hand, a quick and effective communication which they were trained to understand. They reacted in seconds. Three of them took hold of a shocked John, two grasping his arms and one getting a practiced lock around his neck. John struggled violently like a fish on a hook, finally giving in to the panic he had been holding back. Kendra felt a surge of pity for him as they dragged him away. She would apologize to him later, but for now she had a mission to wrap up.

"No!" John's shrieks echoed back to her as he was taken to the holding cells. She tried to ignore him, the accusations he flung at her burning into her soul as she marched to the reception area to rendezvous with the teams. "You can't do this! Let me go!" The rest faded into incomprehensible screams as he was dragged down the stairs. Glancing about she saw that the teams were looking at one another uncertainly. Evidently John's performance had unnerved them. She tried to shut out the accusations she could still hear ringing in her ears, but the force of them had hit her hard.

She swallowed and looked around at the Recallers, some nowhere near ready yet, who were watching her curiously. Trying to appear less defensive than she felt, she launched into her speech, covering her unease with a cool, professional appraisal of the situation. She hoped it sounded more confident than she felt, and that it would go some way toward dispelling the sense of unease that had swept through them all.

Brice pelted down to the cells as fast as his legs would carry him, which he had to admit was not especially fast. Cursing his lack of fitness and Kendra's attitude, he forced himself to redouble his efforts. The mission would soon be starting and he couldn't afford to be late.

Kendra had already shown that she was willing to do anything to get the job done, and this time the stakes were even higher. Failure this time would mean disaster for her and for the organization. He was convinced he was doing the right thing, but in his heart he simply wanted John Davis dead. The helicopter had malfunctioned right on cue—he wasn't the technical guy for nothing—but the cocky little cretin had survived it with barely a scratch. No one had felt a Shift, certainly not Brice, and in any case if Davis was so powerful he would have been able to stop the crash from happening in the first place. Pure blind luck had kept Davis alive, and it galled Brice to his very core. Why should fate conspire in favor of this arrogant man when people like Brice were overlooked? Fate could be cruel, but Brice could play that game too.

Kendra had told him that she was afraid she would fail to kill this Shifter, but now she had the perfect opportunity to succeed. She could save her career, she could save all the other scumbags she had allowed to escape over the years, and all she had to do was throw enough firepower at the subject as soon as she so much as blinked. Brice did not approve of Kendra's long-term plan to play judge over the guilty and innocent, to decide who deserved to die and who didn't. That decision had already been made by her superiors. He didn't understand why she was so worried about it. As far as he was concerned, he had it on good authority—his own—that the people they tracked and destroyed were abominations. Dangerous and uncontrollable. Yes there were drugs, yes there were surveillance options, but in the end the best thing to do was to eliminate them completely. One did not contain a plague, one eradicated it.

Brice put Kendra's sentimentality down to her gender. She didn't approve of killing, even when it was the correct and only option, and that was because she was a woman. Brice could understand that. Women felt compassion where men saw reason. He couldn't hold that against her, especially since she had made the right decision about the more dangerous subjects. Her heart was weak, but her head, thankfully, was strong. She wouldn't let anything get in the way of this kill, even her precious new recruit.

Brice had heard Davis screaming as Kendra ordered him removed and the man had sounded crazy. He obviously had some kind of connection to this Shifter and didn't want any harm to come to her. He saw the organization as his enemy now and his rationality was shot to pieces. This meant he would leap at the chance to defend the Shifter from them, which could end in only one fate for him.

As he neared the bottom of the steps Brice could hear the repeated clang of metal on metal, accompanied by grunts of desperation. The sounds were explained when Brice rounded the corner. Davis stood in the center of his cell, sweat coating his face and causing his brown hair to appear far darker as it clung to his forehead. His chest rose and fell rapidly as he stood bent at the waist with his hands on his knees. He hadn't noticed Brice.

As Brice watched, Davis rallied with a strangled cry and snatched up what appeared to be the lid from the cell's toilet. Holding it in both hands, he launched himself at the bars, smashing the lid against them with his full weight. His onslaught had no effect on the solid metal. As the reverberation died away Davis collapsed to the floor, his energy spent. He put his head in his hands and slumped against the bars.

Brice would have laughed if he had been in a laughing mood. The sight was truly pathetic. Didn't Davis know that the person he thought he was trying to help was the complete antithesis of himself? He was caught in this Shifter's web and was just too stupid to realize it. *Well*, thought Brice maliciously, *now he can be caught in* my *web if he likes being a puppet so much.*

Trying to keep the contemptuous sneer from his face, Brice stepped forward and reached through the bars to tap Davis on the shoulder. Startled, the younger man leaped to his feet and stumbled away from the bars. He stood eyeing Brice suspiciously while his composure returned. His arrogant expression returned as he took in Brice's appearance.

"John," said Brice, letting an edge of desperation creep into his voice, "I know you don't trust me, but I need you to tell me where the Shifter is."

Davis was clearly surprised. He wasn't so good at masking his emotions. "You expect me to tell you where she is? If you don't know, I'm not going to help you."

Davis looked as though he was about to speak again. Brice cut him off with a violent shake of his head and allowed his eyes to widen. "You don't understand. They're going to kill her. I can't let them do it! I read the file, John, I know she didn't mean any harm, but Kendra, she ...." He trailed off and shook his head again, looking intently at the floor to suppress the smile that was itching to slide onto his face.

"What? She … what?" Davis clearly wanted to believe him, although he must have been suspicious.

Brice raised his head with a resigned sigh. "She's authorized full force. She's going to kill her on sight. The whole team's mobilizing and they'll be leaving in a few minutes. When I confronted Kendra she told me I was off the team because I wasn't reliable. I thought if I could get there first then maybe I could stop them, or help the girl."

The younger man was staring at him with a look of hope so desperate, so pitiful, that Brice could barely hold back a snarl. Luckily Davis appeared to be looking through him rather than at him. Brice saw his expression cloud. "She told me she would consider trying to help her. She lied to me, *again*."

Brice nodded sympathetically. "She uses everyone, John. No one has any value to her. That's why if you want to help the girl you have to tell me where they're going. We don't have long."

Davis's gaze refocused on Brice. "You'll never get there in time. Let me out and I'll go. I can help her. Please, Brice, let me out." His voice sounded calm again, rational, which would have been a problem if he was using his brain to think through the unlikely scenario of Brice actually coming to help him. As things stood, however, he was intent on getting to the church and would probably arrive at just about the right time.

Brice nodded vigorously, a genuine delighted smile forming on his face. "Okay, I'll just grab the keys." He hurried over to the cupboard at the far end of the corridor, almost giggling to himself over his masterful manipulation of the hapless young man in the cell. Collecting the keys, he first attended to the back door of the cell corridor, which led directly outside to the back of the building. Davis should easily have enough time to make it to the church before the mission began. Kendra was probably only just finishing the briefing. It would take time to get everyone in place, and they were trying to keep it quiet, so they wouldn't be moving too fast.

The bolt-hole was ready. Brice ambled back to the cell and

inserted the key in the lock. Davis feverishly watched his hands fiddling with the lock, his frustration visible. Feeling as though he was winding up a clockwork toy, Brice smiled to himself. This was all far too easy.

The door slid back and Davis jumped through, casting a querying look at Brice as he did so. Brice motioned in the direction of the door he had unlocked and stood back to let him pass. Davis ran off down the corridor and into the night without a word, leaving Brice to marvel at his success. Heading back to the door, he locked it again and hung the keys up on the wall. He thought if worse came to worst he could pretend he had released Davis out of pity. No one would suspect him of any other motivation. By that time it wouldn't matter. Kendra would be relieved that the Shifter was dead and Davis's fate would be of little concern to anyone.

———————

The briefing was complete, the plan set. They would approach the church from all sides, offering the subject no escape route. Kendra could barely remember the last time she had come up with a plan so deadly, so airtight. There was no chance that Jenna would escape.

Her heart ached at the thought. With gritted teeth she closed her mind to her emotions, steeling her resolve for what she knew had to be done. Nothing else mattered. Kendra marched out at the head of her Recaller team, the most heavily armed team of her closest and most trustworthy Recallers. She had to ensure that no one would fire before her and she had given explicit orders to that effect. She was sure her team would obey. She glanced at her watch to check that she would arrive exactly on time and not before the failsafe teams were in place.

She saw the glance Brice gave her and the reassuring nod as he hefted his semi-automatic rifle. He looked so trusting, so eager to please her on this most vital of missions. Brice wouldn't let her down. Everything was set, the plan was flawless. She nodded back at Brice, setting her face in a cold and professional expression, hoping against hope that the sentiment would find its way into her heart.

John ran blindly through the driving rain, ignoring the slap of sodden clothes against his chilled skin. He could barely see the ground in front of him and hoped to God that he was running in the right direction. By his estimation cutting through the fields should be shorter, but so far he seemed to be heading into nowhere. The grass he ran on was rough, as if rarely walked on, and in the darkness he could hardly see where it led. The church should be just on the other side of the field. He didn't have far to go.

His pulse was pounding wildly in his ears. He was deaf to it, though, just as he ignored the fiery pain stabbing his side, as he concentrated on placing one foot in front of the other, forcing his aching limbs forward across the unknown terrain. He had no idea how long he had been running, but was dimly aware that what had started out as an adrenaline-fueled sprint had quickly waned to a pathetic jog. Now it was no more than an ineffective lope. Panic welled up inside him as he pushed on, his desperate body telling him he couldn't possibly get there in time. He would be no use if he arrived in this condition.

Blinking and shaking his head, he glared at the dim countryside around him, determinedly ignoring the voices in his head. One was harder to resist than the rest. It was a soft, quiet, insidious intonation that wouldn't be ignored. It sounded disturbingly truthful.

You've been lied to, it hissed. *You've been manipulated throughout this entire affair by those you trusted the most. Nicholas lied to you. Kendra wanted to use you. Brice tricked you, and now Jenna is manipulating you. You know this. You know the only one you can trust is yourself. Why are you running to her side when you know she lied to you, when she killed your friends? Why do you willingly believe her when you know she's a murderer and a betrayer?*

His resolve faltered as the voice repeated his fears over and over, pounding in time with his tortured heart, and he knew it was right, at least at some level. He tried to focus, but he couldn't stop the feeling of uncertainty building like a chill in the pit of his stomach. What was he running to?

None of them deserve your help. None of them deserve your loyalty. Whatever happens, they brought it on themselves.

The voice fell silent. John's focus and resolve snapped back into place and he felt his veins flood with new energy. He forced his unwilling body across the last hundred yards of the rain-swept field. It didn't matter who was manipulating who. It was irrelevant if he was playing someone else's game or by someone else's rules. Some rules were fundamental. Some rules formed a personality's bedrock, and the rule he was obeying now was his own.

They were going to attack Jenna and she would probably be killed. He couldn't let that happen. No matter what she might have done, no matter what evil she might have caused, no matter how many people might be saved, and no matter what good might come of it, he could not and would not stand by and let her die. If it was someone else's plan to lure him to her side, then so be it. He would be betraying himself and his own principles if he allowed an innocent life to be endangered for any reason. He could take no comfort from avoiding a trap at the expense of a life.

John gritted his teeth and ran on, desperate to reach the church before Kendra. He could see lights up ahead, but they seemed so far off. He steeled his resolve and pushed on.

TWENTY-THREE

CHAPTER

Kendra marched at a steady pace, refusing to allow her nerves to overcome her professionalism. She had chosen the straightforward frontal approach. The other teams would be closing in from the sides and back. It was an awkward operation as she had refused to authorize vehicles and especially helicopters. If this was indeed the same Jenna she had known at school, then she had been able to convince Kendra she was dead, convince John she was his age, and even convince an elderly doctor to sacrifice himself for her. She was easily powerful enough to use deception, illusion, and brute force against them. Kendra herself had been the victim of those powers when Reynolds was killed.

Kendra's mind was as clear as she could make it, her resolve as strong as she could manage. Her entire being screamed that this was the very person who had inspired Kendra's mission to save those who could be saved, and that to hunt and kill her now would undermine all the good she had ever done. Following that logic to its conclusion was a disturbing exercise. If Kendra had decided to save the innocent by destroying the threats, then her decision had to be based on the assumption that she knew the difference between the two. Jenna had been classed as an innocent, a minor threat, not worthy of the pain Kendra had put her through in her relentless mission to catch her. This time, however, she had classed Jenna as the most dangerous foe she had ever encountered.

Had all those she had let escape become deadly? Had some she had destroyed been innocent after all?

She wrenched her thoughts back to the present, reaching up to wipe the stray hairs from her soaked forehead. She had done what she thought was right. She had placed herself in a position to help those who could be helped, and now she must kill one to keep those others safe. It was a harsh and vicious decision, yet no different to the others she had made throughout her entire career. Kendra did not have the luxury of feeling sentimental about the sanctity of life. John Davis had screamed that she had no soul. He had accused her of being cold and heartless. John was free to think that way, but he did not understand her dilemma. He had seen her files, but he had not understood them.

She would have to explain to John when she got back that she hadn't *wanted* to do this. Perhaps that might salve her lacerated soul. Perhaps in time he would understand her, maybe forgive her. Perhaps in time she could forgive herself.

Brice glanced at Kendra as they marched calmly down the long road to the church. His mood was light, almost excited. Soon the Shifter would be dead and Davis would be caught in the crossfire. He would make sure of that. Things would be back to how they should be. His failures with the house and the helicopter had already been forgotten.

Kendra looked incredible in the rain, he thought. Her clothes were plastered to her skin because she had eschewed a coat in favor of easy access to her weapon. The effect was quite a sight and Brice had trouble keeping his eyes off her. The weapon in his hand was cumbersome, slick with water to the point that he thought it might not work properly when fired. One of the condescending young upstarts he was marching with had assured him that the rain wouldn't be a problem. Brice sneered at the memory of the smiling young man turning back to his colleagues, making some kind of comment which had them all laughing. Perhaps an accident might happen tonight, Brice thought, especially since it was so dark and wet. Mistakes might easily occur.

He chuckled lightly as he walked along. It wouldn't do to attract attention to himself by doing something stupid in full view of the others. He would have to trust fate to deal with that particularly unpleasant individual, as it often did. No, tonight was about Davis and the Shifter. Davis was a nasty, arrogant thorn in Brice's side, just like so many others he could think of. People like that were a cancer on the world and a plague infecting society. There seemed to be more of them than decent people who just wanted to get on with their lives without having to share their world with these cankers.

Brice considered it lucky that he was intelligent enough to outsmart all the arrogant scum walking the streets, pretending the world was built in their image and for them alone. He could see them coming, he knew what they were like, and he would eventually be the last one laughing because he saw the truth of the world.

He smiled happily as he hefted his gun, seeing the church coming into view. Soon it would be over, and soon he would once again be Kendra's favorite.

The church was just ahead and John almost sobbed with relief when he saw he was alone in the graveyard. He staggered the last steps to the building. He had to reach Jenna and help her escape.

He rounded the building and glanced to his left, toward the front part of the graveyard where it joined the winding road down which he had wandered earlier. He could see shapes in the darkness, moving silently, the lightning glancing off metallic objects in the shadows.

They're here!

STEVEN D. JACKSON

John stumbled toward the church door, his limbs and mind exhausted from the lateness of the hour as much as the grueling journey. As he neared it the door creaked open and Jenna slipped out, running over to him as he gave up and fell to his knees on the steps of the old building.

"John! My God, what happened? I saw you from the window. Are you alright?"

As she helped him up, he shook his head and grinned stupidly at her, absurdly pleased to have arrived in time. His breathing was so heavy he could barely speak. He gulped in great breaths of air as he pointed in the direction of the approaching Recallers.

"They ... they're coming ... Jen, you ... gotta run."

She let go of him and took a few paces to his left, staring at the approaching lights. He stayed where he was, completely spent, hoping she would do something like Shift them out of harm's way. His breath began to slow and he glanced at her, suddenly fearful. She had her back to him, calmly facing the Recallers.

Suddenly he felt the tingle of pressure in his head, softly, very softly. He knew she was about to make a Shift. He smiled, knowing that he had reached her in time and that it would be a matter of moments before the Shift happened. The tingle increased slightly, and then faded. He tried to relax, opening his mind to the possibility that something was about to change, allowing her to do whatever she had to.

The tingle vanished. Jenna let out a soft cry and doubled over, hands to her face. She stumbled backward into John as he reached for her. His eyes widened. She had failed. Kendra's words came back to him.

"... *combined ability ... resistant to her powers* ...."

Horrified, he stared at Jenna's ashen face. She couldn't save them, she couldn't save herself. She held onto him, breathing deeply as he cradled her in his arms and watched, as if in slow motion, Kendra's death squad approach. In an instant, he made up his mind. Pushing Jenna behind him, he stepped forward defiantly, shouting at the approaching TRD and her henchmen.

"Kendra! I won't let you do this! I swear I won't let you get away with it!"

His voice sounded choked and unconvincing even to him. He felt Jenna stiffen as he called Kendra's name. The figures came inexorably closer. Jenna slowly extricated herself and smiled sadly up at him. Then she put a finger to his lips and gestured for him to step back. Without a word she turned to face the Recallers.

Kendra, now clearly visible in the light from the church, held up a hand to halt the procession. Her face betrayed nothing as she faced Jenna across the graveyard, slowly drawing her gun from its holster. Jenna raised her chin, staring defiantly at the Detective from atop the church steps. Her hair blew in the wind, whipping around her and lending her an ethereal quality as she stood before the church.

"I didn't think you would come in person," Jenna said, her tone, cold and harsh, carrying easily over the sound of the rain. "I thought you'd had enough of chasing me."

"You let me believe you were dead." Kendra's shouted voice was accusing. "You let me blame myself for years for a death which never happened."

Jenna laughed, a short bark with no mirth behind it. "Why would you worry about one when you've been responsible for hundreds? Or was it because you didn't get to pull the trigger on me yourself? Perhaps you thought I cheated you out of your prize for a hunt so well executed."

John was shocked. Where was this vicious tirade coming from? The bitterness and anguish he could hear in Jenna's voice was deeper than he would have believed she could produce. Why was she goading Kendra?

The Detective let out a brief yell of anger and raised the gun to aim at Jenna, her face contorting with a strange expression which could have been anger or anguish. "I devoted my life to helping people like you!" she shrieked over the pounding

STEVEN D. JACKSON

rain, her voice losing all trace of calm professionalism as she gave in to her emotions. "How dare you stand there and accuse me of that?"

Jenna regarded her coldly, raising her arms out to her sides. "Then what are you doing here, Sarah?"

"You know what I'm doing here. You brought me here! This has all been your plan." The Detective paused, looking down and shaking her head slightly. When she spoke again, her tone was more controlled "But you know how this ends. I have to take you down. I can't let you go."

Jenna nodded, keeping her arms raised. The rain pounded the graves mercilessly as the moment lengthened.

"No!" John shouted, pushing past Jenna to stand in front of her. She scrambled out from behind him and tried to push him back as he struggled, confused. "You don't have to do this, you can just—"

An ear-splitting crack ripped the night air, thundering over the sound of the rain as it hammered earth and stone. Jenna fell back, a gasping cry of agony escaping her as she collapsed to the ground, clutching her stomach. John whipped around just in time to see Kendra, with a primal scream of anger, deliver a powerful backhanded blow to the short, fat man standing beside her who had fired the shot. The man fell back, apparently unconscious, his weapon flying out of his hands to land behind him just in front of the ranks of armed Recallers. With a surge of loathing, John recognized Brice.

The other Recallers leaped into action as John turned to lift Jenna and carry her into the church. Laying her on the cold stone floor of the old building, he jumped back to the door and bolted it shut before any of the others could reach it. The silence in the church grew weighty as the echoes of the slamming door faded. The thick stone walls muffled all but the softest hint of the driving rain and the shouts of the Recallers.

Turning back to Jenna, he carefully lifted her and carried her to the front of the church. He could see that she was bleeding profusely as he laid her on the cushioned pew in the front row. He had never seen so much blood coming from a living person's body. Cursing himself for not doing it before, he ripped off his jacket and pressed it to her stomach, feeling a dread certainty that she was going to die. There was simply too much blood. Already it surrounded them, the cushions upon which she lay now sodden and red, a puddle beginning to form on the floor beneath her.

Weakly, Jenna pressed her hand to the jacket and looked up at him. He could barely see her through a blur of tears, and he only slowly became aware of the desperate sobbing sounds he was making as he tried to staunch her bleeding. Her hand closed on his and pushed it weakly away. Looking down into her eyes he saw no hope in them, and the sight tore him apart. Her clammy skin terrified him, her pallor a deathly grey which caused her eyes to seem vividly green. He felt a horrific guilt that he had done this, he had failed her. He had told her to wait in the church, he had brought her to this place, and he was the one and only reason why she now lay dying in a church far from home. She looked so terrifyingly alone, her breath coming in short gasps as she finally found his gaze and held it.

His sobs gave way to outright tears as he looked into her beseeching eyes. She reached up a trembling hand to the side of his face, smiling feebly at him and trying to form words. John clasped her hand and leaned toward her, trying to hush her and to stop her doing anything that might hasten what he felt so powerless to prevent. She would not be dissuaded and closed her eyes as she began to whisper, her hand still loosely clasping his.

"I don't even ...." Her voice was so faint it was almost lost in the crashing sounds from the door. The Recallers were trying to get in. It wouldn't take them long to find the back entrance, but John didn't care. Nothing mattered now. "I don't even ... know what's mine ... what's real ... anymore." Her breathing became shallower and she struggled to pull in air. "This ... this is ... real. This ... matters ...."

She smiled suddenly, a surge of strength coming from somewhere as she opened her eyes. "I couldn't control it, John," she whispered, a desperate look on her face. "I couldn't stop it. It hurt people—" A flash of agony twisted her mouth and she cried out. John tried to speak, but the words wouldn't come. Her eyes closed again as she murmured, "I wanted to help you. I ... I'm sorry I ... I'm sorry I hurt you."

Her eyes remained closed as she stopped talking, her breath returning to shallow, rapid gasps. Her face was so clammy and grey it scared John even to look at it. "Forgive me ... John."

John bent over her. His lips brushed hers in a delicate but heartfelt kiss as he knelt at her side and cradled her head in his arms. He could feel her breathing light against his face. "There's nothing to forgive, Jenna," he whispered, his voice almost too choked for speech. "I'm so sorry I did this to you ... so sorry ...." He tried to say more, but his throat constricted. Suddenly a terrible pain sliced through his head and he fell back with the force of it. He tried to cry out, but the agony in his head and the pounding of the Recallers at the door swamped his senses. He couldn't even tell if he was screaming or not.

His vision swam, the church sliding out of focus, being replaced with an indistinct greyness. The pain in his head increased, pulling him down into darkness.

TWENTY-FOUR

CHAPTER

The sound of a heavy wooden door slamming open brought him back to reality. He was cold, lying on a hard stone floor as the sound of approaching footsteps filled his ears, pounding through his head. Hands grasped at him, pulling him roughly upright as a woman spoke in a low and strangely detached voice. "You do not have to say anything, but it may harm your defense if you fail to mention when questioned something which you later say in court."

The situation made no sense, and something else was wrong. He grinned suddenly, summoning the strength to speak. "It's something which you later rely on in court, idiot." His voice came out sounding slurred and he had no time to reflect on why he was being arrested—if indeed he was being arrested—because a fist suddenly slammed into his stomach, driving the wind from his lungs. The pain was incredible, but he was prevented from falling by the hands which gripped him under the arms.

"Keep it up, smartarse. Give me another reason." The voice was cold, and strangely familiar.

John jerked his head up in shock, staring at Kendra, who stared back without a hint of recognition. She regarded him coldly, as one might an insect, before turning and heading out of the church, indicating to the others that they should follow. She was in police uniform, as were all the others. John recognized their faces from the organization, but none of them were armed and no one was dressed for rain.

Feebly he struggled against the arms half-dragging him toward the open door, and then stared in utter bewilderment at the glorious sunlight pouring through. "What the hell is going on?" he said, not caring what any of his captors thought. He twisted his head back to look at the front row pew and was unsurprised to see that Jenna's body had vanished. The cushions were clean and dry. What was happening here? He had thought that Shifters couldn't Shift when injured, let alone dying. Perhaps she wasn't dead. Perhaps she had managed to save herself. He clung desperately to that thought as he was bundled into the police car. Whatever else was happening, perhaps Jenna was safe.

Or perhaps, the insidious voice in his head whispered, perhaps the Shifts are undone when the Shifter dies. Maybe it was all her creation. The organization, Kendra, Shifters, everything. Or maybe it was her last act to move her body and undo the organization?

He had to accept that the chances of Jenna being alive were low. Something inside told him that she had made a monumental Shift with every fiber of her being, pushing past the Recallers' barriers and changing everything but him. He knew that he was unaffected, as had happened with Tom, but now Kendra was a policewoman and not a Transition Recall Detective. The organization didn't exist. Was that Jenna's final gift to him, or to Kendra?

John sat on the small metal chair, his hands cuffed behind his back. He gazed at his own reflection across the brightly lit, unadorned interrogation room. The two-way mirror was obviously a little bent. His face was slightly too wide. He wondered why they had cuffed him so he couldn't put his arms on the table in front of him, especially as he had yet to be charged with anything. He wracked his brain, trying to remember whether the police had to charge him before they cautioned him or if they could charge him afterwards, and whether he had the right to speak to a lawyer before the first interview. It was so long since he had done criminal law that he couldn't recall. He only had the vague belief that someone somewhere hadn't followed the right procedures, and that it probably made absolutely no difference.

The door opened and Brice stepped into the room. He too was wearing police uniform and looked extremely agitated. He locked the door behind him and sat down on the chair across from John. He stared at John warily for a few moments before asking in a timid voice, "Do you recognize me?"

John nodded, silently regarding the man he hated more than any other. Apparently Brice had been spared the Shift too. Of all the disgusting people John could have something in common with.

"There was a Shift," Brice said hurriedly, obviously relieved to find someone else who remembered. "I Recalled it, but no one else did. I couldn't stop it, though, I just remember ...." He trailed off, looking distressed. "Now I'm a police officer. I don't even know where we are or what I'm supposed to do! They told me to talk to you about a girl's death. They said you shot her." He looked nervously at the door and leaned forward, his desperation clear. "But I know it was me! I shot her and you know I did, but you are the prime suspect! They were talking about where you might have gone and I told them to check the church. I made up a story about seeing you go in there. I don't even know why they are after you or where she was supposed to have been shot! I'm just so, so confused ...."

John sneered, loathing the man more as he spoke. "And you, of course, have the gun, don't you?"

Brice went white. He stood up, shaking, running his hands around his body in a faintly grotesque manner. Finding a gun in the holster at his back, he pulled it out and stared at it. "But this isn't the one I used." His voice was soft, his expression disbelieving.

"Well, of course," John said casually, "I didn't see what kind of gun you used."

Brice dropped the gun and stared at him in horror, backing away while his mouth opened and closed in an almost comic manner. "You ...? You ...?"

"Apparently," said John. He smiled at the fat man. "When you came in you didn't have a gun, and it just struck me that you would be the last person I'd want to speak to. Unless of course this was all being done for my benefit, because that would mean I was the one in control."

Brice stared at him.

"Oh, don't worry," John said, taking malicious satisfaction from the abject terror on Brice's face, "I wasn't always in control. Call it a parting gift from a dear friend of mine."

John reached forward, placing the evidence bag containing the gun on the table. He straightened, adjusting his cumbersome police uniform. Removing his gloves, he placed them on the chair behind him and walked toward the door. He paused as he inserted the key in the heavy lock, looking back at the fat, sweaty abomination handcuffed to the chair facing the mirror.

"I suggest you make a start on your defense, Mr. Brice. I think you'll find the prosecution has all the evidence they need to put you away for a long time." He frowned thoughtfully. "I'm not even sure whether the death penalty has been abolished just yet."

Brice began to scream, rattling his chubby wrists against the cuffs as he struggled to escape the chair. John calmly opened the door and stepped through, pausing only to savor the pitiful squeals coming from the grotesque excuse for a human being whom Jenna had handed him on a platter.

And speaking of crockery, he mused as he wandered through the crowded police station, *I wonder if I can fix that coffee cup?*

EPILOGUE

Something smashed to the floor by his foot.

John jumped away from the kitchen sideboard, dropping the spoon in a panic. In spite of himself, he let out a yelp. He glanced over his shoulder, fervently hoping his rather girly scream hadn't been overheard. He would look faintly ridiculous if someone found him standing in his sunlit kitchen on a calm Sunday morning and freaking out at the sound of something delicate smashing.

"Oh no. No way ...," he whispered to himself in disbelief, groaning as he looked at the floor.

Coffee dripped mockingly off the fragments of porcelain that had once been his new coffee cup. He glared accusingly at the rapidly expanding puddle and shook his head.

"Unbelievable," he muttered incredulously.

The puddle reached his foot. Out of defiance, he remained where he was, as if daring the insolent liquid to come any farther.

He sighed. Now he really did look ridiculous.

"Was that you?" asked a voice from behind him. John didn't look up, contemplating how even with the gifts he had been passed some things just had a way of going wrong.

"You screamed," the voice continued, clearly on the verge of laughter.

"Shut up, Chris," John replied, his eyes narrowing in concentration.

THE END

Steven D. Jackson lives in Hampshire, United Kingdom, where he works as a director of a law firm in Southampton. Shifter is his first novel. You can find Steven on Facebook and contact him at steven.d.jackson25@gmail.com.

Lightning Source UK Ltd.
Milton Keynes UK
UKOW051827250712

196561UK00002B/6/P